model

UNDERCOVER

NEW YORK

Carina Axelsson

sourcebooks
jabberwocky

For Ellen, Marina, and Victoria

Published by Sourcebooks Jabberwocky, an imprint of Sourcebooks, Inc.
P.O. Box 4410, Naperville, Illinois 60567-4410
(630) 961-3900
Fax: (630) 961-2168
www.sourcebooks.com

Originally published in 2014 in the United Kingdom by Usborne Publishing Ltd., an imprint of Usborne House.

Library of Congress Cataloging-in-Publication data is on file with the publisher.

Source of Production: Worzalla, Stevens Point, Wisconsin, USA
Date of Production: November 2014
Run Number: 5002866

Printed and bound in the United States of America.
WOZ 10 9 8 7 6 5 4 3 2 1

The Big Apple

I'm on my way to *Chic: New York*, the fashion magazine—or more specifically, to their head office located just off Times Square in New York City. And before you start thinking this is another one of my mom's hard-core plans to get me modeling…it's not.

You see, I'm not in New York City on my way to *Chic* as a model. I'm on my way to *Chic* as a *detective*.

Not that I know many details yet about the case I've been asked to solve.

The call from *Chic: New York* came two days ago, just as I wrapped up solving my first big mystery during Paris Fashion Week.

"Axelle, I thought you might be interested to hear about a call I've had from New York," my modeling agent, Miriam, said on the phone Saturday afternoon, her breathless voice a conspiratorial whisper. I remember the exasperation I felt as I stood, ice cream in hand, on a bridge over the Seine, trying to formulate an excuse to get out of whatever modeling job this was surely about.

But the call wasn't about a modeling job, and my

exasperation quickly turned to excitement when I heard her continue: "Have you ever heard of the Black Amelia? It's the most famous black diamond in the world. *Chic: New York* is—was—using it on a cover shoot, but…it's missing. It hasn't been seen since yesterday. *Chic* would prefer not to involve the police just yet, so they are wondering if you'd be interested in accepting the case."

Interested? Are you kidding? Do fashionistas wear black? Do I like French fries?

The *Chic: New York* team must have heard about me solving the mystery of missing French fashion designer Belle La Lune —and that I'd managed to find her before the French police! I was thrilled that *Chic* had asked for my help and accepted the job right away. But before jetting off to the Big Apple, I went home to London with Mom to repack my suitcase, and to see my dad and Halley (my West Highland white terrier). And so this morning I caught a direct flight out of London.

Sitting in the back of the enormous black Cadillac Escalade SUV (sent by *Chic*) that had picked me up at John F. Kennedy International Airport, I stretched my legs and stifled a quick yawn before pressing my face against the window. I silently ogled the view as the driver, whose name I'd learned was Ira Perlman, deftly wove his way through the late-morning Manhattan traffic.

In case you've never been there, New York City looks like a film set. As we navigated our way out of the Queens-Midtown Tunnel, all around me I could see shiny skyscrapers, pavement crowded with a gazillion people, and honking yellow cabs. And even if it had been my first time in the Big Apple (I'd actually been with my parents a couple of times before), the grid-like street layout would still have felt familiar from various films and television shows (like *Law & Order*—my grandma loved the U.S. version and watched it for years, in between *Midsomer Murders* and *Miss Marple*). The city seemed to vibrate with a frenetic energy all its own.

I watched as plastic bags blew across the streets and leaves fluttered in the early spring wind. Cool, sharp gusts were blowing in off the New Jersey shore. I had to admit that my mom had been right to insist that I pack the new trench coat she'd bought me. ("Burberry!" she'd chirped. "And only half price!")

Apparently my mom was psychic too, because at that moment my phone rang. Bracing myself for the onslaught of questions, I answered.

"Axelle, darling! How was the flight? How's New York City? Wonderful, isn't it? I wish I was with you! Your baggage didn't get lost, did it?" The questions came so thick and fast that I didn't even get a chance to respond. Finally I heard, "I have to go now, Axelle, I have to meet a client"—Mom is an interior designer— "but I'll call you later. Your father and I are so proud of you. Modeling in New York City!"

Modeling! Argh! My mom was *so* in denial! *When*, I asked myself, *will she finally understand that all I want to do is solve mysteries? And that modeling and high heels and hair spray mean nothing to me?* At least, nothing more than offering the perfect cover for figuring out fashion crimes, like tracking down a missing designer or a famous black diamond. My mom's big dream has always been for me to model—like, *real* modeling, not *undercover* modeling. And clearly—annoyingly!—even after I cracked last week's big, juicy case in Paris, modeling is *still* her dream for me.

Grrr!

I took a deep breath to control myself and said as lightly as I could, "Well, I have to go now too, Mum. I have an appointment at *Chic*—*about the case.*"

"Yes, well, have fun! Maybe you'll shoot a cover—I'll keep my fingers crossed! Bye for now, darling."

As I slipped my phone back into my pocket, it vibrated. I pulled it back out and read my new messages. There was a cute one from my dad and another from my BFF at home in Notting Hill, Jenny. Ellie B (non-modeling name: Elizabeth Billingsley), the new friend I'd made last week in Paris, had also sent me a text welcoming me to the Big Apple and asking if we could have dinner together later. She'd just flown into town for New York Fashion Week, which was starting on Wednesday. The last message was from Miriam, my agent, checking that I'd arrived safely and that the car *Chic* had promised had picked me up from the airport as planned.

Miriam—Miriam Fontaine, Paris-based agent

supremo—had been super helpful and kind since the events of last week. I've known her my whole life because she was my fashion-editor aunt's oldest friend, and her agency had represented me when I modeled (undercover) at Paris Fashion Week. After the story of how I'd found Belle came out, Miriam made sure I was all right, fending off the press and keeping my mom calm. She also—together with *Chic*—organized this trip to find the Black Amelia.

But in the aftermath of all that had happened, I'd occasionally caught her looking surreptitiously at me through slightly narrowed eyes. While she didn't say anything, I knew she'd been completely surprised by the fact that *I'd* solved the mystery of Belle's disappearance— even though Miriam knew I'd been obsessed with solving mysteries since, like, forever.

Fortunately for me, Miriam also had an agency in New York City and was happy to continue representing me as a fashion model here. Because, yes, I'd decided that the best course of action for solving this crime was once again to go undercover as a model. It was the easiest way for me to infiltrate the closed world of fashion, especially during Fashion Week when no one in the business would have time to spare for my questioning. But to work as a model, I needed the help of an agency. And who better than Miriam and her well-respected team? I knew I could trust her to be discreet, and I knew she'd help me keep up my modeling pretense.

Hervé (my booker at Miriam's agency in Paris) had also sent a message wishing me luck and saying something about an option for a magazine editorial in Paris.

I quickly looked through my messages again. No, there was definitely nothing from Sebastian.

But had I really expected there to be?

My throat tightened at the thought of his cool gray eyes and the warm smell of his leather jacket—not to mention our last conversation. *Argh!* I fiddled with the buckle of my La Lune shoulder bag for another moment. Then, pushing Sebastian out of my mind, I looked back out the window.

Once we turned north onto Third Avenue, I was fascinated by the speed at which we flew past the bisecting streets: Thirty-Eighth Street, Thirty-Ninth, Fortieth, and on and on. Ira, the driver, was seemingly unfazed by kamikaze bike messengers or the enormous potholes pitting the street like a bad case of acne. Even the yellow cabs coming at us out of intersections or from behind other cars didn't seem to concern him.

At that moment my phone rang again. It was a local number. *It must be Miriam's New York office*, I thought as I answered.

"Hi, Axelle. This is Pat Washington, your booker here at Miriam's NY," said a loud, energetic voice. "I can't wait to meet you. Miriam and Hervé have told me so much about you. I just wanted to be sure you've arrived safely and are on your way in…" I barely said I was before she kept talking. "Great, because you are going to be busy—very busy. I'm just waiting for *Chic: New York* to confirm you for a shoot tomorrow, which is fabulous. You've also got several show castings lined up."

Very busy? Fleetingly I wondered if she knew I was here to solve a crime or—

"Jared Moor," Pat continued, "should confirm for tomorrow—I'll let you know later today—and I'm still waiting to hear back from DKNY, Jorge Cruz, Diane von Furstenberg, and The Isle. But don't worry, there'll be others."

Great, I thought. *And when am I supposed to solve the case?*

"As for your *non-modeling* business," she continued pointedly, as if reading my mind, "we can discuss that in more detail when you get here."

Her brisk dismissal of my true reason for flying this far made me slightly nervous. Somehow I'd have to make it clear to her that I needed time to follow up on leads and clues—but surely Miriam had done that?

"Although," Pat continued, "if you've looked at your printed schedule—did Ira give it to you? Yes? Good. Well, then you'll know that you are going straight to *Chic* for a go-see before coming here. You'll be seeing Cazzie Kinlan herself! She wants to meet you and maybe see you in some clothes before tomorrow's shoot."

As Pat continued talking about the coming week, I looked into the folder Ira had pointed out when I'd climbed into the car. Pat was right. There was a printed schedule…but behind it was a slim envelope addressed to me. Inside was a letter from Miriam. And according to the letter, the go-see at *Chic* was actually a briefing from their editor-in-chief about the case…so either Pat had no idea why I was *really* going to *Chic*—despite her earlier allusion to my "non-modeling business"—or she was being discreet. But before I could finish reading the letter, she cut through my jet lag with the following loud announcement:

"And, Axelle, I hope you look good, girl. *Chic* magazine is at the top of the fashion pyramid—you have to look your best going in there. Clean hair, some cute little outfit—"

"Yes, but I just got off an international flight! I hardly—"

"Girl, I don't care if you just came in from Mars. You better freshen up and get it together. A model has to look like a model—got it? I'll see you here after *Chic*. I'll introduce you to everyone and then we'll have lunch. Now look sharp, girl!"

Look sharp? I hung up and slumped back into the soft leather seat. Great. I'd just arrived, and already I had a fashionista breathing down my neck!

"Are we nearly there?" I asked Ira, picking up Miriam's letter again.

Ira nodded, his long, frizzy orange hair bobbing. He was wearing Ray-Ban aviator sunglasses and a gold-and-diamond pinky ring that glinted in the sunlight every time he moved his right hand. "Yup. Traffic hasn't been too bad this morning and I was able to avoid the construction work around the Chrysler Building, so I'd say we've made pretty good time." As he turned left onto Seventh Avenue, he continued with a sideways nod of his head, "That's the famous Times Square. The *Chic* offices are a little farther down on the left. The tall silver building, you see it?"

I nodded, eyes glued to the window as I took it all in. So far on our drive through Manhattan, the loud, brash, and bold attitude of the city was exactly as I'd remembered it. But at Times Square that attitude was amplified by, like, ten—and those enormous billboards loomed over everything. I couldn't think of an equivalent at home in London. Trafalgar Square? No way. Too grand and Old World. Piccadilly Circus? Yes, that came much closer— but without the darker Batman-Gotham vibe.

I caught Ira smiling at me in the mirror as he parked. "You know, Axelle…" (Unlike Pat, Ira pronounced my name like the car part, instead of the *correct* way, which is to rhyme it with the verb "excel.") "I've been to Europe. I've seen a lot. London, Paris, Madrid. They got a lotta nice things, those cities, but not one of 'em has Times Square. You know what I'm saying?"

I sure did.

"Anyway, it's quarter after twelve, Axelle. I was told to be sure you weren't late," he said with a nod toward the silver skyscraper. "Must be important."

"It might be," I answered, shrugging my shoulders as visions of the missing diamond sparkled in my mind. "Anyway, thank you, Ira, for getting me here on time."

"No problem, kiddo. I'll be out here waiting for you. Good luck."

"Thanks, Ira," I said. I quickly ran my hands through my hair and popped a mint in my mouth. *So much for looking sharp,* I thought. Then I grabbed my shoulder bag and stepped out onto the sidewalk.

The Briefing

The muted hush beyond the steel and glass doors stopped me in my tracks. Times Square and all of its colorful, noisy chaos were instantly relegated to another world.

Of course, *Chic* was another world—even within fashion.

I put my phone on silent and went to the reception desk. After giving my name, I was directed to the elevators. The Sid Clifton Building—that's the building I was in—houses all of the magazines published by Sid Clifton Inc., including *Teen Chic* and *Chic Home* and a host of other titles. And if the large portrait hanging in the lobby was anything to go by, Sid Clifton wasn't just a corporation, but a real person too.

The people going in and out of the lobby seemed to be a mixture of gray-suited corporate types, fierce-looking older women in elegant trouser suits or power dresses, bike messengers in full sportswear, and lots of young, glamorous journalist or junior-editor types with Starbucks cups in hand. I also saw a few models, their large shoulder bags bumping against their hips as they bounded through the lobby, long hair streaming behind them.

Before entering an elevator, I took a quick look at myself in the large mirrored wall behind the reception desk. Skinny jeans, my new super-cool detective-style trench coat, little black sweater, and Converse sneakers with DIY decorations (pointy silver studs). All topped off with a large gauzy scarf my mom had bought me over the weekend.

"Modal and cashmere," she'd explained. "It'll keep you warm. New York can be quite blustery in spring. And it'll add a touch of color." She was right; I liked the way it looked. I pinched my cheeks for a bit more color, added some lip gloss, and stepped into an elevator.

Thankfully, it was empty. I was starting to feel nervous—very nervous. "Calm down, Axelle. Relax," I told myself, taking a deep breath. Naturally, I'd jumped at the chance to take on this case...but now that I was here—*flown in from London by* Chic!—the enormity of what I'd accepted suddenly hit me like a weighted handbag. There was no way out of this. And if I didn't solve this case pronto, my reputation would be reduced to that of a one-trick pony.

"Get it together, Axelle. Get it together," I repeated. My grandma had always said, "You'll be the world's best detective one day, Axelle." I took another deep breath and, with a quick look skyward (or elevator ceiling-ward at least), I prayed for her to help me.

I stepped out on the eighteenth floor into the *Chic* lobby. It was a sophisticated, serene space of white and cream. Elegantly framed *Chic* covers decorated the walls, and straight ahead, in large brass letters on the creamy marble wall behind the receptionist's desk, was the word *CHIC*. A few models were sitting in the reception area, their long legs stretched out, phones or iPads in hand, shoulder bags slouching beside them on the white sofas.

I was halfway across the room when a young woman in teetering heels and a short skirt came out to greet me. "Axelle? Hi, I'm Amy, Cazzie Kinlan's assistant," she said, holding out her hand.

Cazzie (also known as Cassandra Kinlan) is the young British-born editor-in-chief of *Chic: New York*. She's widely considered to be one of the new fashion stars of her generation—and she was the one who'd called Miriam to put me on this case.

I followed Amy through a labyrinthine warren of white offices and corridors. Shoes and dresses were everywhere: on heavily loaded racks, exploding out of rooms, spilling off shelves. And like busy ants, a sophisticated, stylish assortment of women and men strode purposefully from place to place.

"We're nearly there," Amy said before stopping at a white door and softly knocking. "Ms. Kinlan?"

Then, before I knew what was happening, I was sitting in a comfortable white armchair, about to take on my second case.

I hadn't known what to expect when meeting Cazzie…but I suppose I'd imagined someone like my Aunt Venetia (who until recently had been editor-in-chief of *Chic: Paris*, and whose skin was thicker than last season's wedges).

Instead I was confronted with a waif-like young editor who was clearly anxious. A nervous, agitated energy came off her in waves.

She was standing near the large corner window opposite where I sat. She wore silky, calf-length pajama bottoms—at least that's what they looked like to me—with a pair of purple python-print stilettos. A flimsy camisole top worn under a tiny, black fitted jacket completed her look. Her brown hair fell to her shoulders like mine, but there the similarity ended. Hers was stick straight and with zero frizz. It probably looked amazing no matter what she did. She had wide hazel eyes, and her fine, unadorned features reminded me of what Miriam had mentioned in her notes—that Cazzie had once been a model.

She gave me a brief once-over as Amy quietly left the room. Then as soon as we were alone, Cazzie crossed the floor, introduced herself, and got straight to the point.

"My life is on the line."

When she saw my eyes widen in shock, she sighed and slumped like a rag doll into her large white desk chair.

"I'm sorry, Axelle. I don't mean that literally—I'm not personally threatened in any way," she quickly clarified. "But I feel as though I might as well be. You see, *I* was responsible for the diamond. It was my idea to use it, and it went missing on a shoot *I'd* organized and personally styled. And it was whisked away right under my nose. Poof—gone! Just like that…" She turned and looked out the window as she continued.

"Axelle, if this diamond isn't found, not only will I have made a mockery of *Chic*—I can assure you that no one will ever loan the magazine anything of value again—but my personal reputation will be in tatters. The fashion world will never let me near another magazine or photo shoot again! I might just as well start looking for a new job—in another business."

Turning back to face me, she continued, "I don't need to tell you that the last thing I want is to have the police snooping around. The risk that people will start talking is far too high. That's why I called you. I'm counting on your discretion. This story cannot leak! Please, Axelle, you must find the diamond—but I'm afraid you'll have to do it on your own."

From the many snippets of gossip I'd heard Aunt Venetia share with my mom over the years, I knew how unforgiving the fashion world could be. I had no doubt that Cazzie Kinlan's livelihood and reputation were in dire straits. Furthermore, if this story went public, *Chic* would also suffer a severe blow. No surprise then that Cazzie was willing to try anything to avoid the police—even if it meant going with a sixteen-year-old fashion detective as untried as a new pair of shoes: me.

Then, before I could ask a question, she held out her cell phone. "I received this yesterday—Sunday. I wanted to show it to you right away. I know I sound paranoid, but I didn't want to discuss it with Miriam over the phone in case…" She stopped and drew a deep breath while I took her phone. "It's from an unknown number."

I read the brief text message.

Are you having a good weekend?

"For a split second," Cazzie said, "I thought it must have been sent by a wrong number, that the message wasn't intended for me. But then I had this strange feeling in my stomach, and I knew…I knew it had to be the person…the thief." She shivered. "I can almost hear them laughing when I read it."

"Have you received anything else like this?" I asked.

Cazzie nodded. "Sort of. It came early this morning—unknown number again. If you scroll down, you'll see it. I don't really understand…"

You're about to start the ultimate treasure hunt.
Answer correctly and you'll find what you want.
But be warned: by the time you find it, it'll be the least of your worries…

Now I could hear the laughter too. The image of a deranged joker, head thrown back and cackling, came to mind. The first message *could* have been dismissed as a mistake, but this one was different; it was threatening.

Did "you'll find what you want" refer to the Black Amelia? And what did the sender mean by "the least of your worries"?

"I tried texting back." Cazzie quickly ran her hand over her face before continuing. "But my message didn't go through. It was like the number was blocked or no longer existed."

Hmm…so if it was the thief, he or she was probably using a phone with a disposable SIM card to avoid being traced. But what did these messages mean? Nothing seemed to link them directly to the theft of the Black Amelia, but there didn't seem to be any other explanation. Not that I'd tell Cazzie…

"Who knows?" I asked. "About the missing diamond, I mean? Who have you talked to about it?"

"Besides you and me? Only Miriam. I haven't even told my boyfriend—although he's sensed something's up. I've been jittery, to say the least." The dark circles under her eyes definitely attested to that. "But I haven't told anyone here at the magazine and apart from whoever took the diamond—and, like I said, you and Miriam—I doubt anyone else knows. If they do, it didn't come from me."

Then she pushed a nondescript black office folder

across her desk toward me. In her soft English voice, she explained, "These are the notes Miriam told me you would need."

I looked her in the eye as I took the folder.

She nodded, a faint smile at the corners of her lips. "And, yes, I wrote them myself, per your instructions. Good thing you included that warning—I've fallen into the habit of letting my assistant, Amy, write everything up for me."

When I'd accepted the case, I'd been meticulous in the detailed instructions I'd asked Miriam to pass on to *Chic* regarding what I would need—and secrecy had been a major factor.

"You should find everything you wanted: a list of those present at the shoot, their job descriptions, a brief bio of each person, the studio's address, and a few more details I thought might be useful to you."

"And the shoot?"

Cazzie nodded. "For tomorrow? It's been confirmed and everyone will be able to make it. That's a fashion miracle, considering how busy everyone is before the Fashion Week shows that start on Wednesday. We'll be the same group at the shoot, and just like last Friday, there'll be no assistants and I'll do the styling myself."

In my instructions, I'd asked if there was any possibility of *Chic* organizing a reshoot: the same group of people, the same studio, the same time frame as the shoot last Friday. I wanted to—*needed* to—re-create as closely as possible the circumstances surrounding the Black Amelia's disappearance. Because I didn't yet have any tangible evidence to go on, I hoped that being in the studio the diamond was stolen from— and meeting the group that had been present when it happened—might yield some clues. Plus, without a doubt, a reshoot was the most discreet way for me to ask questions without raising any suspicion. I could ask the group about last Friday while "working" with them, as opposed to tracking them down individually and trying to question them.

So it was great news that Cazzie had taken my request seriously and made the reshoot happen. "Not a problem," she said when I thanked her. "I have plenty more clothes to photograph for the magazine's upcoming issues, so it was easy enough to convince everyone that I needed them again—even last-minute."

I opened the folder she'd given me and slowly perused the papers inside. On top was the list of those present at the shoot:

<u>Studio 7, Juice Studios,</u>
<u>Friday 9 a.m.–5 p.m.</u>
Cazzie Kinlan: editor
Peter Van Oorst: photographer
Trish Fine: makeup artist
Tom Urbino: hairstylist
Chandra Rhodes: model

Misty Parker: model
Rafaela Cruz: model
Brandon Hart: photographer's assistant/digi-tech

Hmmm…it was a small group. As I ran my eyes down the list, I realized that Brandon Hart was the only assistant. That wouldn't have struck me as odd, but after modeling in Paris all last week, I knew that all the key players—photographer, stylist, hairstylist, and makeup artist—have assistants on photo shoots…and yet there was just the one on Cazzie's list. Normally Cazzie would have had a junior stylist along with her, surely? And hadn't the photographer used more assistants than just his digi-tech guy? And what about hair and makeup? I asked Cazzie about this.

"You're right—normally there would have been a fair number of assistants on hand. Trish, Tom, and Peter would certainly have had them. As for me, I don't normally style the shoots. I did it this time around because the idea of using the diamond had been mine—and I knew it wouldn't have been loaned to us if I wasn't personally involved. So for the sake of the diamond and its security, I wanted to keep the number of people in the studio as limited as possible, hence no assistants—for any of us. I thought the fewer people who knew about it, the better… Not that my idea worked." She broke off, her voice strangled with fear and worry. She stood up and paced the length of the large window, her stilettos sinking quietly into the plush white carpeting.

I skimmed through the rest of the notes as Cazzie continued to pace. Hmm…there was one detail I hadn't thought about, one that now seemed glaringly obvious—and necessary.

"Cazzie?" I asked, standing up. "Do you mind if I use your computer?"

She stood by the window. "Of course not. Go ahead."

I quickly crossed to her desk. I wasn't sure I'd find what I wanted, but it was worth a try. They rented out space, after all. I googled "Juice Studios NYC," then clicked on their web address, and—bingo—there it was: a diagram of Studio 7's floor plan. In fact, their website showed a floor plan for every one of the seven studios they rented. I emailed Studio 7's plan to myself so I had a copy of it on my phone.

From the detailed floor plan I saw that the studio was shaped like an *L*. A curtain could be pulled across the entire opening where the two rectangles met, creating a long area (the longer bit of the *L*) where the photo shoot took place and hair and makeup were done, and a short curtained-off space at the bottom that was used as the dressing area.

Both a "normal" door and a large delivery door (for taking equipment in and out of the studio) were at the top of the main studio area. I asked Cazzie if the doors had been left open during the shoot.

"Once the day got started, the delivery door remained shut—I'm sure of it—and the normal entry door was only used by the group…" As she spoke, Cazzie was looking over my shoulder at the floor plan. "Well, with the exception of our lunch delivery, which came from the cafeteria downstairs. But they only dropped our lunch off and left."

Then, moving her finger across the floor plan, she said, "In this corridor just outside the studio is a bathroom. That's the one we used. So I don't think anyone from our group left the seventh floor—at least not that I know of. And no Juice Studio assistants came up from downstairs. Peter sent Brandon down if he needed anything. Incidentally, Peter was the only person I said anything to about the diamond before the shoot."

"When did you tell him you'd be shooting with it?"

"A few days earlier. But again, I trust Peter completely, and besides, it's hardly the first time we've shot valuable jewelry together. Anyway, I don't remember anyone else coming into the studio once we started shooting."

"Juice Studios must keep a log of people who go in and out of the building… Do you think I can see it? Just for that day?"

Cazzie chewed on her bottom lip for a moment. "The visitors' log is kept at the studios' reception desk—it's the one everyone signs when they come in or leave. I'm sure I can get hold of it, but I'll have to do it without raising suspicion. Leave it to me. I'll send it to you as soon as I have it.

"What scares me," she continued after a moment, "is that I've known almost everyone on that list for a long time. I mean, Trish, Tom, Peter, and I have known each other since our teens, and I've known all three girls since they started modeling. And Brandon is someone I've started working with a lot, thanks to Peter. If you'd asked me on Friday morning if one of them could steal a diamond, I'd have laughed and bet my life that nothing like this could happen—even with the diamond in plain sight.

"Of course, for all I know, someone else may have come in, someone I didn't see. I was in the dressing area half of the time, getting the girls ready, so..." She shrugged before continuing. "But like I said, Peter and I made a point of reducing the amount of traffic through the studio."

"And when did you notice the Black Amelia was missing?"

Her shoulders slumped as she answered. "Not until I was packing up to leave, when I checked the case it came in. Everyone else had already left. At first I thought it was one of Chandra's practical jokes. I know it sounds odd," she quickly added when she saw my eyes widen. "But if you knew Chandra, you'd know it's exactly the kind of joke she likes to play. She loves magic and card tricks—she always has.

"I can't tell you how many times she's kept the crew entertained when we've been on location somewhere, waiting for the weather to change, or at the airport, delayed by a late flight. She's especially good at making things disappear." Cazzie paused for a moment. "I really thought it was one of her jokes. I even went so far as to call her…"

"And?"

"She answered, but she didn't say anything about the diamond. She just talked a bit about the day and then asked what I wanted."

"So what did you say?"

"I was terrified of broaching the subject and ended up not saying anything. After all, if she hadn't taken it, how would it sound if I started asking her about it?"

"As if you were accusing her…"

"Exactly. And of course she would have realized that the diamond was missing, and I couldn't risk that getting out. Anyway, after I got off the phone with her, I realized that she couldn't have taken it."

"Why?"

"Because in some little way, Chandra always brings your attention to whatever she's taken. I think she likes to see the surprise on your face. And anyway, I doubt even she would be bold enough to steal a diamond as a joke. Then again, she didn't seem to give much thought to its value—unlike Misty and Rafaela, the other models shooting that day. They both asked a lot of questions about the Black Amelia…"

Cazzie paused for a moment before continuing. "I

was sick to my stomach when I didn't find the diamond. I can't tell you how I panicked. I searched the entire studio, every corner, every centimeter, but it was gone." She let out a long sigh.

"And when you searched the studio, did you notice anything unusual, something that may have slipped your eye earlier in the day?"

"You mean like the proverbial loose thread from the thief's jacket or a crumpled note with a name on it?" She shook her head. "Sadly not—and believe me, I looked. I even stayed on while the cleaners put everything in order. They do it in the evening so that the studio is ready for the following morning. I stayed on until it was spotless, white and shining. By this point I was frantic. I didn't know what to do—I went home and fretted all night. And then, in the morning, the story about you finding Belle was all over the news and I thought you could be the answer to my prayers. I called Miriam right away."

I really hoped I could live up to her faith in me. I flicked through the folder until I came to a photo of the Black Amelia.

"Yes, that's it," she said, "although, needless to say, it's even more spectacular in real life."

I pulled the photo out. The diamond was at the center of an ornate piece of jewelry; the picture showed it modeled on someone's hand. Fine strands of white gold set with tiny white diamonds formed rings around the middle and index fingers, then stretched down across the top of the hand where they encircled the Black Amelia. From the bottom of the black diamond another strand of small white diamonds dropped to the top of the wrist, where it joined a fine multi-strand bracelet. The effect of the large, black glittering stone set into such a delicate ornament was exotic and unusual. Once seen, it could not be forgotten.

"By the way," Cazzie said as I gazed at the image, "in the folder I've also included a brief history of the diamond. I doubt that has any direct bearing on its disappearance, but since you are trying to find the diamond, I thought knowing something about it might help you."

"How much is it worth?" I asked.

Cazzie shook her head. "A lot. You'll see in the articles I've included that when it was last at auction it set a new world-record price for a black diamond."

"But if the diamond is so valuable, wouldn't it have had its own security guards?"

"Argh! Don't remind me!" Cazzie said. She started to pace the room again. "This is the bit that kills me. Just thinking about it…" She turned to face me. "Normally the diamond would have had at least a couple of guards with it, but it belongs to a young guy named Noah Tindle. Have you ever heard of him?"

"Did he create Tindle Computers?"

Cazzie nodded. "Noah is a friend of mine; or more specifically, his wife, Vanessa, is a very good friend of mine. She's a model and always says that I'm the one who got her career off the ground. So anyway, Noah owns the diamond. In fact, he owns quite a few gemstones. He has one of the largest private collections of gemstones in the world. All of his stones are unique, both because of their cut and color, and because of their provenance. Noah only likes stones that have dramatic love stories behind them."

She actually cracked a small smile when she saw my surprise.

"I know—it doesn't quite fit the image of a computer geek. But since marrying Vanessa—I introduced them, by the way—he's been refining his collection to include only gemstones like the Black Amelia.

"Anyway, to get back to your question, yes, normally the diamond would have had a couple of security guards with it. But because I'm such an old friend of Noah's and Vanessa's, and because they were thrilled that the diamond would be used on the cover of *Chic*—Noah especially, because like many of these computer types, he's eager to be seen as interested in more than just software programs—they weren't particularly worried about the diamond's security. They knew it would be safe with me.

"They actually live in California, but Noah has been here for most of the last month, putting together a deal, so he had Vanessa send the diamond to him and he literally handed it to me early on Friday morning before the shoot, on his way to the airport. He was flying back home to see Vanessa and do some work at his HQ, so we made arrangements—thank God—that I was to keep it in the *Chic* safe for the entire week he's gone. He'll be back from California on Friday evening. I have to—*you* have to—find it by then. I feel like such a coward, not telling him anything, but how can I? How?"

She stood at the window, watching the traffic far below for a moment before continuing, her voice a whisper. "But if we don't have it back by Friday evening, then I'll have to tell Noah and the police—and Sid Clifton, the owner of this building and the magazine." There was a pause before she turned to look at me, shoulders heavy with fear and fatigue. "Please, Axelle," she begged, "please, you have to find the diamond. I didn't steal it, but somebody in the studio at that photo shoot did. And if I don't get it back…"

We both left the rest unsaid.

✳ ✳ ✳

Ira was waiting outside for me as promised. I slid into the car, and we continued downtown to Miriam's agency on Mercer Street. We sped through Midtown in no time, with Ira speaking as quickly as he drove. I was given a running commentary on the city all the way down. The traffic lights remained green for us until we hit Houston, the wide street that bisected the city east to west and that, according to Ira, was the "Ho" in SoHo (an acronym for "South of Houston"). After the brazen scale and slick, shiny facades of the buildings around Times Square, I was unprepared for the super-trendy and almost quaint feel of SoHo. A warren of one-way, narrow streets like the rest of the city, SoHo was pulsating with life—but on a more human scale.

As Ira pulled up to the curb on Mercer Street, I also saw a marked difference between Miriam's agencies. In Paris, Miriam's was housed in a large, grand two-hundred-year-old stone building on a wide, elegant boulevard, while here, the agency's downtown location gave it a cool, funky vibe. The redbrick exterior and large loft-style windows looked friendly and unpretentious—an impression that was reinforced when I got out of the elevator on the top floor and found myself in the agency's lobby.

Jay-Z was playing over the music system, and models came and went, while a few photographers stood by the large wall of zed cards that acted as a room divider. Through large glass doors to my right I could see an enormous roof terrace with wooden decking and an assortment of small ornamental trees, high grasses, and colorful flowers—just like a meadow, only on a rooftop!

The sophisticated artsy-crafty vibe caught me by surprise. After speaking with Pat and hearing her admonition to "Look sharp!" I'd expected something less…fun.

At that moment I caught sight of a tall woman with

short black hair waving at me from across the room. She stood on the other side of an enormous booking table, and she was backlit by the large windows I'd seen from the street below. Could she be Pat?

"Hi, Axelle," she said loudly as she took her headset off and came toward me, "and welcome to New York City." Her booming voice left me no doubt that, yes, this was indeed Pat. She was wearing a loose-fitting gray-and-black-striped top with three-quarter-length sleeves, black leggings, and flats. A pair of dangly earrings shook under her closely cropped Afro, which was short at the sides and a bit longer on top. She was in the process of giving me that fashion once-over I was starting to get used to. It's as if most fashion people can't talk to you until they figure out what kind of stylistic box to put you into.

"Not bad, Axelle, not bad. You've got that whole London, slightly boho, slightly edgy thing going... But what's with the glasses? Nobody told me you need glasses. And do they have to be so big? I mean, I know geeky is in and all, but still..."

She said the word "glasses" as if it was some kind of disease.

How could I explain that I'd worn them so long—even though I didn't really need them—that I didn't feel like myself without them? They gave me the anonymity I felt I lacked, especially now that I had some fashionable clothes and a model haircut. With my giant specs on, I could move around more freely, discreetly—and that was what a detective needed, right?

"Umm…my eyes dry out quickly with contacts so my optometrist told me to wear my glasses as much as possible," I lied.

I felt Pat's eyes bore into me while she mulled over my excuse.

"Well, as long as they come off for castings, fittings, and bookings," she finally said. "Got it? Good. Now let me quickly introduce you to everyone, and then let's go get some lunch. We have to talk and you must be starving."

Yes, ma'am, I thought as I followed her to the booking table.

After Pat had introduced me to all the bookers, we made a quick trip to the floor below, where I met the accounting department, signed my contract with the agency, and was made aware of the labor laws in place for child performers—which is how anyone modeling under the age of eighteen in New York State is classified.

"Because you are only sixteen, these laws protect you from being exploited, too much overtime, that sort of thing," explained Pat.

For a moment I panicked—then calmed down after realizing that the laws pertained to my modeling only, not my sleuthing.

But unfortunately Pat had caught my momentary anxiety. "That's the spirit, girl! I love that you want to work adult hours. But don't you worry, I'll keep you more than busy. When you aren't doing castings and bookings, I'll personally instruct you on a bit of fashion history, perfect your runway walk—you know, sharpen you up."

I was about to say something about needing some time to solve the case when I remembered Miriam's parting comment to me when we'd last spoken. I could almost hear her breathless voice:

Axelle, I need hardly tell you how sensitive this matter is. Secrecy is paramount. For that reason, I am the only person aside from Cazzie Kinlan who is aware of your true intention in being in New York I have mentioned to Pat, however, that you might need some time to yourself.

Might need some time to myself? Argh! I was here to solve a case. The modeling was only supposed to be a way for me to infiltrate the fashion world and get close to the suspects. Despite what Pat seemed to think, it wasn't supposed to be—nor would I ever let it become—an all-engrossing career.

"Work is all part of the game if you want to hit the top, Axelle," Pat continued. "and I want you to."

What a nightmare! Pat had no clue (no pun intended) about my real reason for being here. And she seemed even more ambitious for me than my mom (if that was possible).

I fell silent as the implications of this situation whirled through my mind:

A major case to solve on a very tight deadline + A booker who wants me to be a supermodel and is oblivious to the case = ARGH!

And some people think being a model is tough, I thought. *They should try being an* undercover *model.*

Just as I was starting to feel like a wet, wrung-out, jet-lagged rag, Pat finally said something that perked me up—perhaps the only thing that could have perked me up from the state I was in.

"I think it's time for lunch. Do you like hamburgers, Axelle?"

***

Lunch was a block and a half from the agency at Balthazar, a French-style brasserie with red awnings. From my banquette seat I watched as the restaurant hummed with a lively mix of fashionistas, stylish out-of-towners, and one or two famous faces. And the hamburgers and fries were as good as Pat had promised—she obviously enjoyed a good burger as much as I did. She attacked her cheeseburger with gusto, ketchup quickly replacing her lipstick. *At least*, I thought grudgingly, *we have that much in common.*

Our lunchtime chat, however, reinforced my earlier impression that I was going to have to take the term "undercover model" to a new level if I planned on solving this case under Pat's eagle eye.

"Axelle, your modeling career is on the cusp of some-thing big. B-I-G, girl. We'd be silly if we didn't push it. Not every model is given the opportunities you had last week in Paris. And now I want to expand on that here."

"But I wasn't in Paris just modeling, you know—" I said pointedly. I was about to continue but she cut me off.

"Oh, I know about finding Belle La Lune and all," she said with a breezy wave of her hand. "I saw it in the papers. But now you're here to model. And listen, Axelle"—I waited as Pat leaned forward on her elbows, her eyes boring into me—"you can't let these golden modeling opportunities just fly past you. You'll regret it later—trust me. Of course, what you do with your time off is your thing. Miriam told me all about you needing a little time to yourself; I know you have a school report. But *my* thing is to see that you're working, girl, *working*."

A little time to myself so that I can work on my school report? Thanks, Miriam!

In exasperation I stabbed my last few fries into the ketchup on my plate. I mean, as an excuse, a school report hardly afforded me any coverage—and Pat's next comment confirmed this.

"Anyway, even if I keep you too busy, you'll still have plenty of time to write your report on your flight back to London. I used to do my school reports the night before they were due, and school was much tougher back in my day. You kids all have it very cushy nowadays."

Grrr! If I hadn't known better, I'd have thought she was working for my mom!

During lunch, Pat passed me a set of keys for Miriam's flat. Miriam and my parents had decided that I should stay with her while she was in NYC for the Fashion Week shows. (My mom had absolutely, flatly, and loudly refused to let me stay with Ellie at Ellie's friend's apartment. "Not until I know her better," she'd said. What I actually think she meant was, "Not until you're five hundred years old.")

While initially I'd chafed at the idea of staying with Miriam—she could be as much a stickler for style as my Aunt Venetia—I was now pleased. Any place that provided a safe haven from Pat and her plans was fine with me. Plus it offered discretion—staying in a hotel, or even a model's flat, could have led to questions if I had to go out at odd hours or wasn't dressed like a model.

Miriam was due to fly in from Paris tomorrow afternoon, just in time for the shows—and not too soon to help pull Pat off me.

✳ ✳ ✳

Pat and I walked back to the agency, where I was given my details for the following day's castings—and also for the newly confirmed *Chic* shoot.

"You see, Axelle, this is what I was talking about at lunch. I mean, how many new models do we get in here every year? And how many of those models—*on their first day here*—are booked by *Chic* magazine? How many?" Without skipping a beat, Pat answered her own question. "None. N-O-N-E. That's how many."

If only she knew, I thought, my nose deep in my printed job details.

As Cazzie had promised, the group for tomorrow's shoot was indeed the same as Friday's. Same hair, makeup, models, digi-tech guy, and photographer— and Cazzie too, of course. It was a testament to *Chic*'s power and prestige that even during the super-busy lead-up to Fashion Week, everyone had made the effort to confirm. Of course, working on a *Chic* shoot was the ultimate proof that you were at the top of the fashion game—and no one wanted to miss that.

Before I left, Pat double-checked that I had all the agency telephone numbers, email addresses, private mobile numbers, Miriam's home address, and so on. And just like in Paris, I was told to call the agency twice a day, every day, no matter what—and to check my emails throughout the day. "Hervé told me you'd sometimes forget to call him, but I'll be watching you, Axelle. You'll be sharp in no time!"

I left before Pat could come up with any more plans for my career advancement.

✳ ✳ ✳

Ira was parked outside the agency, waiting to take me to Miriam's. As per Cazzie's instructions, he was to drive me until I'd safely arrived "home," which in this case was Miriam's apartment. We crossed the West Village and Chelsea before turning onto Tenth Avenue. Traffic was moving well, and in no time we were zooming past the back of Lincoln Center—home to many New York City fashion shows.

"You see those white tents?" Ira asked. "Those are the show tents. You're gonna be walking in 'em soon."

The tents were enormous, and as we flew past, I saw security guards, workers in construction helmets, deliverymen, and people with walkie-talkies going in and out of them. Signs saying "BACKSTAGE CHECK-IN" and "COLLECTIONS & EQUIPMENT" were posted at different entrances.

"We're only a minute away from Miriam's. She's got a fancy address," Ira told me. "Lots of famous people on her part of the avenue. You'll like it. And you'll be just across the street from Central Park. It's lovely at this time of year. The trees are just turning green, and the flowers will start coming up fast now."

Finally he came to a stop outside a large pink-colored stone building. As I craned my neck upward, I could see two muscular peachy-colored brick towers reaching for the sky. Windows, balconies, and turrets vied with one another for the best view over the park just opposite. Suddenly the car door opened and a man dressed in livery said, "Welcome to New York City, miss."

The doorman led me inside and across a sleek art deco lobby with polished marble floors and dark wood paneling on the walls. We took an elevator to the twenty-second floor, and as soon as I stepped into the corridor, the door opposite opened.

"*Bonjour, mademoiselle,*" said a small, smiling woman in a tweed skirt, with glasses on a chain around her neck. "I am Nicolette, Madame Miriam's housekeeper. And *merci*, Sam, for bringing *mademoiselle*'s luggage in." She smiled at the doorman.

Miriam's apartment was sumptuous yet welcoming. From the large windows of her dining room and living room, Central Park was neatly delineated, a magical block of green surrounded by a high "fence" of stone and steel skyscrapers. There was a kitchen at the back— along with a couple of rooms for Nicolette, who lived in so that she could look after the place while Miriam was in Paris. Miriam had the large master suite and I had use of her guest bedroom.

Large Tamara de Lempicka prints hung on the walls. They made a colorful counterpoint to the elegant palette of soft beiges, rich greens, and luminous blues of the walls and fabrics. Mahogany art deco furniture gave the apartment a slick, urban sophistication.

My room was furnished with light-green silk curtains and thick carpet underfoot. My window looked over

Seventy-Fifth Street. To the right, if I craned my neck, I could just see the leafy greenness of Central Park. An old-fashioned marble bathroom adjoined my bedroom.

After showing me around the kitchen and being assured that I was fine, Nicolette retreated (she had dry-cleaning to pick up for "Madame Miriam"), leaving me in peace. For some minutes I stretched out on my bed and closed my eyes as a deep drowsiness overtook me. (It was nighttime in London and my body knew it.) After a few minutes, I forced myself to look at the time: it was just past 4:00 p.m.

I'd made arrangements with Ellie, who'd flown into NYC yesterday, to meet downtown for a quick dinner at 6:30 p.m. That gave me a little more than two hours to spend on my own, and tired though I was, this wasn't the time for a nap. I had a case to solve.

So, where to start?

I knew I'd have to wait until the shoot the next day to look into the circumstances of the disappearance properly. But in the meantime, if I had to find the Black Amelia, it might help to know exactly what I was looking for. I'd seen the photo Cazzie had given me, but I'd never seen a black diamond in real life—so that seemed like the most logical place to start.

And according to my guidebook only one place in the city had a gem collection large enough to include such a stone: the American Museum of Natural History.

***

I slipped out of the apartment building and followed the directions Sam had given me—not that it was complicated. The museum was only a few blocks uptown from Miriam's.

Central Park, in all its early-spring green glory, was on my right. Straight ahead, looming into view, was the large, imposing building that housed the finest dinosaur fossil collection in the world, along with tribal art, taxidermy, insects—and gemstones.

I climbed the stairs to the columned entrance and purchased my ticket. After studying the museum map for a few moments, I turned into the Hall of Biodiversity— but not before stopping to admire the sheer size and awesome stances of the fighting dinosaur skeletons soaring over the visitor entrance. They were amazing!

The museum was vast, and after being directed to keep going straight until I'd walked under the hanging canoe and then to turn right at the giant mosquito, I finally found myself in the Morgan Memorial Hall of Gems.

It was like walking into a cave. The low-ceilinged space was dimly lit, the minimal lighting aimed squarely at the gems inside the glass cases. Thick carpeting muffled any footsteps. Up a few stairs, in a small room off the hall, I found what I was looking for. The Isabelle W. A. black diamond—all 82.06 carats of it—smoldered in the spotlight.

It didn't dazzle like a white diamond—in fact, it seemed to attract the light and pull it inside itself. Flashes of green, black, and white glimmered from deep within the large teardrop-shaped stone. It reminded me of a wild animal in a cage: it had come from a faraway world and seemed sad to have been pried from it.

I was bent over the case, quietly admiring the diamond, when I heard someone behind me say, "She's a beauty, isn't she?"

I turned and found a museum assistant just behind me. Her thick black hair brushed the shoulders of her uniform, and a pair of enormous round glasses was perched on the end of her nose. "You know, black diamonds are notoriously difficult to cut. That's why the big ones are so rare—they break easily due to their internal crystalline structure. By comparison, cutting a white diamond is like slicing through butter."

"That's interesting," I said—and I meant it. I straightened up, thinking. So large, black diamonds were difficult to cut, while white diamonds were easy to cut. Hmm…I was reminded of something I'd heard on the news about how thieves often stole large diamonds and then had them recut into smaller stones so they could sell them without being traced. But according to what the museum assistant had just said, that tactic wouldn't work well with black diamonds.

She was about to turn away when I posed the

question, just to be sure. "So you couldn't have a black diamond cut into new, smaller diamonds, then?"

She turned back around to me, shaking her head. "No. Not a black one. Not easily anyway—they are *tough*." She smiled at the black diamond in the case as if it were an old friend.

"And what about trying to sell a famous black diamond? A stolen one?"

She shrugged her round shoulders. "I would say that trying to illegally sell a stone like any of the ones here"—she nodded to the case—"would be impossible. A famous diamond would be recognized by collectors and specialists at once."

She was about to walk away again but something in me had started to hum. Not wanting to lose the thread of my thoughts, I quickly asked her, "So stealing a famous large, black diamond to resell it wouldn't make sense because it would be immediately recognized on the market?"

She nodded. "You sure have a lot of questions."

Ignoring her comment, I kept thinking. I was trying to grasp at something. I didn't yet know what, but I nearly had it. *Black diamonds were difficult to recut, and famous ones difficult to resell...*

She started walking away again.

I followed behind her as I finished my thought: *So why risk stealing a black diamond to make money?*

My mind was racing. Everything she'd said was

ringing in my ears, waiting to be made sense of. And that would only happen if I could sit for a moment.

I thanked the lady for the information she'd shared and turned to leave.

"You're not planning on stealing one, are you, honey?" she asked, smiling at me, hands on her broad hips.

If only she knew—I was trying to *find* one. I shook my head. "I just find it interesting."

"Yeah, me too—even after working here for over twenty years. Well," she said, "if you have any more questions about the stones, you just come by and ask for Vera." She pointed at her museum badge.

I thanked her again and left.

Hurriedly I walked out of the Hall of Gems, through the Hall of Human Origins, and back under the hanging canoe. I didn't stop until I came to the Hall of North American Mammals. There I found an empty bench next to a grizzly bear family and sat down.

Before coming to the museum, I'd assumed that the diamond had been stolen for money. Someone who needed cash had stolen the diamond to sell it—and maybe that was still the case.

I had no idea how the text messages Cazzie had received fit in—if they were indeed from the thief. Perhaps they would lead to a demand for money, or…?

With my new knowledge, more sinister possibilities now came to mind. Because *if* the Black Amelia had been stolen by someone who knew about diamonds and how difficult it would be to break up or sell a famous black one, then maybe that person hadn't stolen the Black Amelia for money, but as *blackmail*...or even as *revenge*.

This theory raised the question of whether Cazzie, or even Noah, had done something to hurt or offend someone. Perhaps someone from last Friday's shoot? Or had someone else walked into the studio unnoticed? Someone from their past?

A shiver ran through me as I realized that I'd probably taken on more than I could handle here. This case had seemed so straightforward: a bold theft within a confined space, with a limited time frame and a short list of suspects. And yet, with no apparent clues and a new sinister twist, the case now seemed to be anything *but* straightforward.

Who's Who

I left the museum in a daze, the new possibilities whirling through my mind. I caught the subway at the Eighty-First Street station just outside the museum and headed downtown.

The subway system was much like the Tube at home in London—even the underground mugginess was similar. There was rush-hour traffic on the train, so an empty seat was a luxury I wouldn't find at this hour. As I stood holding an overhead handle tightly, I reached my free hand into my shoulder bag and pulled out the paper Cazzie had given me with the brief biographies of the people present at the shoot.

At thirty-two, Cazzie was one of the oldest on the list. Only Tom Urbino, the hairdresser, and Trish Fine, the makeup artist, were older, and not by more than a few years. All were successful and at the top of what Pat called the "fashion pyramid." Even Brandon Hart was considered extraordinarily lucky to be the person responsible for carrying out all of Peter's retouching.

I couldn't imagine why someone from this highly

successful group would have stolen the diamond. Then again, my first big case in Paris last week had taught me that some people harbor dark secrets that fuel powerful, hidden motives. Was the diamond being used for blackmail? And if it was, why hadn't a demand been sent yet? Or were the brief, unexplained messages Cazzie had been sent leading to that? Or was this all about revenge? But by whom? And why? Again, the thought that maybe someone else had snuck into the studio came to me. But how would they have known that the diamond was there—or even been able to get close enough to it without anyone noticing? And again, *why*?

I nearly missed my stop because of thinking so much. Just as the doors slid shut, I bounded out of the train and came up for air at the West Twenty-Third Street station in Chelsea. Ellie was staying at a friend's apartment nearby, and I hurriedly started walking the short distance to the restaurant where I'd arranged to meet her.

My phone suddenly rang. I looked at its lit screen—it was Pat.

"Axelle, where are you? Why haven't you called? I'm about to leave for the day. I hope you've been resting. You've got to be fresh for *Chic* tomorrow."

"Yes, thank you, I did rest," I replied—which was sort of true, if you can call doing research in a museum resting. "And now I'm on my way to meet Ellie B for dinner. We want to discuss the upcoming show castings.

And," I quickly added, "I thought I would ask her for some tips for tomorrow's shoot."

"That's great! I'm really starting to feel your passion for fashion! Keep it up, Axelle. Keep it up."

Pat quickly gave me the address details for the next day's now-confirmed Jared Moor show casting, although she still didn't have an exact time. She said she'd have to call me later with that. Then she told me about a few more castings for later in the week that still needed to be confirmed.

"Like I said this afternoon, we just have to be careful that we respect all of these new laws for underage modeling. The old days are over. No more eighteen-hour days during the shows, even if you want to—as I'm sure you do," she said loudly. "I could strangle our mayor!"

And I could thank him, I thought as I put the phone away. I'd need every spare moment I could get for this case.

✳ ✳ ✳

Ellie was already at the restaurant, standing in line waiting to order. She'd come directly from a shoot and still had traces of heavy makeup around her big blue eyes. She was also trying to finger-comb her teased, honey-blond hair into a normal shape.

"*W* magazine," she answered when I looked at her, eyebrows raised, after hugging her. "A sort of goth-meets-haute-couture story. Everything here is yummy," she went on, pointing to the large chalkboard with the day's specials written on it. "And it's all vegan and gluten-free."

Typical Ellie, I thought, smiling to myself despite the thought of vegan cuisine. At least I'd had that delicious hamburger for lunch. And anyway, I was happy just to see her.

It was hard to believe that I'd only met Ellie a week ago in Paris, when I'd gone with my aunt to Miriam's agency to hear the latest news about Belle La Lune's dramatic disappearance. London-based Ellie had made the bookers coo with pleasure just by walking into the agency. That was the kind of effect she had on people. No surprise that she was a rising superstar within the fashion firmament. But what had struck me first was how nice and friendly she was—sharp too, I'd noticed as she bantered back and forth with the bookers.

I'd hoped that she'd be willing to help me go behind the scenes of the fashion world so that I could find Belle La Lune. What I hadn't counted on was her suggestion that I model—although, in retrospect, it had been a brilliant idea. I couldn't have come up with a better ruse for sleuthing among the fashionistas if I'd tried, although she'd had to push hard to persuade Miriam's agency to take me on.

So between giving me advice for my first photo shoot and helping me search the La Lune mansion for clues—not to mention teaching me how to walk down the runway!—Ellie and I had become fast friends. I was thrilled (and more than a little relieved) that she'd be in New York all week for the shows.

As we lined up to order, Ellie promised to show me the ropes for Fashion Week, just like she had in Paris. But she said doing New York Fashion Week was basically the same as doing Paris Fashion Week—only the vibe was different.

"How so?" I asked.

"Well, it's New York. You know: loud and fast. That whole elegant, delicate Parisian thing is, well…Parisian. Fashion here is sportier, more free—I love it. And by the end of the week, once the shows are in full swing, the city will be crawling with the biggest players in the music industry—rappers, pop stars, you name them— and most of Hollywood follows too. You'll be fine," she added quickly when she saw the panic on my face.

"So how's it going?" she asked after we'd placed our order and found an empty table near the front window. She asked in what sounded like a breezy, nonchalant way, but I knew her better than that. I knew where this was leading, but I was going to try to divert it—for Cazzie and *Chic*'s sake, and for Ellie's too. The last thing I wanted was for her to become inadvertently entangled in this case.

"Umm…well, like you said, the city sure is fast paced…"

Ellie rolled her eyes and sighed before fixing her

gaze on me, eyes smiling. "You know what I'm talking about."

"I do?"

Ellie leaned in close. "Hello? Axelle? It's me, Ellie. Did you really think I'd believe that you'd fly all the way to New York just to model—like, *real* modeling? You must be here on a case."

I said nothing.

"I mean, your mom could barely get you to go to the fashion shows in Paris before last week—and you only live a two-and-a-half-hour train ride away. So, New York? Honestly?"

I knew how determined Ellie could be. She'd continue to needle me until I'd told her everything—or something, at any rate. On the other hand, I knew that she could keep a secret…and if anyone could give me good insider information on the suspects I was dealing with, that would be Ellie. But still, I didn't want to put her—or her career—at any potential risk.

So I decided on a compromise. I admitted to her that I was working on a case, but I didn't go into any details about the Black Amelia or what exactly had happened. I only mentioned the group of suspects (at least the ones I knew about so far), where the crime had happened, and that something of value had been taken.

Ellie let out a long, soft whistle as she leaned back in her chair and looked at me. "Wow. The people you've just mentioned all work in the upper echelons of fashion. I mean, the *very* top. You can't climb higher up the fashion ladder. Rafaela, Chandra, Misty, Cazzie, and Peter—even Trish and Tom—are all big names who go to the *Vanity Fair* Oscar party, win awards at the CFDA gala, and have hundreds of thousands, if not millions of followers on Instagram.

"They're all big-time. I'm only halfway to being where they are. And, by the way, don't let Brandon's status as a digi-tech guy fool you. Both his parents are famous fashionistas. His work for Peter has always been something of a hobby for him—a way to meet models, the rumors say."

She stopped for a moment as if remembering something. "The only one on that list who might still remember what it's like to do something as mundane as grocery shopping is Chandra Rhodes. She's known for being quite detached from the fashion world—despite being at its epicenter whenever she decides to agree to a shoot. Something, by the way, she supposedly only does so that she can maintain her sailboat and the enormous loft she has here in the city."

Ellie took a bite of her salad before continuing. "I know Misty wants to get into film, and Rafaela counts some of the biggest pop stars as friends. We work together during the shows, but otherwise they're on a whole other level from me. They regularly appear on covers and have major contracts.

"As for Peter, I have started to work with him. He's

lots of fun and makes you look amazing. And Cazzie I know too. She's been booking me more and more, which is great. I think she has a soft spot for fellow Londoners." She paused for a few seconds before asking, "Do you have any leads?"

"No—far from it, at this point. And if there was any tangible evidence at the scene, it's since been cleaned away, so all I'll be able to go by are background research and a reconstruction of the minutes leading up to the crime. I thought this case was going to be so straight-forward… Anyway, I can't wait for the shoot tomorrow so that I can finally meet the group and hopefully sink my teeth into something solid. Right now it all feels a bit shadowy."

"Well, I'll definitely keep my eyes and ears open for you. Is there anything specific I should be on the look-out for?"

I nodded slowly. "Anything about any of their whereabouts last Thursday—the day before the shoot— and Friday evening. And the weekend too. Nothing in particular, just where they were, who they saw, or what they were up to. And any gossip you hear about their careers or finances, or even their personal lives, might be helpful."

"Fine. Consider me your extra pair of eyes and ears. By the way, how great that you're getting a *Chic* booking out of this. You'll get some great tears for your book! Pat must be delighted," Ellie said with a laugh.

I rolled my eyes. "I thought that being over three thousand miles away from my mom would give me a break from having an overzealous fashionista constantly on my back. Little did I know."

"Well, Pat is an amazing booker. She wants us all to succeed."

"I noticed."

"You'll just have to be creative about dealing with her."

"Thanks." Annoyingly, Ellie always put a good spin on everything—even Pat.

I suddenly had an idea and, before popping the last bite of my vegan, gluten-free burrito into my mouth, I said, "Ellie, I saw on my map that Juice Studios isn't far from here. Do you have time to show it to me?"

She nodded as she speared another piece of her chick-pea fritter with her fork. "And at the same time I can show you the best place in the city to watch the sun set."

✳ ✳ ✳

Ellie wasn't kidding—the sunset was spectacular from the High Line, an old, unused railway line that had been turned into New York's first elevated public park. The old tracks now support everything from large flowering shrubs to thigh-high wild grass, contemporary sculpture, tables, and benches. Not to mention people: some sat, others walked, and a few even played music.

After climbing the metal staircase that led from street level up to the old railway, we stood for a few moments to admire the large orb of brilliant orange that seemed to hang in the sky, replete and sated after a day's work. The honking, screeching brashness of the city was muffled by the unexpected sound of the wind rustling through the tall grass and leaves.

"So...?" Ellie and I were walking side by side, and while she didn't elaborate on the "so," I knew what she was asking about: him. *Him* being Sebastian Witt—the super-cute, tousle-haired, leather-jacket-wearing son of the chief inspector who'd been investigating the case I'd just solved in Paris—and the guy I'd kissed only three days ago.

When I remained silent, she pushed. "How is he?"

"He's fine, I assume." I tried to sound as nonchalant as possible—while thoughts of Sebastian's gorgeous smile and cool resourcefulness under pressure whizzed through my mind. I might have given his broad shoulders a passing thought too.

"You *assume?*"

She stopped in her tracks and turned to me, her head tipped to one side the way Halley, my West Highland white terrier, does when she's watching me and trying to guess my next move. However, unlike Halley, Ellie can speak.

"What do you mean? Haven't you spoken to him? Isn't he here?"

"I don't know."

She observed me through narrowed eyes. "Last I heard, you and Sebastian had snogged for hours on a bridge in Paris. And now, three days later, you don't know where he is? Have I missed something?"

Good question...

On Saturday afternoon—my last day in Paris—Sebastian and I had kissed at sunset on a bridge in Paris. I know that sounds impossibly romantic, but the reality was that I'd needed an intense week of dodging serious danger and near death—with him by my side for much of it—to finally admit that he was not only a good friend, but totally kissable too.

So far, so good.

Now comes the tricky part...

Once I went home to London, Sebastian and I had continued to text. He was planning to meet me in New York. Like me, he still had another week of school vacation. Luckily, his father thought it would be good for Sebastian to see New York, plus he had an aunt he could stay with. We'd planned to meet as soon as we both arrived in the city. Sebastian didn't know for certain that there was a case to solve here, but I knew he had a sneaking suspicion. He'd been with me when I received the call from Miriam about *Chic: New York* and the Black Amelia. And while he'd been careful not to ask me anything, he knew (like Ellie) that I'd never get on a plane to model in NYC if there wasn't a mystery involved.

I took a deep breath before turning to Ellie. "On Sunday—yesterday—while Mom and I were making dinner, Mom left her phone on the kitchen counter while she ran up to her bedroom to get something. And then her phone lit up with a text message—from Sebastian!"

"Oh no...don't tell me... You looked, didn't you?"

I nodded. "I had to. I know I shouldn't have—but how could I *not*? Honestly, could you have ignored that?"

Ellie shrugged her shoulders. "No, probably not...but it depends. I mean, they could have been planning a surprise party for you or something. You never know."

I rolled my eyes. "Trust me, this was no surprise party. I read their messages, and... Oh, Ellie, I was so angry with them! I was fuming! Apparently my mom was trying to convince Sebastian to keep an eye on me while we were in New York, to make sure that I modeled and kept any detective work to a minimum. According to my mom, my 'modeling career is far more important than any detective case'—*and Sebastian agreed!*" Just thinking about it made my anger flare. Lips pursed, I stopped talking to let the breeze cool me down.

"Oops," Ellie said. After a moment she continued, "But what did he tell you? He must have had a good reason for saying what he said. I mean, he knows how much your detective work means to you—he helped you solve your last case."

"Yeah, well, I confronted him about it over the phone and he didn't deny talking to my mom." I took another deep breath. "And after I'd heard that, well, it wasn't as if I needed to hear more. I told him we shouldn't talk anymore."

Ellie looked at me, her wide eyes incredulous, but she didn't say anything.

"Anyway, I'm sure it's for the better," I said, mustering as much finality as I could.

"What do you mean by that?"

We started walking again.

"Well, imagine: if I did still like him, and he was here with me, he'd only be a distraction. I mean, have you ever tried working with someone when all you want to do is kiss them? Not that I want to kiss him anymore, but you know what I mean."

Ellie laughed. "Sure. My last boyfriend was a male model, and we worked together sometimes, but I wasn't inordinately distracted."

"That doesn't really count," I answered. "I mean, it's not like while modeling together he'd be distracting you from potentially life-threatening situations or keeping you from saving someone. Not unless a huge light was about to fall on you or the photographer suddenly croaked on set or something. But what are the chances of that happening?"

"Do you have to be so dramatic? And by the way, modeling can be dangerous. Like when I had to model faux fur coats in the Nevada desert last summer. A model fainted from heatstroke on set."

I rolled my eyes. "That's not the same thing. Anyway, like I said, it's just as well that we aren't together. If I don't solve this case quickly, my reputation as a detective will be flatter than a gladiator sandal. I don't need to have a distraction who spies for my mom hanging around me."

"That's what you *think*."

"That's what I know."

"What was it you told me last week, Axelle, about evidence?" Ellie asked. "Something about how, as a detective, it's stupid to jump to any conclusion until you've gathered all the evidence possible, because otherwise you risk making a major mistake."

I didn't say anything.

"Well, you might want to consider applying your sleuthing techniques to the non-detective parts of your life too."

"Thanks, Nancy Drew."

She shrugged her shoulders. "Suit yourself, but I bet he comes to New York. He might already be here looking for you. And then what will you do?"

"Work on my case."

Ellie rolled her eyes. "Duh. I mean, with or without him?"

"He'll probably be too busy sending my mom feedback to have much time to help me out."

Ellie looked at me intently before asking, "Seriously, suppose he does show up and can help you—don't you think that you'll want his help?"

"Maybe."

"And I bet you'll forget all about him spying for your mom once you kiss him again."

"No I won't."

"No you won't forget he's spying for your mom, or no you won't kiss him?"

"Both."

Ellie sighed. "Well, I still think he's totally into you—and I know you're into him. Even if you won't admit it."

"What I'm really into right now is solving this case," I told her, changing the subject once and for all.

✳ ✳ ✳

"That's Juice Studios over there," Ellie said a few minutes later, pointing to an old redbrick building on the corner of the street below us that ran perpendicular to the High Line. "The one with all the big windows."

Juice Studios was housed in a former factory building at the corner of Seventeenth Street and Tenth Avenue. It sat calmly, serenely commanding its corner of the block. Seen from afar on a quiet evening, the building didn't look like one of the city's most popular fashion photography venues. According to what Pat had told me at lunch, not a day went by—weekends included—without a magazine editorial or some major fashion campaign being shot on the premises. I looked on as a fashionista exited the studios and quickly disappeared into a waiting black Escalade. Then I continued to watch as the last rays of daylight lit up the studio's industrial windows and made its redbrick facade glow orange in the setting sun. A minute later, the sun was gone.

In the twilight, the studios—vast, empty, and painted white—sat like silent film sets, waiting for the models and fashion teams to bring them to life the following morning.

And if those walls could talk, I thought, *I'd love to hear what they could tell me.*

"Axelle, I have to get going or I'll be late," Ellie said suddenly. "I'm supposed to be at Ralph Lauren for a fitting in twenty-five minutes. If you're going home to Miriam's, we can share a cab uptown. You can drop me off and then keep going."

✳✳✳

Once the yellow cab had dropped Ellie at the Ralph Lauren building, it was only a matter of minutes before it deposited me outside Miriam's.

The elegant lobby in Miriam's building made a distinct contrast to what I'd seen in the last few hours. Comparing the tall, stately art deco building to the low brick buildings of SoHo and the blackened old warehouses of the Meatpacking District—not to mention the funky charm of the High Line—was like comparing a pair of comfy old jeans to a haute couture dress. They both were good, but very different.

Earlier, Nicolette had told me that she retired to her rooms after seven in the evening, so after taking the elevator up, I let myself into the apartment with the key Pat had given me at lunch.

The apartment was quiet, yet alive. As I stood in Miriam's high-ceilinged, wood-paneled living room and looked out the floor-to-ceiling windows, Central Park West, Columbus Circle, and Fifth Avenue lay before me like spangled ribbons teeming with life. Thousands of lit windows punctuated the vast cityscape, glowing like faraway fireflies. It was magical. Even from this height, the city vibrated with a hushed frenzy that was addictive to watch.

But sleep was beckoning—it was now 2:00 a.m. London time. Slowly I walked to my room and checked my messages. I quickly sent texts to my mom and dad, and Jenny too. Still nothing from Sebastian, I noticed.

But that was what I wanted, wasn't it?

I knew Ellie hadn't believed that—and Jenny had thought I was beyond hope. "What?" she'd said last night in London, when she'd come to help me pack. "You're finally wearing heels and have a decent haircut, *and* you've snogged the cutest, hottest guy in Paris— and now you don't want to talk to him? Please, will you one day make sense to me?"

Of course, when Jenny put it like that, she made my

decision sound silly. But it wasn't that simple, I thought as I stomped off to the bathroom.

After a long, hot shower I slipped between the cool sheets of my bed and stretched. For the umpteenth time I pushed Sebastian out of my mind. Then I pulled out Cazzie's notes, trying to focus on the Black Amelia. But it was hopeless. Within moments, I was asleep.

The Black Amelia

I woke up early. By 5:00 a.m. local time—which was 10:00 a.m. London time—I was wide awake. I got out of bed and went to find my laptop. It was time to get to work.

I turned it on and grabbed the folder Cazzie had given me. Carefully I perused the brief biographies she'd compiled for everyone on the list she'd given me yesterday and then transferred her notes to my laptop. Then I started to look for more information on the group. But with the enormous amount of career news, photos, magazine stories, and blog posts online, I could have spent a day researching just one of the group, let alone all of them.

Hmm, I thought, *maybe when Sebastian*—Argh! I cut myself off right there. *Stop, Axelle. He's helping Mom, remember?* Before any of Ellie's admonitions from last night started ringing through my mind, I told myself that I would just start with basic background research and do more when I found the time.

I quickly jotted down the few things that caught my

eye, then moved on to the Black Amelia. I made sure to add the information I'd gleaned at the museum to the details I already had on the diamond from Cazzie, and then I did a quick web search, pasting anything I found interesting into my notes. Together it all formed a fascinating kaleidoscope of the diamond's tumultuous past.

After a couple of hours I got out of bed and moved to the desk. Slowly I pored over everything I'd put together…

As with most famous diamonds, the Black Amelia's history is no less dazzling than the stone itself. Originally discovered deep in the Brazilian jungle by a nineteenth-century American explorer, the diamond—then in its rough, uncut state—was double its current size of eighty-three carats. According to legend, it was stolen by the explorer from a sacrificial altar, along with a hoard of other jewels and gold.

However, before leaving the jungle, the explorer became ill with a deadly virus and perished there. The diamond was taken by his valet, who hid it in a secret pocket sewn into his jacket and took it back to his hometown in Portugal. But knowing that the value of such a rare diamond would enable him to start a new life and fearing for his safety as long as he kept it, he decided to leave for the Flemish city of Antwerp, the diamond capital of the world.

There he sold the stone to a famous diamond

merchant who finally cut it. Because black diamonds are so difficult to cut, it took the merchant four years and much of the original carat size was lost. But the resulting stone was still the largest black diamond anywhere in Europe at that time. The merchant then sold the diamond, now set as a brooch and christened the "Eye of Brazil," to a rich banker, and for the next one hundred years it lay quietly in a family vault.

In the 1960s, however, the diamond was put up for sale at auction in London. There a famous British stage actor bought it for the woman he was in love with, the Mexican actress Amelia de la Roja.

Amelia had the jewel reset as a pendant and wore it everywhere, until it became as famous as she was. At this time the press began calling the diamond the Black Amelia. Meanwhile, Amelia de la Roja married and divorced the British stage actor twice. Then, after they'd both retired from the screen and stage, they married for a third time, thus starting the legend that a woman in possession of the Black Amelia could never fall out of love with the man who'd given it to her.

When Amelia de la Roja died, the diamond was again sold at auction—this time to raise money for the charities she'd named as beneficiaries of her estate. The famous punk rocker Kean Feral bought it for his wife, and to commemorate their love, he promptly had the stone reset in an elaborate hand chain bracelet. When Kean Feral later died of a drug overdose, the diamond passed into the hands of tech billionaire and gem collector Noah Tindle.

I got up to stretch. At least my online research had confirmed what the museum assistant had told me about black diamonds being difficult to cut. The idea of the diamond being stolen for resale now looked weaker than ever... In fact, so far, I couldn't think of a reason why anyone would want to steal such a famous jewel. Nor, I thought as I returned to my desk and scrolled through the brief biographies I'd compiled, was it easy to imagine anyone from this small, elite fashion group as a thief. And yet one of them must have taken the diamond...

Peter Van Oorst: Photographer, Dutch citizen, thirty years old, has been living in New York for twelve years. Started as an assistant to a number of well-known fashion photographers before branching out on his own, after which success came rapidly. He's often described as the leading fashion photographer of his generation. Smiling in all the photos I saw on Google. (I'm not sure that means anything, though.) Girlfriend is a junior fashion editor.

Trish Fine: Makeup artist from New York, thirty-five years old, famous for the way she does smoky eyes. Internationally in demand and launched her own makeup line three years ago (together with a major cosmetics firm). Assisted various well-known makeup artists in NYC, then moved to Paris for a few years to hone her skills before returning to NYC. In promotional photos, she wears her long orange hair teased at the top, goes heavy on the eyeliner, and pouts. Single.

Tom Urbino: Italian, from Milan, thirty-seven years old. Famous for his "natural" looking hairstyles. Also known for liking to work with whatever is at hand, such as olive oil, hand lotion, or seawater. Tom claims this gives hair a more "organic context." Manages to wear cowboy boots, cowboy hat, and beaded jewelry without looking overly ridiculous. Has his own mega-salon in NYC and an olive-oil-based hair product line. Lots of photos on Facebook of him partying.

Chandra Rhodes: Model, seventeen years old, from California. Shoulder-length, sandy-blond hair and gray eyes. Loves to sail and surf. Took six months off to sail with her father and sister, and sent regular blog dispatches from around the world. Has just signed a contract to represent a major cosmetics firm. Is developing her own vitamin-packed smoothie mix. Splits her time between a beach house in Northern California and a loft in NYC. Boyfriend is a carpenter in California.

Misty Parker: Model, eighteen years old, from a farm outside Cleveland, Ohio. Wholesome looks with corn-yellow hair and cool blue eyes. On her way to accumulating more covers than any other model. From the beginning she has been selective about the work she accepts. She is now poised to launch a major acting career. Keeps a large, long-haired cat, which has become an Instagram sensation, in her SoHo apartment. Not romantically linked to anyone at the moment.

Rafaela Cruz: Model, nineteen years old, born in New York City, parents from Cuba. Long, dark brown hair and caramel eyes. Strong, fun personality (judging from her Twitter feed and Instagram photos). Popular with other models and, crucially, fashion designers. She opened more shows last season than any other girl. Rumored to be dating a hip-hop artist. Just bought herself an apartment in the West Village.

Brandon Hart: Native New Yorker, twenty years old, studied photography at Columbia University. Does digi-tech work for fun. His father is a majority shareholder in a large luxury fashion brand conglomerate, and his mother is a former supermodel. He works exclusively for Peter.

*Cazzie says: "Brandon is gorgeous. I've asked him a million times to model, but he's absolutely not interested."

**I say: I couldn't find anything online about him apart from his digi-tech work, his Instagram account, and stuff on his parents. Bit of a dark horse in this lineup.

Cazzie Kinlan: British citizen, thirty-two years old, has been working as editor-in-chief of *Chic: New York* for six years but has been living in NYC for twelve years. Live-in boyfriend, workaholic. Travels to the shows in Paris, London, and Milan for the prêt-à-porter and haute couture. Seems to earn a good income, including a clothing allowance. Other perks include a business expense account, chauffeured car (Ira), and phone. Good reputation.

My phone rang, abruptly pulling me from my thoughts.

"Axelle? Are you sleeping?" It was Pat. Why was she calling me so early? The agency didn't even open for another hour! "I'm calling to make sure you're awake. It's eight o'clock—and you have to be at Juice Studios for your *Chic* shoot in an hour. Hasn't anyone told you that fashion never sleeps?"

"But I do," I said, stifling a yawn.

"That's not funny, Axelle." Did she ever soften up? I wondered. She seemed to have more hard edges than my grandma's old crocodile handbags—no matter what time of the day it was.

"Good thing I called," she continued. "Now wake up and take note. I got an email late last night confirming

69

the time for your show casting at Jared Moor. It's at five o'clock. I'll email that to you so you don't forget, and then *blah, blah, blah…*" I tuned her out because I'd just received a text. I put Pat on speakerphone and read the following message:

Can you meet me now? I'll be at the coffee shop at the corner of Seventeenth Street and Seventh Avenue. Cazzie

"Axelle? Are you there?"

"Yes. Yes, I am!" I said, dragging my attention back to Pat. I quickly noted the few other details she gave me concerning my day and then finally managed to get her off the phone.

What could Cazzie want? I thought as I pulled on my robe and headed to the bathroom. I quickly texted her to say I'd be with her in thirty minutes, then jumped into the shower. Ten minutes later—notes in my bag and fresh NYC bagel in hand—I was on the street and running at full speed to the subway station.

✳ ✳ ✳

Cazzie was standing outside the coffee shop waiting for me. She was clearly distraught; my wet hair and overall dishevelment didn't even garner a second glance. *What's good about rushing while dressing is that at least you don't look like you've tried,* I reminded myself. In the minefield of fashion, trying too hard was even worse than not trying at all. On that positive thought, I followed Cazzie as she led me, her teetering red stilettos softly clicking, to a corner table in the back.

"I'm sorry to call you so early but you have to see this—and I don't want to deal with it at Juice when we're working together," she said without preamble. "It came about an hour ago. I'm feeling a bit sick."

Taking her phone I read the new text message:

Clever Cazzie, clever Cazzie. So they say, but are you really? Let's find out! You'll be sent three riddles to answer. Let's hope you get them right!

The light, breezy tone, coupled with the threatening undercurrent of the message, brought the image of the deranged joker back to mind. It had been sent at seven thirty this morning—not long before Cazzie contacted me.

"Scroll further down," she said. "I quickly wrote back because I wanted to get a reaction. I don't know if it was the right thing to do…but it's too late now."

Cazzie had written:

I need to see the diamond by Friday.

The answer was unnerving:

Shut up! I'm the one in control now—not you, you stupid fashionista. You'll see the treasure if and when I want you to. Now you've upset me so I'll have to delay your first riddle. That's too bad—for you. I was going to send it later today, but now who knows? Maybe you won't see anything by Friday. That's my choice.

In the meantime, enjoy the fashion shows!

The vagueness of the messages was infuriating—which I guessed was the point. Whoever was doing this was clearly enjoying their new power. But why? And would the riddles reveal some kind of ransom or demand? At least this person definitely seemed to have the diamond... So could this be leading to blackmail?

"Blackmail?" Cazzie asked when I said as much. "But they've insinuated that I'll see the diamond again if I 'answer correctly.'" She was rereading the texts she'd been sent.

"The riddles they say they'll send might actually be demands for ransom. If so, they might be assuming you'll give in to them. At least that's what it sounds like to me. I see the number was 'unknown' again."

She nodded. "I'd love to trace it, but I can't possibly show this to anyone, can I? Someone might start asking questions. And anyway, I know from past experience at the magazine that something like this is almost impossible to trace. I'd have to call the police, and that's something I absolutely cannot do—not yet anyway. Look how I've angered them just by responding. Who knows what they'd do if they found out I'd called the police? But maybe if I play their game there's a chance I can get the diamond back by Friday."

She roughly pushed her empty coffee cup away and turned to look out the window, letting out a long sigh. Today she was wearing a pair of distressed skinny jeans and a Chanel tweed jacket with something silky and white peeking out from underneath. The black circles under her eyes matched her jacket.

"I'm dreading the shoot later," she finally said. "The thought that someone in that group has probably taken the diamond, that they could be the one taunting me with these messages—and then having to rub shoulders with them all day…"

"Play it cool. Whoever is doing this—whether they're one of the group or not—is hoping that you *will* crack. They're trying to scare you. As they've just pointed out, they're in control. So don't let your behavior remind them that they are." I waited a moment before continuing. "Can you can think of anything you've said or done to any of that group, anything to make someone angry enough to try blackmailing you? Or to seek revenge against you?"

She shook her head. "Honestly—no, I can't think of anything. Like I told you yesterday, I've known Peter, Trish, and Tom for years and consider them good friends. I've known the models since they started, and I know Brandon, who I really like, through his mother. She was like a mentor to me when I started modeling. I've never had a fight or even a disagreement with any of them. Honestly."

"Hmmm…maybe it isn't against you personally," I said aloud as another possible theory formed in my mind.

"What do you mean?"

"Well, if the thief isn't after you personally, they may be trying to blackmail *Chic* by using you. After all, if you have to go public with this, *Chic*'s name will be dragged through the mud."

Cazzie looked at me, eyes wide.

I sighed. "Anyway, it's just an idea."

"I'm not sure that makes me feel any better," Cazzie said. She was becoming visibly more drained with each passing moment.

"I'm sorry, but don't worry. I'm sure we'll corner them—whoever they are," I quickly added. "And at the studio today I'll have a chance to ask questions about Friday. I should get something to go on from the answers."

"I hope so," she said with another sigh. Then, after a quick look at her watch, she got up to leave.

As I watched Cazzie walk to her waiting car, I hoped my confidence about cornering the culprit would turn out to be well founded. Bravado alone wasn't going to solve this case—and with both my and Cazzie's careers on the line, I had to hope there was more to me than empty promises.

Cazzie had offered to take me with her in her car to Juice Studios, but I said it would be better if I walked. I didn't want to give anything away by the two of us showing up together.

After pushing open the glass door of the studios, I went to the reception desk and gave my name and the details of the shoot where I was expected, then signed the logbook. From there I was directed toward the elevators and caught one going up. I stepped out into the lit corridor that led to Studio 7.

The studio had the entire seventh floor to itself. I passed the bathrooms and, at the end of the corridor, opened the door into the studio itself. I blinked as I stepped into the light-flooded space. From the inside, it looked as it had from last night's vantage point on the High Line—all large industrial windows and well-worn wooden floors—only now it was coming to life.

Giant lights were being moved into position, their skeletal frames reminding me of the dinosaur fossils I'd seen yesterday at the museum, and a caterer was just leaving after setting up the buffet table with a yummy-looking selection of breakfast muffins, fruit, and croissants. Just to the right as I walked in, at the top end of the studio, a gray paper background was being clamped into place.

The morning sun shone brightly, and a buzzing, busy atmosphere permeated the studio as it was made ready for the shoot. It was hard to believe that such a dramatic theft had taken place in this room just a few days earlier.

Thanks to my early-morning study session with my computer and Cazzie's notes, I recognized everyone from the group on sight—not that I let on. And Cazzie came forward to say hi as if we hadn't just been talking together a quarter of an hour earlier.

She introduced me to Peter Van Oorst, who set his camera down to shake my hand. He was dressed in black jeans, gray T-shirt, black leather jacket, and sneakers. A pair of large glasses with thick black frames (a bit like mine) completed his look. His light, sandy-brown hair was long and pushed back from his forehead. It was also greasy in that über-cool fashionista kind of way. Did it look like that because he hadn't washed it in two weeks, or was it because he just had a lot of product in it? Or both? I couldn't tell.

"Ah, last week Paris, this week New York," he said with a big smile. "Your modeling career is definitely getting off to a good start, isn't it?" Then he leaned closer to me and said, "And hopefully, here in New York, you won't be sidetracked by another mystery—although what incredible luck that you found Belle! But that's what happens when you're in the right place at the right time, isn't it?" He pulled back and winked.

Instantly the morning chatter focused on my mystery-solving exploits last week in Paris, although fortunately for me, everyone seemed convinced that luck alone had led me to Belle. Of course, I'd be lying if I didn't say I was annoyed that everyone (my mom included!) so readily believed that finding Belle had been nothing more than a fluke…but then again, that's what I'd told the press after it happened. And continuing with that pretense made sense. After all, the longer everyone continued to believe that Paris had been a one-time case of exceptional luck, the longer I could continue to work as an undercover model.

I kept this in mind when Trish and Tom arrived a minute later and tried asking me more questions. Again I answered as discreetly as I could and, lying through my teeth, clarified that I was in New York City purely to model.

Fortunately, between the *Chic* booking and the various castings I had coming up—which I made sure to mention—this was entirely believable. And Cazzie, taking her cue from me, helped to steer the conversation away from any detective talk. Soon everyone's focus was back on fashion—and the shoot of the day.

Cazzie thanked everyone for coming to the studio to shoot a last-minute *Chic* editorial. "I'm sorry, but as you know, some of the Paris dresses we'd planned on shooting last Friday didn't make it to the studio in time, and we'd love to have them in the magazine. So as soon as I saw that they'd finally arrived, I booked us back in here. I really appreciate you all juggling your schedules for this. Hopefully we'll get a great editorial story—and maybe even another cover for the next edition—out of our work today."

The part about the dresses coming in late from Paris was true—Cazzie had told me as much. But did *Chic* really need to photograph the dresses with the same group of people? No—Cazzie could have booked any photographer and model she wanted. It was just a seren-dipitous excuse to gather Friday's group together again for my sleuthing benefit.

Within minutes, Tom started working on Rafaela, while Trish began putting makeup on Chandra (who'd just arrived on an early-morning flight from Miami). Cazzie led Misty and me to the curtained-off dressing area—but not before I loaded a plate at the buffet table with croissants, fresh fruit, and an enormous banana muffin.

I followed Cazzie as she pushed past the linen cur-tain that acted as a room divider. As the plans showed, the dressing area formed the shorter section of the large L-shaped studio. To the right as you walked in, a lightweight but opaque fabric blind was stretched across the large east-facing windows, providing cover for the models who were changing clothes. Under the windows was a long trestle table for the stylists' equip-ment and accessories.

Opposite the windows—immediately on my left as I walked past the dividing curtain—a full-length mirror was mounted directly onto the wall. And next to the mirror was another, smaller trestle table. Cazzie indicated that I could use this one too. I set my shoulder bag down on the table next to hers. On the far corner of the same table, conveniently within reach of the clothes racks that stood against the far wall, sat the steam iron for taking the wrinkles out of the garments.

Cazzie wanted us to try on a few outfits and walked to the clothes racks to choose them. *Good*, I thought, *this is my moment to get started by asking Misty some questions*. Although starting a conversation wouldn't necessarily be easy. So far she couldn't seem to draw her eyes away from her own image in the mirror.

Misty's skin reminded me of the alabaster urns we had in our living room at home: smooth, white, and cool. Her movements were measured and poised, and even without makeup and with her long, wavy, blond hair falling naturally, she was mesmerizing to watch—just how you'd imagine a screen star from an earlier era to look. I could understand why she was being predicted as a natural for film. In fact, I knew from my online research that she was about to start acting in her first movie role.

I moved closer to her and finally asked, "How was the shoot last Friday? Cazzie told me a little about it. She said the photos look great."

Misty turned her blue eyes to me and shrugged her shoulders. "If they really looked good, we wouldn't be here reshooting," she answered.

"That's not true, Misty," Cazzie interjected as she brushed some lint off a jacket. "This isn't a reshoot. Friday's shots really *do* look good—but as I explained earlier, we felt strongly about also doing an editorial with the Paris fashion show dresses that arrived late. If they'd arrived sooner, we would have shot them on Friday. But shooting them today works out well anyway—it allows us to do totally different hair and makeup."

Cazzie's excuse for gathering all of us together sounded so convincing that I was beginning to believe it myself.

"We're going to do six shots today—and another cover try," Cazzie continued as she looked right at me.

Cover try? Why was she looking at me as she said that? I wasn't supposed to be in the cover try, was I?

Cazzie saw my panic and laughed. "Don't worry, Axelle. You won't be in the cover shot. Surely Pat said you'd be doing our 'Style for Less' section."

I nodded. She had—but I'd forgotten.

"You'll be doing three shots, and although these pages go near the front of the magazine, we keep the text to a minimum and each shot gets a full page—so you'll definitely get something for your book out of it. The pages usually end up looking like they could have come from the back of the magazine."

Ellie had told me that magazines often booked new girls they liked for their "Style for Less" pages to try them out. If a magazine was happy with the results, that could lead to the model being booked for the prestigious editorial stories at the back of the magazine.

I turned back to Misty, ready to try again with my questioning, but just as I started to speak, she put her headphones into her ears and said, "I have to listen to my music now. We'll talk more later." Then she sauntered out with a wiggle of her hips.

Cazzie shook her head. "Don't worry about Misty," she said. "She's always been like that—self-obsessed. And I think it's become worse with her film career taking off. Although," Cazzie continued as she peeked out through the gap between the wall and the hanging divider curtain, "it could be that she just wanted to talk to a certain someone."

I looked out through the same sliver of space as Cazzie and watched as Misty sauntered toward Brandon. At least I presumed it must be him—he was the only one I hadn't met properly yet. Judging from his profile and tall build, he was as good-looking as Cazzie had said he was. He'd been busy setting up the lighting when I walked in.

"It seems she's still after him."

"Have they been together?"

Cazzie nodded. "Briefly, a few months ago. Brandon put an end to it, but Misty still likes him—so they say. And by the looks of it, that may be true. Anyway, I'll call her back in a few minutes to try on some things. I'll start with you instead, Axelle."

I turned and followed Cazzie back to the clothes racks. We were alone now, so as I started changing out of my clothes, I asked her to show me where she'd kept the diamond during Friday's shoot.

"Actually," she said, "I kept the diamond in the Juice safe downstairs until we needed it. I felt secure knowing it was there. We're hardly the first magazine or client to have brought a valuable jewel onto the premises, and the safe is there for that purpose. Plus I had Ira outside in my car. I'd asked him to keep an eye open for any suspicious-looking characters going in or out of the studios, just in case. I didn't mention the diamond to him, though—and he didn't ask any questions. So I felt totally secure about keeping the diamond downstairs.

"Anyway, we didn't shoot the diamond until after lunch—it was the last shot of the day. Just before the girls went on set, I ran down and fetched it." She nodded toward the studio door. "Nobody came with me, and nobody knew where I'd gone—except possibly Peter. He must have guessed. But like I said yesterday, apart from Peter, none of the others knew that we'd be shooting such a large and famous diamond."

"Speaking of which," I said, "didn't anyone ask any questions about the diamond once you brought it on set and they had a chance to see it?"

Cazzie nodded. "Absolutely. Especially Rafaela. She's very into jewelry. If you check out her Instagram account, you'll notice that at once. I remember that

Misty wanted to try it on. But Chandra isn't so into that sort of thing. She thought it was nice but really didn't pay much attention to it. Peter and Brandon thought it looked amazing—which it does—and were eager to see it on set under the lighting they'd set up. Tom thought it could make a good hair ornament—he would. And Trish was only concerned with doing up Chandra's hand. You remember how the diamond is set in a hand chain?"

I nodded.

"Trish had to apply makeup to Chandra's hand to even out her skin tone—although we didn't cover her wrist tattoo. I liked the contrast between that and the diamond."

"And did you say anything about how much it's worth? Or who it belongs to? Anything like that?"

Cazzie nodded. "Yes, stupidly I did. I'm kicking myself about it now, but at the time I really didn't give it any thought. Again, I was working with a group of people I know well—and like. I didn't spell things out for them in terms of the Black Amelia's value, but we did talk about how much it *might* be worth, and, yes, Noah and Vanessa Tindle's names were mentioned." She paused for a moment.

"And I did mention that I'd been personally entrusted with the diamond." She winced as she said it. "Interestingly, considering I've only ever seen him wear beads, Tom was the only one who knew anything about the diamond—or at least he was the only one who openly said that he remembered reading something about it in some magazine article. He told us a bit about its past."

"So the diamond was in the safe until you ran down to fetch it after lunch?"

Cazzie nodded. "Although, actually, it wasn't directly after lunch. First Trish and Tom retouched the makeup and hair, and then I got the girls dressed. Then I went down. It was at around 3:00 p.m."

"And then?"

"I came back up here with it in my handbag. That one," she said, pointing to her Mulberry satchel bag sitting on the trestle table next to mine. "I came straight back in here with my handbag, and then I took out the diamond—it was wrapped in a velvet pouch inside a clasped box. It's a custom-made leather case—easy to open—and the diamond slid right out of the velvet pouch into my hand. I called Chandra to me and fastened it onto her hand. We stood exactly where you and I are standing now."

"And then Chandra went out on set wearing the Black Amelia?"

"Yes. And we took the photos."

"And then you put it back into the safe?"

Cazzie wrinkled her brow. "No…I was going to, but after I took it off Chandra's hand, Rafaela wanted to quickly try it on, and I let her. Then I removed it from her hand and slipped it back into the velvet pouch and then into the case. I put it in my handbag because I intended to go straight back downstairs and put it back in the safe. But then I stopped at Brandon's computer. Peter and Brandon were looking at the shot we'd just done, and I wanted to have a quick peek..."

"And during all of this, you're sure your handbag didn't leave your arm?"

Cazzie nodded. "Positive."

"And did anyone see you put the diamond in your bag?"

"Well, Chandra and Rafaela, obviously. Misty too. I'm not sure how much the others saw, but theoretically any of them could have seen me slip the diamond into my handbag."

"And did anyone get close to your handbag at this time?"

Cazzie shook her head.

"So after taking a quick peek at the shot you'd just done, you took the diamond back to the safe downstairs?"

Cazzie shook her head. "That had been my intention, but as I turned to leave, I smelled something burning and thought it was the iron—we leave the iron on all day for freshening up the clothes you girls wear. Anyway, I ran in here to check, but it wasn't the iron. It was a fire."

"A *fire*?"

She nodded. "There was a fire in the building next door. Suddenly we heard an alarm going off, followed a few minutes later by police and fire sirens. I tell you, it really made us jump, because this corner of the city is always so quiet. Nothing ever happens here."

"Hmm… Well, I want to hear about the fire, but first let's backtrack a bit. What did you do with your handbag when you dashed in here to check the iron?"

"I set it down there. Just as it is now." Cazzie pointed to the far corner of the small trestle table that was against the left-hand wall of the dressing area. "On Friday, like today, I also had the iron set up on that corner of the table. My handbag was literally right next to me as I checked on the iron."

"So no one could have tampered with it while you were in here?"

"No way. Impossible. No one came near it."

"Right. So you dash in, set your handbag down, and check on the iron, which is okay. And then?"

She paused for a moment as if rewinding the event in her mind. "And then, as I was turning the iron off, the fire alarm rang."

"And what did you do when the fire alarm rang?"

"I ran to the windows to see what was going on," she said, pointing back into the main studio beyond the curtain divider.

"What? You didn't look out of these?" I pointed to the windows just opposite where we stood.

Cazzie shook her head. "Those blinds are fixed. The owners of the studios don't want to take any risk of having models 'unintentionally' photographed from one of the neighboring buildings. So I went back out into the studio area."

"Right. So you left the dressing area to look out the windows of the studio, leaving your handbag—with the diamond in it—on the trestle table?"

"Yes."

"And what did you see from the windows?"

"The firefighters were busy battling the flames in the building next door. People were evacuating it, and we saw someone being wheeled into an ambulance. We wondered whether we'd be evacuated from the studios too, but they called from downstairs to say that the fire was well contained and under control. We didn't have to worry."

"So while you were standing at the windows you wouldn't have noticed anyone come into the dressing area after the alarm went off?"

She shook her head. "I feel like such an idiot. But there really wouldn't have been much time for anyone to come in here and take the diamond from my bag. And while we didn't all run to look out of the windows at the same time, I think I remember everyone being there together in the end."

"Was the curtain drawn across the dressing area like it is now?"

"Yes, it was. That much I'm sure of. It was pulled closed the whole day for privacy. We pushed the folds aside a bit to come in and out—like we did just now when we came in."

"And how long after the alarm rang did you come back here to fetch your handbag?"

"About five minutes later, I'd guess. Like I said, there wouldn't have been much time for someone to come in here and take it."

"And when you came back, did you check to see if the diamond was still in your handbag?"

"Sort of… I did have a quick glance in my handbag, and I thought I saw the diamond's box, so I didn't look further. And from that moment on, I kept my handbag on my arm. It didn't seem necessary to take the diamond back to the safe anymore because everyone was getting ready to leave.

"We'd finished for the day, and we were all a little distracted and restless after the fire scare. The girls quickly changed into their own clothes, and Peter and Brandon packed up their equipment. Trish and Tom did too—and Chandra very sweetly helped me pack up the outfits. Then one by one, everyone left. By four thirty, I was the only one here."

What she'd told me yesterday about how she'd searched the studio after everyone left now came to mind. I imagined Cazzie here alone, looking for the diamond as the cleaners worked around her.

"So let me backtrack again. When you came back here after looking out the studio windows, you thought you saw the diamond's box in your handbag."

Cazzie nodded. "Yes, but I only saw the corner... It wasn't until after everyone had left and I took the box out of my handbag that I realized it was actually the case for my sunglasses—they look so similar!" Her voice started to sound panicked just talking about it. "I was sick to my stomach—especially as I realized that the diamond must have been stolen in those few minutes when we were all looking out the window. At least that's what *I* think... What about you?"

I bit into my croissant and considered, while Cazzie took a long breath. "It certainly does seem that way," I agreed after a moment.

"Does knowing that help a lot?" she asked.

"Well, everything helps one way or another," I said with more optimism than I felt. "At least we've narrowed down the time frame for the theft. That's something."

But now I'd have to account for everyone's time for those crucial five minutes...and somehow I'd have to do it without arousing any undue suspicion. *Easier said than done*, I thought as I pushed past the curtain divider, aiming to start with hair and makeup.

But as I stepped out into the studio, I was met by a smiling Brandon. He really was gorgeous. And he had a light meter in his hand.

"Hi, I'm Brandon," he said as I stood there, mouth open—and probably with croissant crumbs stuck to my lips.

"And I'm Axelle," I said, pulling myself together and shaking his hand.

Brandon Hart was tall, dark, and handsome. With his chiseled chin and cheekbones, long brown-black hair, and warm, laid-back style, he looked more like a Hollywood actor than a computer geek. As the digi-tech guy, it was his job to import the photos taken by the photographer to his computer and then adjust the shots' color, exposure, and so on, in real time in the studio. (Although Brandon was so good that he also did Peter's post-editing of the images after the shoot.)

He was wearing jeans and scruffy sneakers, topped off with a white shirt and a well-worn aubergine-colored velvet jacket. A large sports watch peeked out from under his jacket cuff. He must have known he turned heads, and yet he seemed totally indifferent—careless, even—of his looks. His easy manner was natural, and when he spoke to you, his chocolate-brown eyes were intense but warm. Basically, Brandon was super-cool.

I glanced at Tom and Trish, but they were still working on Chandra and Rafaela. Misty was sitting next to them, tuned out, earbuds in. I did see her turn her head slightly and look at Brandon and me as we spoke, but she turned away when I caught her eye. Peter was doing light checks at the other end of the studio, and Cazzie had followed behind me with the clothes she'd selected.

I was about to ask Brandon about the fire last Friday when he beat me to it with a comment of his own.

"Peter wants to think that you're here to solve a case.

He says it would make a great fashion story—trench coats and trilbies." He was smiling. "But I told him it couldn't be true—because detectives are generally about fifty and bald."

I rolled my eyes. "If Peter took a look at my modeling schedule, he'd see that solving any kind of mystery will be impossible for me. I'm going to be crisscrossing town all week."

Brandon laughed. "I'll tell him that." He continued to look at me through his thick lashes, his dark eyes friendly and warm. "And will you be doing many of the shows?"

"Well, I have a lot of options and fittings sched-uled at the moment. Let's see how many of them confirm." Out of the corner of my eye I saw Misty watching us again.

"And have you been to the Big Apple before?"

I nodded. "Twice—with my parents. The last time was some years ago."

"Well, do you think you'd—" But Brandon didn't get a chance to finish his question, because at that moment Tom called over and waved at me. It was time to start with my hair.

* * *

The next hour flew by under a cloud of hair spray. I was asking so many questions that Tom finally said, "Axelle, your mouth has been open since you sat down. If you keep going like this, by the end of the day you'll have as much hair spray in your mouth as you have on your hair." He had a point, but I'd gathered loads of information *and* managed to discreetly record it on my phone.

Not that it all had any direct bearing on the case. I was too concerned about arousing suspicion to ask specific questions about last Friday. But at the very least, the snippets I'd gleaned from Tom and Trish added a couple more time-and-place details to what little information I had concerning the shoot.

One potentially important detail was that Peter and Brandon seemed to have their backs to the dressing area during the crucial few minutes when I believed the diamond was stolen. They were seated at Brandon's computer editing the photos they'd taken and only got up to look out the windows after the others repeatedly called them over to watch the action below.

Trish and Tom told me about the person they'd seen being wheeled into the ambulance—an old lady, apparently. And while I didn't think that had any direct relevance to the case, it gave me a useful reference point. Finding out if the others had noticed her would tell me when or if they were at the window. Fortunately, it was an unusual enough occurrence that anyone who *had* been looking out the window when the fire alarm went off couldn't have failed to notice it.

Trish and Tom's chatter also added much-needed

nuances to the character sketches Cazzie had prepared for me. And that was important. As my grandma liked to say, "Observation is key. Your grandfather would repeat that to himself whenever he was stymied by a case." (He was a detective with Scotland Yard.) "Remember, Axelle: the most minute detail can sometimes lead you to the biggest clue." In other words, don't ignore the small stuff.

✳ ✳ ✳

My hair and makeup finished, I went back into the dressing area. Chandra was there and seemed to be searching her iPad for something. Her tousled mane, sun-streaked from surfing, had a controlled wildness to it. Apparently that look was Tom's specialty. Rafaela was strutting around the dressing room too. She still hadn't changed out of her own clothes, and her lithe figure was encased in black leather. Her long, dark hair had been straightened flat and moved silkily at the slightest provocation. Both were waiting for Cazzie, who was bent over Brandon's laptop in the main studio near the set, checking the lighting with Peter.

"Hey, how lucky were you last week? Finding Belle and all?" Rafaela greeted me. "That must have been exciting. Maybe you should be a detective."

I pretended to laugh off her comment and then said something about how fab the studio space was in an attempt to distract her.

There was something wild about Rafaela, I decided as we chatted. Being with her was like being with a talking tiger. She had the tawny feline eyes, high cheekbones, and easy movement of a big cat—only instead of stripes, she had tattoos. I tried counting them as she asked me about finding Belle La Lune, but I gave up when I reached number eight. Then I quickly brought the conversation around to the safer subject of the Paris shows. Both Chandra and Rafaela had been there. In fact, all three of us had done the Lanvin and Chanel shows, though I'd been so busy trying to find Belle that I hadn't noticed them, beyond passing them once or twice on the runway.

Chandra seemed tired, and unlike Rafaela, she was clearly reluctant to chitchat. Then again, she'd flown in from Miami early this morning. She sat quietly in a chair, iPad still in hand.

Without making much of an effort, I managed to get Rafaela onto the subject of the fire alarm, and she readily answered my questions. When the alarm's wail had pierced the air, Rafaela had apparently been sitting in the studio while Trish applied makeup to her eyelids.

"At first I thought, *Cool, something interesting is finally happening around here*. But it was just an old lady who'd had a heart attack and some fire that wasn't even burning anymore."

Ignoring that, I asked, "But weren't you scared when the alarm first went off? I would have jumped."

She shrugged her shoulders. "All I saw was darkness," she said mysteriously.

"*Darkness?*"

Rafaela slapped her black leather trousers as she laughed. "Ha! Got you, Ms. Detective! Of course I saw darkness. Didn't I just say that Trish was retouching my eyelids? That means my eyes were closed!"

Very funny.

"Right. One–zero to Cuba," I said.

"Hey, you're funny too." She laughed.

Luckily Cazzie came in at that moment to start dressing Rafaela. Which meant that I could turn my attention to Chandra. She was wearing what must have been a pair of her boyfriend's jeans, cinched at the waist with a military belt and worn with a tiny, white T-shirt under a red-and-black-plaid flannel shirt and black Dr. Martens. She was dressed halfway between Miley Cyrus and a lumberjack.

She also wore a ring on her right thumb and a few fine gold chains. The boyish clothing, however, did nothing to disguise her natural femininity. In fact, the clothes emphasized it. I noticed that on the inside of her forearm she had a small dolphin tattoo.

"Hi," she said with a yawn as I sat next to her. She reached her long arms up and stretched, her thick hair brushing her shoulders.

I was trying to figure out how best to ask her about Friday, but she wasn't giving me any openings. Apart from saying hi, she kept her nose buried in her iPad. I watched as she scrolled through photos that contained a lot of blue—blue ocean, blue sky—and was reminded that she'd taken half a year off from modeling to sail.

Was she willfully ignoring me or just tired? I couldn't decide. There didn't seem to be any way to easily broach the subject of last Friday, and I was about to give up when something Cazzie had said earlier sprang to mind.

"Chandra," I said, "Cazzie mentioned that you helped her pack up last Friday after the shoot. She thought that was really nice of you…and, well, I hope you don't mind me asking, but I'm just starting out, as you know, so… Is that something you do often? Help pack up, I mean. Like, is that something I should do too?"

After a moment Chandra looked up from her iPad, mild irritation registering in her gray eyes. "No, it's not something I normally do. I offered to help Cazzie because she was working alone. It's not something we're expected to do—ever. That's for the stylists and editors to do."

Silently she scrolled through some more photos, then looked back up at me and said, "Axelle, I'm happy to talk about sailing or surfing, but I get bored—*really* bored—talking about modeling, okay?" Then she abruptly got up and went over to Cazzie.

I'd known, of course, that models never usually help pack up the clothes used on a shoot. That would be like a dentist offering to drive you home after an appointment. It doesn't work that way. I'd just wanted to know how she'd answer.

And her answer was interesting...

***

While Misty, Rafaela, and Chandra were on set, Cazzie helped me into my outfit, and then Trish and Tom retouched my hair and makeup. Ironically, I was wearing a high-street copy of one of the ensembles I'd worn for the Chanel show in Paris last week. After the other girls filed off set, I went on. Peter shot quickly, and he wanted me to be still—which suited my purposes because it allowed me to reflect on what I'd learned so far.

As I stood on set posing, I thought about how the studio atmosphere had gradually become mysteriously charged over the last few hours. It gave the situation an added edge that seemed to focus me. As I rewound the interviews in my mind, I was particularly aware of the little clues in the way everyone had responded, like a change of vocal tone or what they'd been looking at when they answered.

I felt convinced that with so small a space and so few suspects, this case would boil down to some minute detail. And sure enough, certain patterns began to emerge. It was like panning for gold in a stream. At last, after all the dirt and bits of stone had been rinsed through the sieve, a few tiny gold nuggets were left.

Now I just had to make sense of them.

"That's beautiful, Axelle, beautiful," Peter yelled. "I love your range of expressions! Great! You've gone from pensive to optimistic—and even surprised—with such truth! Beautiful!"

If only he knew, I thought.

Five minutes later, I was finished with my shot. Freshly changed into new outfits, Misty, Chandra, and Rafaela went back on set for their next shot. Trish had made the girls' skin the standout feature this time. They glistened with dewiness and wore little eye makeup and lipstick. The quiet sophistication of the makeup, together with the hair Tom had styled for them—wild, textured, undone—made them look ethereal and otherworldly.

It was especially amusing to see Rafaela and Chandra like this. With their tattoos hidden under rich fabrics and their innate elegance drawn out, they were hard to recognize as the wisecracking and reluctant models of earlier. Their fairy-tale dresses and commanding beauty were set off perfectly by Peter's beautifully lit, dark gray background.

After watching for a few minutes, I walked to the other end of the studio, sank down onto the sofa, and thought about all I'd heard so far. I was feeling optimistic. I glanced at Cazzie's sleep-deprived face and even ventured to think that I'd have good news for her soon. But at that moment we were called to lunch, and while we ate, two things happened that completely erased my feelings of optimism.

A colorful and varied assortment of salads was laid out on the lunch table. We all sat down (I was between Brandon and Peter), and within seconds, everyone seemed to be chatting, fashion being the main talking point, of course. In between the comments and laughter, however, everyone—including myself—checked their emails, messages, and texts, or got up to make calls. At any given moment, half the table seemed immersed in some kind of gadget—which was not unusual. It was only later that I was forced to give that some thought.

Lunch progressed smoothly, apart from Misty giving me some pouty looks (why?) and Chandra seemingly trying *not* to make eye contact with me (why?). Before sitting down, I'd quickly pulled Cazzie aside and whispered that any help she could give in directing the conversation to Friday afternoon would be useful. True to her word, she repeatedly, yet subtly brought the conversation around to when the fire alarm had gone off. Under Cazzie's guidance, everyone—even finally Misty and Chandra—contributed to my knowledge of Friday's events.

Of course, not everybody's time was perfectly accounted for during those five minutes or so when Cazzie's bag was left unattended in the dressing area. A few of the suspects even had relatively vague recollections of that time. Apart from remembering that they'd dashed to the east-facing windows of the studio area to see what was happening below, not all could recall what they'd been doing immediately before the alarm rang, or whether they'd been one of the first or last to reach the windows, or even who'd been standing next to them at the windows. Speaking of which, one small but not uninteresting point came up. Chandra was the only person who did not mention seeing the little old lady being wheeled into the ambulance. Had she simply forgotten?

All through lunch I kept my phone on my lap so that I could quickly turn the recording function on. By the time we reached dessert, I felt I had a good idea of everyone's whereabouts during those crucial five minutes when Cazzie had left her handbag unattended in the dressing area.

When the conversation didn't focus on Friday's events, Brandon, Peter, and Cazzie shared funny anecdotes about their time working with each other. Brandon was a good mimic, and his impressions had everyone in stitches. Finally, with Cazzie and Peter deep in discussion about the next shots and everyone else otherwise engaged, Brandon turned to me as I sat watching the others.

"I'm not sure I believe your denials from this morning. Are you sure you're not here to solve a case? You've been watching everyone all through lunch, observing us as if we're characters in a crime drama."

"No, I haven't!" I laughed, trying to make light of what he'd said. *Not good, Axelle*, I thought to myself. Had I really been so obvious?

"Do you always contradict people?" he asked, amused.

"No, I don't."

"But you just did it again," he said as he leaned into me, dark eyes smiling.

He was right, and I couldn't help smiling back—this time genuinely. "Maybe what you take for a contradiction is simply the truth."

"Not bad." He pushed his thick, nearly black hair off his face with one swift movement and smiled. "I'll accept that."

Misty suddenly called to Brandon from across the table, asking him about his photography. (During lunch he'd told me that he took photos too.) He tried to ignore her, but she only called his name out again—louder. I felt him tense up. He told her that he'd be with her in a minute, and then he turned back to me.

"I was wondering if you'd..." He stopped to fiddle with his jacket cuff. Then he turned his coffee-colored eyes back to me and simply gazed at me for a moment, that smile still tugging at the corners of his lips.

I swallowed hard. The way he was looking at me was raising a lot of questions. Was he on the verge of asking me out on a date? Or was it simply something work-related? He'd been about to ask me something this morning too, so whatever it was, it had to be that, right? Or...?

But once again, he didn't get any further, because at that moment two slim hands, their short nails painted glossy black, placed themselves on his shoulders. It was Misty. And while she seemed quite breezy and light in her manner, I could feel the tension between her and Brandon. Her beauty was dazzling, I thought as I watched her chat with him. Her full lips and slim neck, her heart-shaped face crowned by a mass of golden hair.

But the longer she stayed, the angrier Brandon seemed to become. After a minute, his fists were clenched tightly by his sides. Why? She was only asking him about his photography… Or was something else creating the tension?

Whatever Brandon had been about to ask me was quickly forgotten.

A few moments later, I was called back to Trish and Tom's area. They wanted to quickly refresh my hair and makeup before they started getting Misty, Rafaela, and Chandra ready for their cover try. Before leaving the lunch table, however, I quickly checked my emails and found the following:

> *You're getting in the way. I know you know what I mean—even though you're trying to hide it.*
> *Pull back now.*
>
> *From someone who's watching you.*

I felt a creepy shiver run through me as I read it. The likelihood that someone there had sent me this email during our lunch was unnerving, to say the least. I was clearly being warned off the case, and presumably by the person who had the diamond. I didn't recognize the address it had been sent from. In fact, it wasn't even a proper name—just a short sequence of numbers and letters. I quickly replied, but whoever had sent the message had already closed the account. My email was unable to be delivered.

Funny how whoever it was had sent me an email, but they'd sent Cazzie text messages. Then again, maybe they didn't want us thinking they were one and the same person… But how did they even know she'd asked me to find the diamond? Or had my lunchtime observations been as obvious to everyone as they'd been to Brandon? If the thief was indeed present, maybe the news of my sleuthing in Paris, coupled with my sudden presence here, had been enough for them to guess the truth. In that case, the thief could be fairly certain that I was working for Cazzie. Again, a shiver ran through me.

I briefly wondered how they'd found my email address. But if they were able to open an unrecognizable email account and shut it down that quickly, getting hold of my email address wouldn't be much of a challenge.

Thoughts were still whizzing through my mind as Tom and Trish tweaked my hair and makeup, and then suddenly Cazzie was in front of me. "Axelle," she said, "I have to dress you for your next shot. Peter is getting ready."

Carina Axelsson

Composing myself—the last thing I wanted was for whoever had sent the email to see me looking scared—I got up and walked with her back to the empty dressing area. As soon as we were safely behind the curtain, she whispered, "Axelle, look. I've received another text…and it seems it's the first riddle."

> You are always making demands—unreasonable ones—so now it's my turn. You clearly don't realize how odious you are, holding people's lives in your hands and crushing them with a swift step of your stiletto. But soon you will.
> Time to begin your treasure hunt! Riddle number 1: There are two lions outside, but also one inside—and she has a certain allure. Find it and photograph it. I'll contact you by 6:30 p.m. If you haven't solved the riddle by then, your next one will be delayed by a day, which means that finding your treasure will be delayed too. You won't have much time but that, of course, is the point. Have fun!

While the texts could be read as a prelude to some kind of blackmail demand, revenge also seemed increasingly likely to be a major part of the plan. And, apparently, watching New York's top fashion editor sweat was a good place to start.

"I never should have touched that diamond," Cazzie hissed. "Never! With the commitments and schedule I have, how am I supposed to run around town chasing down the answers to the thief's riddles? But I can't delay finding the Black Amelia—I can't! I need to have the diamond in my hands by Friday when Noah comes back into town!"

"Cazzie," I said, trying to make her focus, "listen. Please stop. Right now you should just concentrate on finishing the shoot and keeping your ears and eyes open, okay? Let me answer these riddles. Just forward any texts to me as soon as you get them."

She nodded gratefully.

"Okay, I need to do my next two shots *now*," I told her. "I don't have a second to spare if I'm going to solve this riddle. Can you talk to Peter and the others for me? Maybe explain to them that Miriam's just called me and asked me to squeeze in a casting before my five-o'clock Jared Moor fitting? So they need to let me do my remaining two shots straight away."

Cazzie nodded and left. Meanwhile, I could barely concentrate. After reading her new text and my email, my mind was buzzing. But once Cazzie returned to the dressing room and helped me get ready, I somehow managed to go back out into the studio and do the photos. I was relieved when, three quarters of an hour later, Peter declared, "I have the shots. They look great!"

I quickly pulled my own clothes back on, then said good-bye to everyone. A claustrophobic creepiness crept over me as I left. The possibility that one of the people I'd just shaken hands with had sent Cazzie and me those threatening texts and email—and stolen the diamond—was disturbing.

Finally I stepped out of the Juice Studios building and into the fresh air. I let the wind ruffle my hair for a few moments and took a deep breath as I watched Ira sitting in Cazzie's car. He was reading the newspaper.

Fleetingly I wondered if he could be behind the diamond's disappearance. Or maybe an accomplice to it, at least? After all, he was privy to many of Cazzie's conversations and her daily schedule. And he had plenty of time to send texts and emails.

At that moment Ira saw me looking at him. He smiled from the car and gave me a thumbs-up. I waved back, then looked at my watch before my paranoia got the better of me. It was nearly half past two now. My next appointment was the casting at Jared Moor at 5 p.m. But first I was going to follow the directions from Cazzie's lunchtime text and see where they led. I had just over two and a half hours to myself.

Time, I told myself, to start connecting the dots.

Two Steps Forward, One Step Back

After a short subway ride uptown, I found myself standing on Fifth Avenue between Forty-First and Forty-Second Streets, right in front of the famous New York Public Library—the only building on the block.

The riddle spoke of "two lions outside." And while I didn't know much about NYC, I did know that the city had a famous pair of lions, Patience and Fortitude, and that these two stone giants lay on either side of the staircase leading up to the entrance of the iconic library. As a child, I could remember gazing up at them in awe when my mom brought me here to visit the library. Now the two lions guarding the imposing building seemed to gaze at me, their stony silence questioning my purpose in being here.

I had no idea if these were the lions that the riddle was referring to, but they seemed a good place to start. Especially because I didn't know of any other place in the city with two lions outside.

What really had me stumped, though, was the part about "a lion on the inside." What could that mean? *Well, Axelle, there's only one way to find out,* I told myself.

I ran up the wide stone stairs and under the impressive columned portico. Once I was in the vast library entrance hall, I gazed up at the stairways rising above me to my left and right, listening to voices echoing around the high marble ceiling. Farther along to my right stood a small stand serving beverages and snacks, and then the entrance to the library shop. Straight ahead, a large gallery space was filled with an exhibition on children's books, and on the left, corridors and stairs led to various galleries, archives, and reading rooms. But no lion—none that was obvious, anyway.

I randomly chose a flight of stairs and stopped at the first-floor landing, unsure of where to turn next. To my left, I saw a library assistant. I stopped and asked about a lion—a *female* lion, remembering the "she has a certain allure" part of the riddle.

"A lioness?" he asked as he scratched his head. "Well…I can't think of one really. I mean, we have souvenirs of our own famous lions, of course—like magnets and things—in the shop downstairs… But our lions are male lions, and you want a female, right?"

I nodded.

"Well, I'm afraid I can't help you, then—unless of course, you want to find books with images of lionesses. I could find plenty of those for you."

"I think it has something to do with fashion…"

The library assistant shook his head. "Then I'm afraid nothing springs to mind. But I'll be here a while longer, so if you have more questions…"

I nodded. "I'll find you, thank you."

I turned and thought about the riddle as I wandered through the building, but I still didn't see any lions, and the books I searched didn't help me either. Time was ticking quickly by. I now had only an hour until my appointment with Jared Moor. What lion—or lioness—could the thief possibly be referring to?

Argh!

I decided to step outside for a bit of fresh air, buying a bottle of juice from the snack stand on the way. I found a chair on the terrace outside, a stone's throw from the giant lions, sat down, and ran the riddle through my mind once more. I felt that both the riddle and its answer would probably be fashion-related, simply because the thief was in fashion (assuming that he or she was one of Friday's group). So who could I call? Who knew their fashion better than I did? I took a sip of my juice as I dialed the number of the most obvious choice. Not only was she *in* fashion, but she truly loved it. She was even something of an amateur expert with vintage couture.

"What's up, Axelle?" Ellie asked.

"I need your help."

"Go ahead. I'm just leaving a casting so I have the time."

"I know this sounds odd, but do you know of a famous female lion? One that probably has to do with fashion somehow?"

"A famous female lion? A lioness?"

"Uh-huh…"

"I can't think of one off the top of my head… Do you mean like a symbol or a real lion or what?"

"Right now, I think it's a lion that is probably in a book. Maybe a fashion book or something. Maybe a woman in fashion who kept lions?"

"I know that the famous muse the Marchesa Casati kept cheetahs…"

"No, I need a lioness. Or maybe a fashion designer who was nicknamed 'the lion.' Or maybe…" I trailed off. Something had just clicked in my head. It was the idea of a nickname… My granny had often read the daily horoscope to me, and the word "Leo" had just sprung into my mind. Leo was a sort of nickname for "lion." What if the lioness the riddle was referring to was a Leo? Like, born in August? Maybe a famous Leo working in fashion? Before I lost my train of thought, I asked Ellie whether she knew of a famous Leo designer or model who had "allure."

"Allure? That's an old-fashioned word, isn't it? So maybe an old designer… Hey, I have it!" she said excitedly. "The most famous Leo in the fashion world is Coco Chanel. She was born a Leo!"

"Perfect. Thanks, Ellie. I'll start there." I said goodbye and dashed back into the library to find the assistant. Within minutes I was standing between shelves full of books with an old, slim volume in my hands: *The Allure of Chanel* by Paul Morand.

I quickly posed the book on a shelf, face out, and

photographed it—and then I sent the picture to Cazzie so she'd have it ready when needed. A glance at my watch told me I had to go if I was going to get to my casting on time. I carefully replaced the book on its shelf and left. As I dashed under the stone portico and sprang down the entrance steps, I prayed that I'd found the right answer to the riddle.

I rushed out of the library and turned right, then right again onto Fortieth Street. Luckily for me, the Jared Moor design studio was less than ten blocks away, and with the way traffic was moving, walking definitely seemed faster than taking a taxi. My mind was still mulling over the first riddle, hoping I'd gotten it right. A wrong answer on my part would delay the return of the diamond—and that was a risk we couldn't afford. But my answer did seem to fit, so... *Time will tell, Axelle*, I told myself.

I rapidly wove my way through the crowds on the pavement and then sprinted across the street just as the cars came galloping past like a cavalry brigade setting off for battle. A thought that had started to form in my mind just before lunch at the studio once again started to bubble to the surface. But, just like at lunch, before I could finish thinking it through, my phone rang, and fashion intruded in the form of Pat Washington.

"Hi, Axelle. Are you on your way to Jared's? You have to be there in ten minutes."

"Yes—"

She cut me off. "Good, because punctuality is vital: V-I-T-A-L. Here at Miriam's, we don't give a hoot about any of that I'm-a-diva-model stuff. Anyway, I have good news!"

Great, I thought. The only thing that would constitute good news in Pat's eyes was exactly what I didn't need: more modeling work.

"You had a big ol' empty spot in your schedule for tomorrow morning…"

Yes, I thought, exactly the empty spot I had planned to fill with detective work.

"…which I've now filled with a test!"

Argh!

Now before you start thinking that Pat was referring to some kind of modeling test—with questions like "Which model was responsible for pulling fashion away from the grunge look of the 1990s?"—she wasn't.

What she meant by "test" was a photo test.

"We need to fill your book," Pat continued.

"Yeah, but I've got stuff I did last week in Paris coming out in French *Elle* and the La Lune advertising campaign—"

"Huh-hum," she coughed loudly. Even over the phone I could imagine her hand going up like the traffic police. "I know," she said, "and that's great. But it's not enough, and it sure isn't *soon* enough either. Tony Moreno, the photographer you're testing with tomorrow, is good, and what's more, these photos will be a strong contrast to what you've shot so far. They'll be natural, something that shows you as you are, not too much hair and makeup. Okay?" She didn't wait for me to answer before saying, "Good."

Great, I thought. *What will she think of next?*

A second later I found out. "And now for the second round of good news," she announced. "Miriam has just flown in from Paris and has arranged for you to accompany her to *Chic: New York*'s big sixtieth gala birthday bash—tonight! You'll leave her apartment together at quarter to eight. And Cazzie—as editor-in-chief, she's the hostess—is delighted you'll be going. You've really made a good impression on her!"

If only you knew, Pat.

"And no worries about the clothes or mask—"

"Mask?" I interrupted.

"Yes, *mask*. The theme of the party is *Bal Masqué au Printemps*. Something about re-creating the famous masked ball the magazine threw when they first launched. Anyway, Cazzie will send something up to Miriam's apartment for you to wear. I'm telling you, she likes you, girl. Okay? Good. So, look sharp tonight, Axelle. Everyone who's anyone in the fashion world will be there. And if you're not the hottest new thing in fashion by the end of this week, then my name's not Pat Washington!"

By the time I'd finished speaking with Pat, I was standing in front of the Jared Moor Building. Following the directions I'd been given, I went around the corner and in through the service entrance at the side. After signing in with security, I took the elevator up to the showroom space, where I was expected.

What then transpired was basically an echo of my experiences last week in Paris. I went in, said hello, changed into a dress, walked in it, said thank you and good-bye, and then left. If they liked the way I looked and walked in their clothes, I'd get booked.

Of course, it wasn't as dry an experience as I just described. I did chat a bit with the design team (they liked my DIY Converses), and I knew the other model at the casting from Paris. The atmosphere was good, with a lot of laughter and high spirits.

Jared himself was young, friendly, and relaxed, despite the frenzied activity going on around him. And dressed as he was—sneakers, black jeans, black T-shirt—he reminded me of what Ellie and I had talked about last night at dinner: the different style vibe between Parisian and NYC fashion.

Like she'd said, "New York fashion always feels minimal and sporty, and has a kind of edgy glamour. But that's the city; it's tough, fast, and fierce. I always feel like there's no time or need for ruffles in the Big Apple—unless, of course, you're Carolina Herrera. She can do a ruffle to die for."

As I eyed Jared Moor's clothes hanging on the racks at the back of the showroom space, I silently concurred with Ellie's musings. The solid-colored, bias-cut dresses and trouser suits hung languid and lean. No stylistic distraction marred their spare, minimal lines; no loud patterns or unnecessary details confused the eye; and yet the clothes had an edgy elegance that made you think they were the perfect thing to wear if you happened to be a pop star stepping out of your own private jet.

Ha! I thought. *I'm starting to sound like one of the fashionistas I'm always shaking my head at!*

Anyway, by the end of the casting I had a feeling I might get booked. Jared seemed to like my "tomboy vibe," as he put it.

As I dressed back into my own clothes, one small thing caught my eye. On the clothing rack next to me, a few of the outfits had tags dangling from them, signaling that they'd already been allocated to specific models to wear for the next day's show. Three of the names jumped out at me: Chandra, Misty, and Rafaela. If I was confirmed for tomorrow, I'd be walking down the runway with three of the Black Amelia suspects!

✳ ✳ ✳

It was six thirty by the time I stepped out of Jared Moor. Pat had told me Miriam wanted to leave her apartment at quarter to eight, so I had just enough time to get to her place and shower and change before heading off to the *Chic* party.

Checking my phone, I saw that I had several messages—including an email from Cazzie.

Hi Axelle,

I'm thrilled you'll be joining us tonight at Chic's birthday party. I'm only sorry I didn't think of it myself! As you know, my mind is not at its best right now. I hope to make it up to you with the dress and mask I've sent up to Miriam's. They should fit you perfectly—and both are spectacular.

Anyway, back to business. The next riddle follows, so your answer to the first riddle was clearly the right one, and the thief was amazed I had the answer so quickly. I have the feeling they are going to make the riddles more difficult as a consequence. I just hope we're doing the right thing. My nerves are frayed and I'm not sleeping. I pray this will all end well. Half the time I want to go to the police and just let them handle it, but then I remember that if I do that now, my career will be finished, over—not to mention the damage I'll do to Chic's reputation. So then I tell myself to just hold on, that we'll—you'll—solve this.

Cazzie x

P.S. All of Friday's group will be at the party tonight.

Then came the thief's message and the next riddle:

How lucky I was that you were stupid enough to bring
the diamond into the studio without security or a locked
box. Just a beautiful stone wrapped in an easily opened
case—in your handbag.

I suppose you trusted us all. But successful people like you
always think you have everything under control, don't you?

Your next riddle:

Donna Karan

Marc Jacobs

Céline

Rhymes with power. Find the…and photograph it. I'll text
you again at 9:30 p.m.

What kind of riddle was that? I thought, as I stared
at the tiny lit screen of my phone. At the rate I was
moving forward, I'd never find the diamond by Friday!
I pushed my phone to the bottom of my shoulder bag in
frustration, then started walking to the subway station
a few blocks away. I set off at a rapid pace and would
have been at the subway in five minutes—if I hadn't felt
I was being followed.

I stopped and quickly looked behind me, but I saw
nothing. And yet the hair on the back of my neck was
up on end. Was the email I'd received earlier making
me paranoid?

I was ready to believe so until I caught my reflection

in the glass frontage of a skyscraper. I was nearly at Times Square now, one of hundreds jostling for space on the pavement…and yet, amid the tumult, I caught sight of a flitting shape a little way behind me. Was it the thief? I stopped and turned, but they must have seen me notice them in the window. As I turned, they followed suit.

All I saw was a blur diving off to the side. I ran back and followed the shape into a button and ribbon shop—no surprise, really, as this was the Garment District. But the space ran all the way through to the other side of the block, where a second entrance gave access. The shop was crowded. I stood looking around, but I was too late.

"Are you looking for any particular kind of button, miss?" an elderly lady with purple hair asked me.

She'd caught me by surprise. I looked at her, my mouth momentarily unable to form words.

"Or ribbon, perhaps?"

"Oh, sorry, no…no, thank you," I finally sputtered. "Nothing for the moment, but thank you." I turned and left.

By the time I finally made it to the subway station, I was starting to feel like the whole case was slipping away from me.

✳ ✳ ✳

Miriam was waiting for me when I walked into her apartment. "*Ah! Ma petite Axelle!*" she said in that breathy, French way she had. "I am so happy you are here! I hope everything is going well," she continued as she hugged me, "and that you are able to put all that happened in Paris behind you." She stood back and, with her hands on my shoulders, held me at arm's length. "You look *très bien*. And Pat has told me that you are taking New York by a storm—although, of course, she doesn't know that your *Chic* shoot today was arranged for reasons other than pure modeling." She smiled as she said this last bit.

"But still, I'm sure Cazzie will use the photos. I've spoken with her and she is very pleased with them. Plus Jared Moor and DKNY have just confirmed—Pat called me a minute ago—and of course you're testing tomorrow with Tony Moreno, which is great. Plus it's looking good with Jorge Cruz and Diane von Furstenberg, and even The Isle is interested, so you'll certainly be busy."

Busy? So far my modeling schedule, which was not even the real reason I was here, was as jam-packed with fashion as a *Vogue* September issue.

We were in Miriam's kitchen now. She was pouring me a glass of juice. Nicolette passed by quickly with what was probably my dress for the evening. *Chic* was emblazoned on the gray and pink plastic sleeve protecting the garment.

Behind her followed Nick Farah, the hair and makeup artist Miriam had hired for the night. "For a gala event like tonight's, Axelle, *il n'est pas* possible that you'll leave my apartment without looking your best—so Nick will do your hair and makeup right after he's finished with me." Miriam arched one of her eyebrows at me when she saw me squirm, and her meaning was clear: fashion was the name of the game for this evening—no exceptions.

"And how is the case going?" she whispered. "It would be great if you could solve it."

"Well…it's more complicated than I thought it would be…"

"Ah! But most things in life are, you know," she said with a French shrug of her petite shoulders.

"Anyway, I'm digging around." *And trying to stay calm*, I thought, as I looked out the window, *even though I've had an email from someone who says they're watching me, and I'm being followed…*

I suddenly remembered the last riddle Cazzie had forwarded, and thinking that Miriam could help me with it, I pulled my phone out of my bag and showed it to her. "Cazzie received the first during lunch at our shoot today and this last one just as I stepped out of Jared Moor. I solved the first riddle, but the second one looks a bit trickier. Do you have any idea why Donna Karan, Marc Jacobs, and Céline are grouped together?"

She pursed her lips for about two seconds before answering. "Well, they belong to the same group… That's the main thing they have in common. Is that the sort of answer you're looking for?"

"The same group?"

"What I mean is, those three labels are owned by the same business group: LVMH. They are headquartered in Paris."

"And can you think of any other reason why those three labels would be grouped together? Like maybe something their designers have in common or something to do with a collection or something? And what about 'rhymes with power'? Any ideas about that?"

Miriam shrugged her shoulders. "I'm sure they have other things in common, if we looked...but the fact that they belong to the same business group is, in my opinion, the strongest link between them. Stylistically anyway, they are vastly different—I can't think of anything on that level. I'm sorry, *ma chérie*, but that is the best I can do for the moment.

"If I think of something else, I'll let you know. As for the 'rhymes with power' part of the riddle, I really have no idea what it could be about. Now, however, we have to get ready. The party starts soon, and besides, everyone from the shoot will be there." She raised her eyebrows before adding, "Who knows? The fashion gods might smile on you and help you find the thief."

I hoped she was right—I needed all the help I could get. I finished my glass of juice, then went to my room to get ready. The cloister-like quietness of Miriam's elegant apartment helped soothe me after a day of being pulled in so many directions. Then my phone beeped with the arrival of a new text message and I fished it back out of my bag. It was Ellie. She'd sent a couple of photos of herself so that I'd know what she looked like in her party outfit. **Or you'll never find me!** she'd written.

A quick look at the photos told me otherwise. Even wearing an über-glamorous floor-length, blue-sequined gown (**Tom Ford!** she'd written), she looked exactly like the Ellie I knew. The dress shimmered in the light and set off her long, honey-blond hair to perfection. As for a mask, her elaborate eye makeup was doubling as one. It looked amazing, and I wrote back to say so.

Ten minutes later, I stood in the glassed off shower area of Miriam's guest bathroom and aimed the water nozzle squarely onto my back between my shoulder blades. Then, after applying some yummy-smelling Kiehl's shampoo and conditioner to my hair (for shine and no frizz!), I relaxed as the hot water ran down my back. But after a minute my thoughts got the better of me and I began to write with my finger on the steamy glass:

Donna Karan
Marc Jacobs
Céline
Same French business group

Argh!

What was it Miriam had said?

HQ in Paris
Luxury group LVMH

Then I added:

Rhymes with power, find the...
    Flower
    Shower
    Cower
    Tower

And suddenly there it was among my steamy scribbles: the answer to the second riddle. *Find the tower and photograph it.* Surely that could only mean one thing: LVMH's NYC HQ.

The LVMH New York headquarters had to be a tower. After all, nearly every building in Manhattan was a skyscraper. So I just had to get a photograph of this one. Before nine thirty tonight. Tricky, maybe—what with the party going on—but not impossible.

As I turned the shower off and grabbed my bathrobe, the adrenaline from my little breakthrough quickly fizzled away. Someone definitely wanted to make Cazzie sweat, but knowing that didn't bring me any closer to knowing which of the group was behind the theft. And worse, whoever stole the diamond was so certain they wouldn't be found out that they were playing games with us! Not that their braggadocio was unfounded, I thought ruefully. From the little I'd managed to figure out so far, their confidence was well placed. They'd stolen the diamond with style.

As I padded along the corridor in my bathrobe and socks to Miriam's bathroom, where Nick was waiting for me, I let these thoughts wind through my mind, hoping to find the glimmer of a motive. Who was reckless enough to steal a famous diamond? And ambitious or angry enough to threaten one of the most powerful fashion editors in New York?

I would have to do more in-depth background checks. With a bit of luck, something might come up.

And if it doesn't, Axelle? After all, nothing has so far, has it? And time is running out...

I banished that last thought from my mind. I'd figure this case out, I told myself. One way or another, I'd solve it.

Makeup and Masks

M iriam and I left her apartment building promptly at quarter to eight. Miriam smelled like Paris, and her vintage cape was so voluminous that it was as if three, rather than two of us, were walking to her car. (Miriam had hired one to take us to and from the party.)

"Good evening, ladies," our driver said. Once Miriam and I (and her cape) were in the car, he continued. "According to the reports coming in from my colleagues, you ladies are going to one big party. *Chic* is pulling out all the stops. They also say it looks amazing on the inside. You're gonna have fun tonight."

It took us five minutes to cross Central Park. The party was being held on Manhattan's Upper East Side at the Metropolitan Museum of Art—otherwise known as the Met. And what our driver had said was confirmed as we pulled up to the monumental entrance of the museum. This was going to be one *big* party.

Under a covered walkway (in case of rain) constructed just for this evening, a wide red carpet lined the broad stone steps leading into the museum (the same steps made famous by Blair Waldorf and Serena van der Woodsen—at least I knew that much, thanks to Jenny). Dozens of paparazzi stood behind security ropes, their popping flashbulbs illuminating the darkness like fireworks. Unlike those celebrities who were so famous that even a mask couldn't disguise their star appeal, Miriam and I passed by unnoticed. I was thankful for the anonymity my mask afforded me. After all, my agenda for the evening was to do some unobtrusive observation—the suspects from the *Chic* shoot would all be there—and then, I hoped, leave early to answer the second riddle in good time.

But my plans ended up taking a very different turn.

* * *

I saw Ellie immediately; she was at the top of the steps having her photo taken. Having walked past the cameras undetected thus far, Miriam and I were recognized as we greeted Ellie. The three of us obliged the hollering photographers and stood together for a minute as the cameras popped all around us. But then Miriam was called away by a beauty editor from *Allure*, and Ellie and I went on without her.

As we entered the museum, my mouth fell open. The large entrance hall had been transformed into a Parisian boulevard! Old-fashioned streetlights towered over us, their large glass globes softly glowing with golden light, and large potted trees, their branches decorated with twinkling fairy lights, reminded me of the Champs Élysées at night (which I guess was the point).

Enormous urns of flowers—tulips, roses, and even sweet peas—stood on pedestals around the room, their fragrance wafting over the excited, buzzing guests, while "magazine vendors" wearing black berets, mustaches, and red handkerchiefs distributed the latest issue of *Chic* magazine among the colorful, noisy throng. Clearly, all of this was in reference to the magazine's Parisian roots.

"It looks magical, doesn't it? We could be back in Paris." Ellie smiled. Then, turning to me, she said, "And you look am-*a*-zing! I love the dress—whose is it?"

"*Chic*'s."

She rolled her eyes. "Duh. You know I mean which designer!"

I laughed. Fashionistas love to ask "Whose is it?" when they see you wearing something they like. The answer, of course, should be "mine"—because, hey, if I'm wearing it, the chances are I own it. Only fashionistas don't mean who *owns* it, but who *designed* it.

"It's Jared Moor," I told her with a smile. "But apparently it's a one-off for a *Chic* evening-wear editorial. Miriam said he doesn't usually use lace," I added as I looked down at it.

The dress was stunning. Dusty light pink—it was nearly nude—with long, sheer lace sleeves and lace panels at the back and front, it was like a romantic poem written in fabric.

"And I love, love, love your mask!" Ellie exclaimed.

"Mask" was actually a big word for the slip of lace that covered my eyes. Made of the same lace as the dress, it was delicate and surprisingly easy to see through. Simply tied at the back of my head, Zorro-style, it actually did look pretty cool.

And despite the fact that I'd felt resistance to Miriam's idea of having my hair and makeup done, as I glanced around the hall I was glad I'd listened. Everyone seemed to have made a huge effort to look their best. Happily for me, apart from pulling and twisting strands with his fingers while blasting them with his hair dryer, Nick had left my hair quite natural. And my makeup was lightly applied.

"You're sixteen—not sixty," Nick had said with a smile when I voiced my surprise. "And this is a gala event, not a photo shoot. At your age, you'd look ridiculous if I did anything more to you."

After hearing that, I'd leaned back in Miriam's armchair and relaxed while Nick finished up.

"And let's see your shoes," Ellie said.

I lifted the hem of my dress to reveal a pair of purple Converse sneakers—this pair covered in glitter-pen doodles I'd done myself. Needless to say, I'd been careful not to draw Miriam's attention to them.

Ellie laughed. "I've yet to see you wear heels off the runway!"

I shrugged my shoulders and smiled. "I never know if I may have to make a quick getaway."

"I'm not sure you could from here anyway. Too crowded," Ellie answered as she turned and pulled me away from the incoming fray—and right into Chandra and Rafaela.

I hardly recognized Chandra. She was supremely elegant in a black, strapless, clingy dress, the whole surfer-dudette look toned way down. Black tulle covered her face, and her hair was loose and sexy. And she didn't seem to recognize me. In total contrast to her reticence at the studio this morning, she enthusiastically greeted me as if she'd never met me—until I opened my mouth to respond. As soon as she heard my voice, she flushed before quickly turning all of her attention on Ellie. Either she didn't like me, I thought, or she had something to hide.

But I didn't have time to think any more about her reaction, because at that moment one of the "magazine vendors" bumped into me, knocking my little evening clutch out of my hand. His arm brushed mine as we both bent down to retrieve it, and then our eyes met and I realized…I knew him.

It was Sebastian!

To say I was surprised would be an understatement.

"You!" I hissed, furious and incredulous in equal measure.

"Shhh!"

"Don't tell me to shush! You're lucky I'm even saying that much to you."

"We have to talk," he said, as he pushed my clutch away from us and toward Chandra's feet. "I need to explain—"

"Would you stop pushing my bag away? And I thought I said I didn't want to talk to you anymore!"

"Yeah, but you didn't say anything about not *seeing* me." He was smiling in that amazing way he had. I felt my breath momentarily knocked out of me, but ignored it. *He thinks modeling is more important than your detective work—and he's become your mother's spy, Axelle. Remember?*

"Touché. Now would you give me back my bag?"

"Will you let me explain? I have a good—"

Rafaela cut him off as she swooped down with one of her toned arms and, laughing, plucked up my clutch. She handed it to me as I stood back up.

"You have to work on your selling technique, Mr. Magazine Vendor," she told Sebastian.

I watched him straighten up. He was wearing a beret, a false mustache, and a red handkerchief, and even had a baguette sticking out of his magazine bag. He laughingly told Rafaela she was right. Then, as he turned to leave, he brushed past me again and said, "I'll find you later."

"What makes you think I want you to?" I whispered.

"Have you solved the case yet?"

I glared at him briefly before pursing my lips. He never missed a beat.

"Well," he said with a smile, his light blue eyes teasing, "then you'll need all the help you can get."

Before I could say a word, he turned and left.

Grrr!

Ellie and the others were still chatting nearby. Rafaela was all gold and bold. With its cut-out panels, her dress seemed to be winning the "barely there" stakes for the evening. She turned to me again, a teasing look on her face.

"It's Sherlock Holmes! Better watch out, Chandra. You and I are under surveillance tonight!" She laughed. "I bet something's happened that you're not telling us about, Axelle. I wonder what it could be…"

Chandra rolled her eyes but nevertheless looked uncomfortable. Honestly, I was kind of freaked out by Rafaela talking as if she knew I was here for reasons other than modeling.

"Just kidding—but hey, seriously, you never know. The lights could go out, and suddenly a fashionista could be found dead! Was the outfit too tight? Or was there one calorie too many in the canapés? Or did a designer poison an editor for not featuring their clothes often enough?" She really seemed to find the scenario funny.

"You're being gruesome, Rafaela," Ellie said.

"Who's being gruesome?" A tall, dark-haired figure suddenly leaned into our group, making me turn.

"Is that you, Brandon?" Chandra asked.

He smiled and was about to answer when Misty came up behind him. "Yes, it's him. I offered to make him a mask, but he insisted on using one of the freebies. He should have listened to me. Now he looks like half the men here." She stopped abruptly, the corners of her mouth turned down. Brandon, meanwhile, said nothing, but I saw him take a deep breath.

What Cazzie had said this morning—that Brandon and Misty had been together for a short time, and that Misty still liked him despite Brandon ending it— seemed more obvious than ever. Misty seemed to follow him everywhere, even when participating in the biggest event of Fashion Week! At what point did too much attention become stalking? I wondered.

"You're wrong, Misty," Rafaela said. "He looks *better* than half the men here."

Brandon made a little bow in Rafaela's direction.

Before Misty got another petulant word in, Peter showed up with his camera in hand. He was in black tie, but unlike Brandon's, his mask was custom-made and dark red.

"So everyone will notice him, no doubt," Ellie whispered to me.

Peter photographed us from a few different angles before stopping to have a word.

"So, what's up? Have you seen how many stars are out tonight? Fashion, music, film, they're all here, and they look amazing—as do all of you," he added with a beaming smile. While he was talking, he was also looking at the photos he'd just taken and playing around with different editing features on the back of his camera.

"Peter, you're so good at doing your own editing that I don't know why you need me," Brandon teased.

"Ah! Because you're the master," Peter answered with a smile. "But now I have to move on. I promised Cazzie I'd get as many shots tonight as possible. Trust *Chic* to invite me to a party to work!" Then he winked and was gone.

The entrance hall was crowded now, and just when it seemed they couldn't fit anyone else in, the beret-wearing "magazine vendors" started motioning for us to move to the dinner tables. And although I made a point of not looking at any of them, Sebastian caught my eye—and he was talking to a model! Leggy and lean, she had her arm around his shoulder and he had his arm around her waist.

Ellie and I pulled away from the others, and I quickly told her about Sebastian. "Do you know who that is with him?" I asked as I pointed him out.

She nodded. "That's Cleo Martel. She's from here—a native New Yorker, I mean. I think she's with IMG. She's really nice. I had no idea she knew Sebastian, though…"

"That makes two of us."

Ellie smiled, her head tipped to one side. "I think you're a tiny bit jealous."

"No, I'm not. But he seems very friendly with Cleo."

"Axelle. You're jumping to conclusions again. Remember what you said about being a good detective?"

"Thanks again, Nancy Drew."

She shrugged her shoulders. "I'm just saying, you don't have all the evidence concerning Sebastian yet, do you?" I was thankful when she suddenly dropped the subject and said, "We have to find out where we're seated. Come on."

We wove our way through the fashionably dressed guests toward the "Parisian flower stall" to find our seating cards. It took a while, because every two steps someone called "Sweetie" or "Gorgeous" had to say hi to Ellie—who was also "Sweetie" or "Gorgeous"—but finally we reached a long table covered with a silk tablecloth striped in light gray and white. On the table were row upon row of alphabetized seating cards. We gave our names to one of the assistants and were handed our respective cards and gift bags.

"I'm at Table 5," Ellie said as she slipped her card into her tiny clutch bag.

I, meanwhile, peeked straight into my gift bag. It was full of luxury beauty goodies and fashionista essentials, like dry shampoo, moisturizers, and nail polish in the latest cool shades. Even a tiny, box-shaped evening clutch—or minaudìere as Ellie called it—was included and, of course, a special-edition issue of *Chic* magazine printed just for the party.

"And I'm at Table 21," I finally said after I'd closed my goody bag.

We wouldn't be anywhere near each other, so Ellie and I made plans to meet right after dinner and then parted ways.

Just as Ellie left, I felt a hand on my arm. It was Cazzie.

"Hi, Axelle. You look fab," she said. So did she. In her black Saint Laurent smoking dress, she looked like she was channeling a rock star—albeit an anxious one. The stress of her situation was clearly telling on her. Underneath her photo-ready makeup, her face looked pinched.

"How are you?" she asked. "I just wanted to quickly make sure you know what table you're seated at." Then, dropping her voice, she said, "Have you seen the others?"

I nodded. "The only ones I haven't seen are Trish and Tom."

"Don't worry, they're easy to recognize. Trish because of her red hair—it's loose—and Tom because he has the most outrageous scarf tied around his head—and he's wearing a poncho over his tuxedo."

I couldn't help but smile at the thought of that.

After a quick glance around us, she leaned close to my ear and whispered, "What about the second riddle?"

I motioned to her to follow me into a gallery that opened on our left. There we ducked behind a large bronze sculpture.

"I have it solved, I think… Now I just have to go and photograph it. The trouble is, when? The thief is going to call soon, so we're running out of time. But can I leave the dinner now? I'm afraid that'll draw attention to me and what I'm doing here. Maybe after dinner I can slip straight away? Or…" I'd just had an idea—one that would save us a lot of trouble—but I had to know something first. "Cazzie, do you trust Ira?"

"Ira? My driver?" Cazzie was clearly surprised by my question. "Yes…absolutely. Why? Do you need him for something?"

"I do—we do—if he's outside."

Cazzie nodded, and I quickly told her that he needed to go to the LVMH Tower and photograph it.

"No problem. I'll text him right away."

"And don't forget that he must send you the photo as soon as he's taken it."

She texted Ira and then looked at me, her eyes exhausted. "They really want to make me run, don't they? I wonder why. I wonder *who*…"

I shrugged my shoulders. "They're angry or bitter, most likely."

"But I don't understand it," she continued. "Everyone in that group is at the top of their game, or well on their way there."

"Yeah, well, for some people, that's clearly not enough. And you can't tell me the fashion business isn't cutthroat competitive, even on a good day. One day you're on top, the next you're not."

Cazzie looked at me, eyes wide, shoulders slumped.

"What else can I do? What if we don't have the diamond on Friday?"

"We will. Try to focus on the party now, and let me know when you receive the next text, okay?"

She nodded.

"Good." Despite my reassurances to Cazzie, I was feeling more uneasy with every passing hour. After all, she'd flown me out here and was depending on me to solve the case by Friday evening to save her job and reputation—and *Chic*'s—and I still had nothing solid to go on.

"The thief said they're going to send you another text at nine thirty tonight, right?" I asked as I had a new idea.

She nodded.

"Then could you do me a favor? When they text you, write back—"

Cazzie interrupted me to say that she'd tried doing that when she received the first one that morning. "But the account had already been closed."

"Yes—because you waited until you'd texted me, right? And you probably spent longer than you think rereading it and worrying about what to do." She nodded. "This time, answer back right away. Send a text with the photo. The thief is here, surrounded by people, so I doubt they'll get the chance to close the account immediately."

"I'm sure you're right. But what do I write?"

"Tell them again that you absolutely need to have the

diamond back in your hands by Friday night—no questions asked—or you'll have to call the police, no matter how much that will hurt your career or *Chic*'s reputation. And say that they'll surely be caught—in which case they won't be doing anything in the fashion world ever again. We need to make them a bit nervous too."

"Right," Cazzie said with a nod. "So either they give me the diamond back by Friday, or they risk having the police go after them."

"Exactly. And try to engage with them. Tease them or something. Tell them they're not very clever—that the riddles were totally basic fashionista knowledge, or something like that. Maybe if we can make them angry, they'll become careless with their answers and reveal more than they should."

"Fine. I'll do it. I'll write something now, in fact. Then I can copy and paste quickly later. I'll forward you the text right after I've answered."

✱ ✱ ✱

In the large space that was designated for our dining and later dancing, the Parisian boulevard theme had morphed into a Parisian garden theme—or, more specifically, the famous rose garden at the Parc de Bagatelle in the Bois de Boulogne Parc in Paris.

Lush columns of cascading pink roses grew from the floor, and overhead thousands of twinkling lights created a starry summer sky. Blue silk lined the walls, enhancing the feeling of a garden at twilight, while the pale green tablecloths shimmered like freshly mown grass in moonlight. While waiting for everyone to take their seats, I scanned the crowd for signs of Trish or Tom or the others, but I didn't see any of them.

Finally dinner started and, considering that four courses were served and two speeches given—one by Sid Clifton, the other by Cazzie—dinner went smoothly and surprisingly rapidly. Then again, with New York Fashion Week about to kick off tomorrow morning, tonight's event wasn't expected to go too late.

Miriam sat opposite me, and the rest of our table was comprised of a *Teen Vogue* editor (who'd started at *Chic*), a buyer for the famous NYC department store Barney's, an accessories design assistant for Ralph Lauren, a model I recognized from Paris last week, and other professionals from Prada, Dior, and Sergio Rossi.

I drifted in and out of the conversations going on around me, offering comments when I needed to, and smiling and nodding to my left and right. But something I'd heard between the first and second courses had caught my ear: "*...they were all so engrossed with finishing the top of the dress that I was able to quickly add my own little flourish to the skirt without anyone noticing, really. When they finally stood back and looked at it, they loved it. Nobody had seen a thing...*"

That snippet circled through my mind throughout

the rest of dinner. Something about it seemed connected with another detail I'd heard earlier in the day. I was starting to get the buzz that meant I was on to something, but I couldn't quite remember what the comment reminded me of. I told myself that as soon as dinner was over, I'd let Miriam know I needed to get back to her apartment—where I could listen to my phone recordings in peace.

Finally Sid Clifton and his wife stood up, signaling to the rest of us that it was time to move on. Some immediately flocked to the bar set up at the far end of the room, while others followed the restroom signs, and still others headed to the rooftop terrace that Sid had also reserved for the night.

I started walking toward the dance floor, on the lookout for Cazzie to let her know my plans, but just then my phone vibrated. Taking it out, I saw a forwarded text message string from Cazzie:

Have you solved the riddle?

Cazzie had answered:

Of course I solved your riddle. Here's the photograph. Honestly, it was a bit of a joke. Should I help you come up with more challenging puzzles?
Anyway, here's my deal: I need to have the diamond back in my hands by 6 p.m. Friday evening—no questions asked—or I'll have to involve the police.

I texted her saying, **Well done**. Now we just had to wait for an answer.

While I was reading the texts, music started playing. A DJ flown in from London was presiding, and as soon as the first few beats exploded over the speakers, the dance floor was full. I waved at Ellie as I passed her. A vision of shimmering blond and blue, she was clearly enjoying herself—and she wasn't short of admirers, I noted.

But then, just as I was stepping away from the dance floor, someone grabbed my hand from behind.

"Hey—" I said, turning and trying to pull my hand back. Whoever he was, he was strong—and he was ignoring me. All I could see of him was the back of his tuxedo as he pulled me into the dancing crowd. He turned to face me, and taking both my hands, he placed them on his shoulders. Next I felt his hands quickly slide down my sides until they reached my waist and cinched it.

Then he leaned into me and whispered, "This is much better than crawling around on the floor trying to talk."

It was Sebastian.

"Well, it didn't look like you were having trouble talking to other people when you were *standing*," I said as I tried to pull away from him. "And by the way," I asked, "how did you go from magazine vendor to pretend guest?"

"I have my methods, Sherlock."

"It's still Holmes to you," I said as I tried maneuvering

my way off the dance floor. But Sebastian kept moving around me, effectively corralling me with his dancing. Annoyingly, everyone around us thought we were having the time of our lives. The *Teen Vogue* editor who'd been at my dinner table danced past at that moment and gave me a thumbs-up.

I waited for Sebastian to make his next move, and as he did, I quickly slid away—right into the path of someone else. It was almost as if he'd been waiting for me.

"Perfect timing," he said as I flew into his arms.

The masked dancer slipped a hand around my waist and moved me away from Sebastian. It wasn't until he leaned close to me that I realized it was Brandon.

"I was hoping to sneak some time alone with you before leaving, which unfortunately I have to do in a few minutes," he said. "We have an early start tomorrow. It *did* take me a while to find you." He smiled. "Anyway, is there any chance I can convince you to leave the dance floor for a quick drink?"

"Actually, Brandon," I said, "I think that's a great idea." I noticed Misty watching us, anger suffusing her features, but she turned away when I caught her eye.

"Who were you dancing with?" Brandon asked as we made our way toward the drinks bar set up in the entrance hall. I could hear the music behind us, and the smell of cigarette smoke blew in on the breeze every time the large front doors opened. "The two of you were dancing quite…athletically." I couldn't tell whether he meant that ironically or not.

"That was…a friend."

Right at that moment my phone vibrated again. I took it out of my clutch and saw it was Cazzie. She'd received an answer from the thief!

"Brandon," I said, "I'm really, really sorry, but I have to go. It has to do with work. I have to give an answer right now, and it could take a while."

"Work? *Now?*" He raised his eyebrows in mock alarm.

"Yes, it's about a fitting for early tomorrow. Like I said this morning, my schedule is packed…"

"I haven't forgotten anything you said." He leaned toward my ear as he spoke, his shoulder brushing against mine.

Great. He was flirting. I took a breath and said, "I'm sorry, Brandon. Maybe I could take a rain check on the drink? I really have—"

"Right, you have to go. Will you be doing the Jared Moor show tomorrow?"

I nodded.

"Then I'll see you there."

"That would be great," I said as I turned to leave.

"You're different from most models—in a good way," he said suddenly. "You're at the biggest bash of New York Fashion Week, and yet I feel your mind is somewhere else entirely."

I shrugged my shoulders and smiled. He stood watching me as I backed away. Despite the relaxed-looking pose he struck—he had his hands in his pockets and his legs firmly apart—his eyes were intense. I gave him a last smile and quick wave before turning and reading the thief's answer:

I'm glad you liked my riddles because tomorrow I'll send you another—and I'll give you less time to solve it. As for your treasure, I'll be the one who decides when you see it. Don't try to outwit me—I have the upper hand now.

I slipped my phone in my bag and pushed my way through the crowds to find Cazzie.

She was looking for me. We bumped into each other outside one of the sculpture galleries, and without a word—just a nod of the head—we headed toward the roof terrace.

"The thief is playing tough. They don't seem scared at all."

"Well, they will be eventually. Anyway, forward the next riddle as soon as you have it. And keep trying to get the thief talking."

Cazzie nodded, then stretched and took a deep breath. "I have to get back to the party. Do you mind if I leave you?"

"No, you go ahead. I'll have my phone by my side at all times."

It was cool up on the terrace, but the view was amazing. Across Central Park, the Manhattan skyline twinkled like the Milky Way—and it soothed me to feel the fresh air ruffle my hair and graze my face.

But after a couple of minutes, I turned to go back in and find Miriam so I could let her know I was ready to leave. I had to get back to my bedroom and listen to my recordings. The snippet of conversation that had jogged my memory at dinner was still replaying in my mind.

As I wandered through the museum, however, the hair on my neck went up like it had on the street after my casting at Jared Moor's. Out of the corner of my eye, I could have sworn I saw something move quickly behind me, but when I turned back to look, I saw nothing. Was I being paranoid?

I walked more briskly but continued to sense someone behind me. I was sure I was being followed—and the frustration of not having gotten anywhere with this case was making me feel reckless. I decided to turn the tables and follow them.

I slowly moved forward a few more steps, letting several party guests walk past me, then suddenly turned. I saw a flash of shadow as my stalker dodged into a gallery. I quickly followed and entered the same gallery, but it was empty. Glancing around, I noticed that behind a sculpture in the far corner was an entrance into another room. I ran toward it, and as I crossed into the new, larger space, I again saw the flash of shadow as it disappeared around another corner.

Picking up the hem of my long dress, and thankful that I had my Converses on, I ran after the shadow. The second room led to another small connecting chamber. I crossed this one too, wondering where the shadow could have disappeared. Then, while checking behind me, I turned a corner—and ran right into Sebastian!

"You again!" I said, not stopping.

"I've been looking for you," he said as he matched my pace, jogging beside me. "Where are you going?"

"Someone was following me. So I turned around and started following them, but I think I lost them in the last room..."

He stopped suddenly. "I have an idea. Follow me..."

I followed Sebastian as we retraced our steps into the room where I'd lost the shadow. Hidden in the wall was another door, which he pushed open. "I was using this door earlier," he said when he saw my surprise. "It leads to the museum's service rooms and corridors. Whoever was following you must have disappeared through here."

I followed as he led the way down a long, well-lit corridor.

"So how far have you gotten with the case?" Sebastian asked, his voice a whisper as we walked side by side.

"I thought you'd be more interested to hear how my modeling career is going," I hissed back, my temper rising. "You know, what go-sees, castings, and bookings I have. I know it interests you and my mother."

He rolled his eyes. "I told you that the text messages you saw are not what you think."

I tried to interrupt but he quickly asked again, "So how far have you gotten?"

At that moment someone from the catering team walked by and smiled at us. They recognized Sebastian and didn't ask anything about me.

"Not far enough," I finally admitted. "This case should have been easy to solve, but it's not quite turning out that way…"

"So can I help?"

I thought of what I'd decided earlier about doing more background checks. Cazzie and her livelihood and everything else that was at stake came to mind: the loss of a famous diamond, *Chic's* reputation, and mine too. I needed to solve this case, and I didn't have much time. I needed help, and I could trust Sebastian—at least as far as the detective work went. Quashing any feelings I had about us, I finally answered him.

"Yes. I'd like to have your help," I said as a couple of waiters walked briskly past us.

He turned and smiled at me as we went down a few steps.

"When do I start?"

"Now."

We finally came to a door that opened onto a staff changing room with lockers lining the walls. But apart from a couple of Sebastian's fellow "magazine vendors," no one else was there.

"And what do you need?" he asked as he stepped back into the corridor and shut the door behind him.

"More background checks. I'll text you the names you need to research. Do you think you can do that?"

"Absolutely, Holmes."

"Thank you, Watson. And tomorrow there might be some running around town. Cazzie's expecting more riddles."

"More riddles?"

But there wasn't time to explain, because as we turned into another corridor, we heard footsteps around the corner ahead of us—and they were moving briskly. I put my arm out to halt Sebastian and then raised a finger to my lips. When we stopped, so did the footsteps. After a few seconds we moved on—and so did the footsteps. A moment later, we heard a door slam just ahead of us.

I motioned to Sebastian to put his phone on silent and then, moving as lightly as we could, we ran around the corner and down the corridor to the door. I opened it quietly and we both walked through into an enormous storage room. It was like a warehouse. High metal shelves lined the walls and stood in neat rows down the middle of the room. There was just enough space between the shelves to pass through with a small cart, several of which were standing to one side of the door.

I nudged Sebastian and indicated that we should split

up, each of us taking a separate direction. I doubted that whoever I was following knew there were now two of us. With any luck, Sebastian and I could corner them in this room.

Sebastian nodded but also motioned to the light switch on his left. Fluorescent bulbs glowed overhead, their sickly light illuminating the room. I considered. Perhaps it would be better with the light off. My phone had a flashlight and I knew Sebastian's did too. I nodded and Sebastian flicked the switch. We turned our flashlights on, and using our hands to cover some of the light our phones made, we slowly worked our way toward the back of the room.

When I'd reached about the halfway point, the beam of my flashlight fell on an opened box of metal or silver polish packed in metal cylindrical bottles. These, I thought as I grabbed two, could be just the trick for scaring whoever I was following into making a mistake.

Knowing Sebastian had his phone on silent, I sent him a text saying that I planned to roll one of the bottles toward the end of the room. **Good idea** was his answer. **Let me move farther forward.**

I counted to ten, then turned my flashlight off and, with a swing of my arm, let one of the bottles roll rapidly under the shelves.

It did the trick.

The bottle hurtled its way across the floor, its metal sides banging nicely against whatever little things lay in its path. In the distance I heard whoever was in here with us resume a careful patter toward the far side of the room. Quietly, I tiptoed forward a few more feet before I stood to listen. The footsteps had stopped, yet the person who'd been following me could only be a little way ahead. I'd have seen the light from the outside corridor spill into the darkened storage room if they'd opened the door to escape.

Without more thought, I dipped my hand low and let the second bottle roll forward loudly. As it banged its way between the shelving units, the footsteps resumed at a frantic pace…until a loud crash, followed by a rustling of cardboard boxes, echoed through the storage room. Someone—or something—had fallen.

I turned my phone flashlight back on and ran toward the ruckus at the end of the room. I got there just as Sebastian was pulling a kicking, wriggling form out from under the shelves.

A moment later I shone the beam of my flashlight onto Misty's angry face.

"You!" I said as I took a step back. A random scattering of tiny details flooded my mind—the glances this morning in the studio every time I'd spoken to Brandon, the flash of black nail lacquer as her hands suddenly grasped Brandon's shoulders during lunch when he was talking to me—not to mention the anger I'd seen in her eyes when we'd been on the dance floor. Did this all have to do with me? Or more precisely, with me and Brandon? Was she jealous?

I was on unsteady ground in second-guessing these kinds of situations. As my BFF Jenny liked to point out, "Axelle, if you spent as much time watching *Gossip Girl* as you do *Sherlock*, you'd learn so much more about life."

For the first time, I was wondering if maybe she had a point.

At least now I knew that Misty had been following me here at the party. This naturally led to another question: had she also been following me earlier today?

Sebastian went to turn the lights back on, while I turned to question Misty.

"Is this all about Brandon?" I asked, watching as she daintily picked herself up and dusted her dress off.

"Does it surprise you?" she hissed, the venom in her voice unmistakable. "You talked to him—fawned over him, even—every chance you had today, didn't you? As if you couldn't get enough of him!" She was glaring at me now, shaking with such rage that I was surprised her eyes weren't glowing red. Everyone had fixations and weak spots, I thought, no matter how successful. But still…to have gone this far, she must have hated me since the moment she saw Brandon talking to me at the studio this morning.

"What are you talking about, Misty? Beyond basic courtesy, I've hardly singled out Brandon for special attention!" She was nuts. Drawing this kind of attention to herself and her obsession was risky. If she kept doing this, someone would eventually label her a stalker, and surely even her career could suffer from that. "Let it go, Misty—let *him* go."

"You would say that, wouldn't you?" she spat.

I had a sudden flashback to the email I'd received at lunch:

You're getting in the way. I know you know what I mean—even though you're trying to hide it.
Pull back now.

From someone who's watching you.

I'd been running with the assumption that the email came from the person who'd stolen the diamond—that they knew I was on the case and wanted to scare me off. But now, as I watched Misty reapply her lipstick with her shaking hand, I wondered if my assumption could be wrong. The words of the email were threatening, no doubt. And while it could still be interpreted as a warning to stay away from the mystery of the missing diamond, with what I now knew—and what Misty had just made more than apparent—the wording of the email could also be interpreted as a warning from a jealous ex-girlfriend to stay away from "her" beloved Brandon.

The question I'd asked myself a minute ago came to mind again: was Misty the same person who'd followed me after my Jared Moor casting?

I decided it was worth lying a bit to see if my hunch was right.

Misty had just snapped her tiny evening clutch closed and was trying to push her way past Sebastian, lips pressed shut, when I said, "Misty, I saw you earlier today, you know."

She stopped and looked at me. "Of course you did. We worked together."

"That's not what I'm talking about. I saw you following me near Times Square this afternoon, after my Jared Moor appointment. You may have tried hiding your hair, but it was you. I saw you as you ran out of the ribbon shop."

Anger flashed from her eyes and twisted her features. She was strange. Seen across a runway, her vanilla-blond beauty eclipsed her bitterness. But now that I'd seen her close up, under the glare of a flashlight and squirming under shelving, she just looked crazy.

"You didn't see me," she spat. "It must have been someone else. Why would I follow you on Times Square? And by the way," she said suddenly, a sly, dangerous smile on the corners of her lips, "*who* followed *me* here? I think that when I tell people what you've done, what you've put me through—following me and harassing me at a gala, scaring me and cornering me—and don't forget I now have the bruises to show for it…well, it wouldn't take a genius to know who people will believe."

If she'd had fangs, I have no doubt she'd have bared them at that moment. Instead she set her mouth into a menacing line and clenched her free hand into a fist. I'd cornered her, and deep down she knew it. At the same time, I had no doubt she'd go through with her threat if I pushed much harder. I still had no proof that she'd been following me earlier—but I'd called her bluff, and she'd told me more with her threatening reaction than she ever would with words.

But I still had a couple of questions I wanted answered.

"The email you sent me at lunch was from an anonymous account. Where did you learn to open and close one so quickly?"

She didn't answer. Her eyes shone with contempt.

"And what about text messages? Have you been sending many of those lately? From a disposable phone, maybe?"

My last question surprised her, and for a fleeting second her anger gave way to confusion. She genuinely didn't seem to know what I was referring to. I was fairly sure now that although Misty had followed me twice today and sent me the threatening email at lunch, she probably had nothing to do with the Black Amelia or the texts Cazzie was receiving.

"And what were you hoping to achieve by following me?"

"Like I said, *you* are following *me*."

"Were you hoping to scare me away from Brandon? Because if you were, it never would have worked."

She snorted and glared at me for a moment. "It would have eventually," she finally answered, all pretense of innocence dropped. "It's worked before." The corners of her lips turned upward again in a sly smile. "Another model. She went back to Europe, terrified someone was stalking her.

"Anyway I don't know what *you're* trying to achieve now," she continued, "because this game is over. I have a party to get back to—or do you want me to make good on my threat?" Then she lifted the sleeve of her dress and pointedly looked at the large bruise forming on her upper arm. After another moment she pushed her way past Sebastian and left.

I motioned for Sebastian to stay back and not follow her, and a few moments later we heard the door we'd come in through slam shut behind her.

"Why did you let her go? She should be reported, even if she does seem to think she has the upper hand. She's completely nuts!" Sebastian said.

"I can't report her because I never saw her following me."

"But you said that you'd recognized her—even with her hair hidden."

"I never saw her. I only guessed it was her after chasing her down just now. And as for saying that she'd hidden her hair…that was also a guess, although a fairly easy one. After all, from afar her hair is her most recognizable feature. It would be the first thing she'd hide to blend into a crowd."

In silence, we quickly did our best to bring some order to the cardboard boxes Misty had overturned as she'd struggled with Sebastian. Then we turned and left. It was time to rejoin the party.

"Earth to Axelle? Can we talk about this case?" Sebastian was walking beside me, mask back in place, as he patted the dust off his suit. His hair was going in all directions, just the way I liked it. I quickly looked away before he caught me looking at him. "So can we?"

I nodded as I took my phone out and started writing him a text with the names of all the suspects.

"Great. I want to hear about the riddles."

But as soon as we stepped out of the service corridors, Miriam spotted us.

"Sebastian! I didn't know you'd arrived!" Miriam said when she saw him. "Axelle, you've been keeping him a secret." She winked at me.

I didn't say anything. Instead I finished writing the text I'd started.

Miriam looked at her watch and then proceeded to nix any plans Sebastian and I had about discussing the case. "It's time for you to go home, Axelle. You need your beauty sleep. You have a big day tomorrow—including your first New York City fashion show. And I want to get back now too. I'm feeling the jet lag." She turned to look at Sebastian. "Can I get my driver to take you somewhere?"

Sebastian mumbled something about meeting

someone. Visions of Cleo danced through my mind, but I left it at that and we all said good-bye.

"*À demain*, Holmes," he whispered. "We'll have to talk about the case tomorrow, but send me the names so I can get started with the background checks."

"I just did. *À demain*, Watson."

✳ ✳ ✳

As I made my way to my bedroom, my phone suddenly vibrated with a text message. Taking it out of my clutch, I saw it was from Ellie.

> I just heard something that might interest you. Apparently, a long time ago, at the very start of her career, Chandra was caught stealing a necklace from a shoot. Supposedly it was hushed up by her agency, and she has since changed her ways. You said your case is about something missing, and she was there, so I thought you might want to know... Not that I think she'd do anything like that now. I mean, why would she? And who knows if she really did it then? It's just a rumor, after all...

Who told you? I wrote back.

> A model I was just talking to. She's older—like thirty or something—and is having a kind of renaissance with her career at the moment. She just shot an Italian *Vogue* cover.

Anyway, she was a bit tipsy and started talking about Chandra when she saw her near us, and she very quickly brought that up. She sounded jealous of Chandra, and I think it made her feel good to know that about her. She claims she was there when it happened.

Hmm...something else to look into tomorrow, I thought, just as my phone vibrated for a third time. This was quickly followed by yet another message—and both were from Sebastian.

The first one read:

Where are you? Are you ready to go? I am when you are.
Seb x

Huh? What was he talking about? But then I read the second one, and the meaning became all too clear:

Sorry, Axelle. That wasn't meant for you—ignore it! I can't wait to get going on the case! See you tomorrow. Seb

My stomach suddenly lurched to my mouth, and for a second I felt sick. *Calm down, Axelle. Calm down. It's Sebastian, remember? Mom's spy.* I had to remind myself that I was still furious with him. The surprise of seeing him at the *Chic* party and the excitement of chasing down Misty together had begun to erode the wall of disappointment and anger that had built up over the last few days. And if I was honest, the feel of his hands around my waist as we'd danced might have had a teeny-weeny bit to do with it too... Not that any of that mattered. Clearly, what mattered to Sebastian now was Cleo.

And why does that matter to you, Axelle? You're not jealous, remember?

Shut up!

After washing the makeup off my face, I pulled my earbuds out of my shoulder bag, thinking that I could listen to the audio recordings I'd made at the studio before I fell asleep. But jet lag got the better of me, and as I closed my eyes, my last thoughts were of the diamond, the suspects, and Sebastian. Their images turned stiltedly in my mind, as if seen through a broken kaleidoscope. Any kind of conclusion—about anything—seemed a long way off. How would it all end? I wondered.

A Passion for Fashion

The loud ringing of my phone pierced the morning calm. Eyes still shut, I answered.

"Wake up, Axelle! You've got to get going to Tony Moreno's studio! I knew this would happen. You let a model go to her first big fashion party, and what does she do? She oversleeps the next morning!"

Pat was like some kind of fashion rooster, crowing at the crack of dawn, I thought as I slowly came to. Strong sunlight seeped in around the edges of the thick curtains hanging at my bedroom window. Clearly it wasn't the crack of dawn—I had slept late.

"Girl, are you listening?"

Thoughts of Misty and her crazy attempt to scare me away from Brandon came back to me…along with something else. But what? What had I wanted to do so desperately last night? Why had I wanted to get back to Miriam's?

"And don't even try to use jet lag as an excuse because models can't. C-A-N-apostrophe-T! Besides, you've come the wrong way for that. It really only works flying east."

Argh! The recordings, of course! I'd wanted to listen to the recordings I'd made at Juice Studios. There was something I'd overheard during the dinner last night…

"Do I have to call Miriam to get you to wake up and speak?"

"No, no, I'm here, Pat." Someone had said something that made me think, and it felt like it could be important… I'd meant to try to find the connection, but sleep had overwhelmed me. As soon as I could, I'd have to listen to those recordings…

Pat rambled on with details about today. First I had to test with Tony Moreno; then I had a break before my first New York show—Jared Moor—at Lincoln Center. Ellie and I would be doing Jared Moor together—along with Misty, Chandra, and Rafaela.

"And it seems you'll have a fitting at some point for Diane von Furstenberg—probably after Jared Moor. That should be confirmed later this morning. And if there's time, I want to give you a short fashion history lesson—something I like to do with new girls. Anyway, you'll be busy, don't worry."

I wasn't, I thought.

I finally said good-bye to Pat and then dashed into the bathroom to shower. I only had forty minutes before I was due at Tony's studio—which, considering he was way downtown, didn't give me much time.

All kinds of thoughts bounced around in my mind. I had to see Sebastian. When had we made plans for? *Had* we made plans? Had he started with the background checks? And why hadn't Cazzie texted or emailed me yet? Or had I missed something in my morning haste? With that thought, I slowed down long enough to take a deep breath and prioritize. First, I told myself I had to make it to Tony Moreno on time—or I'd have Pat breathing down my neck all day!

After making sure I had everything I needed in my shoulder bag, I quickly stopped by the kitchen to wolf down the bagel with cream cheese and glass of fresh juice Nicolette had put out for me. "You're not in New York if you don't have a bagel for breakfast," Nicolette said as I grabbed an apple to take with me. I called good-bye to Miriam, thanked Nicolette, and shut the door behind me.

Downstairs, my phone vibrated as I flew across the lobby.

It was a text from Sebastian:

I've started on the background checks. Meet outside the Frick Collection at 12:30? Corner of 5th + 70th. Does that work for you?

It did. That would be right between my morning test shoot and mid-afternoon Jared Moor show. I wrote back to tell Sebastian that and then raced out of the building's Gotham darkness into the bright Manhattan morning sunshine.

***

The studio Tony Moreno had rented for the morning was on Watts Street in SoHo, in what looked like an old mechanic's garage. It was clearly a conversion, I thought, as I walked past the derelict gas pumps and found my way into the surprisingly sunny studio.

Besides Tony and his assistant, there were a hairstylist, a makeup artist, and a clothes stylist—all of whom, like me, were doing this to get some photos for their portfolios.

After we all had a look at the fun, colorful clothes Gemma, the stylist, had pulled for the shoot, Tony convened a meeting. I sat at the makeup and hair table while Tony, Gemma, Lisa the hairstylist, and Jimmy the makeup artist stood over me, discussing how to capture the look they wanted. From what I gathered, it was going to be girly and pretty—limited makeup and natural hair, paired with colorful, fun clothes and a clean background. There'd be some softer backlit shots later. They pored over the magazine tears they'd brought as inspiration for a few minutes, and then the final details were decided.

The morning passed quickly. After each shot, we'd run to Tony's computer to watch him edit it a bit (he was his own digi-tech guy) and see what we could improve on with the next shot. By mid-morning I'd emailed a couple of the shots to Pat—with Tony's permission—as proof that I was being productive. In the subject line I'd written "Passion for Fashion"—although, for all I knew, Pat would find the irony in that as opaque as a pair of black winter tights.

Because we didn't have long to get enough shots done—we had to give the studio up at noon—and because my "natural" hair and makeup weren't at all time-consuming, I didn't have the usual lengthy down-time or prep time to spend on my "other business." But I popped my earbuds in whenever I could. I reminded myself to concentrate on *how* the robbery was done—as opposed to by *whom*—and over the course of the morning I carefully went through every word I'd recorded yesterday until I finally found what I'd been looking for.

Again, the image of a small nugget of gold glittering in the gravel of a stream came to mind. Buried in the recordings was a random comment that could hold the key to this case—and I wasn't sure I would have picked up on it if the snippet of conversation I'd overheard last night hadn't triggered something in my memory. *Hmm*…I was quietly humming, excited by the thought that I might have a new line of inquiry for my investigations. Without thinking, I pulled my earbuds out and, smiling, looked in the mirror.

"I know," Jimmy said as he made minor adjustments to my hair with the sharp-tipped handle of his comb. "Isn't fashion the most amazing thing?"

***

A little while later, I received an interesting bit of information in an email from Cazzie. She'd copied the Friday page from the Juice Studios logbook and emailed it to me in its entirety. It showed that nobody, apart from the group working with Cazzie, had been logged as going into Studio 7 while the shoot was going on.

Of course, someone could still have snuck in…but even if they had managed to get past the reception desk and walk unseen into Studio 7, they would have needed to know where to find the diamond—and if they hadn't been working on the shoot, that didn't seem likely. The logbook also showed that two cleaners had gone up in the evening to prepare the studio for the next day, as Cazzie had said, and that she had left an hour later than the others in the *Chic* group.

Cazzie wrote:

Difficult as it is for me to believe, I think I have to assume that one of the group is responsible. Juice was careful to respect my express wish that no one—even studio staff—enter the studio without speaking to me first. The logbook seems to corroborate this.

Also, Juice confirmed to me that everyone else listed as coming and going into the Juice building that day was known to them—and I personally

*know and recognize virtually every name in the
logbook for that day too...*

While in some ways the confirmed sighting of a wild
card might have made things easier, at least now I felt
reasonably sure—like Cazzie—that the Black Amelia
had indeed been taken by one of the suspects on my list.
And that, in turn, gave more credence to the idea now
running through my mind.

Fashionable Plans

I left Tony Moreno's studio feeling more positive about which direction to take the case. The random comment I'd found in my recordings played over and over in my mind. I was sure that this previously overlooked detail was a key clue.

I walked to the nearest subway station and caught a train going uptown. After a transfer, I arrived at the station on Sixty-Eighth Street and Lexington Avenue. I was now in the heart of the Big Apple's famed Upper East Side. Under bright, sunny skies, I walked the few blocks to the corner of Fifth Avenue and Seventieth Street.

"So, Holmes, how's it going?" It was Sebastian—and annoyingly he looked good. Why did he seem like a bigger distraction now than he'd ever been on his scooter in Paris? And after I'd decided that he shouldn't *be* a distraction!

"Axelle?"

Not that I was about to let him know that.

"Where are we?" I said, swiftly changing gears in my head.

Of course, I knew that we were on the corner of Fifth Avenue and East Seventieth Street—about ten blocks south of the Met where we'd been last night—but I didn't know anything about the huge house behind us.

"Well, that's the Frick." Sebastian nodded in the direction of the mansion. "They have an amazing collection of eighteenth-century French decorative arts," he said. "If it had been raining, I would have suggested going in there. According to my sources, it's quiet and guaranteed to be fashionista-free—especially during Fashion Week.

"But I thought if the weather held—which it has— we could cross the street, grab a hot dog, and go into the park." He smiled at me—that heart-stopping, totally cute smile of his. "And it won't take long to walk to Lincoln Center from here. You wrote in your text this morning that you're doing the Jared Moor show."

"I am, at two thirty at Lincoln Center. You're as resourceful as ever, Watson," I said as we crossed Fifth Avenue.

"Yeah, well, don't let it distract you." He flashed me his smile, then laughed.

Very funny. Now he was a mind reader too.

As we walked to Central Park, I quickly filled Sebastian in on the basic information concerning the case. He'd been with me in Paris when I'd received the initial call from Miriam, so he had an inkling about it. But until now, he'd heard none of the details—apart from receiving the list of names I'd texted him last night.

We bought hot dogs and drinks from the vendor on the corner, then went into the park. And while the weather wasn't anywhere near hot—it was a crisp early-spring day, after all—there was no breeze, and the strong midday sun was actually nice. Within five minutes we were seated on a bench beside a large, round pond—the same one where the mouse Stuart Little raced his boat in the movie I must have watched a hundred times when I was tiny. Central Park was beautiful, and even I had to admit it was a worthy rival for Hyde Park, my all-time favorite park at home.

"So," he asked, "who shoots first?"

"How about I play you my recordings?"

"Sounds like you're asking me on a date."

"Trust me, if I were, you'd know it."

"Ouch—but I like your sense of authority."

I ignored that and handed him one of my earbuds, while putting the other one into my own ear. We started on our hot dogs as we listened.

"Well, there's not a lot for you to go on, is there?" Sebastian asked a while later as I put the earbuds back into my shoulder bag.

I shrugged my shoulders and said nothing.

He narrowed his eyes and watched me. "Don't tell me you've managed to extract something from that—or do you have something else to go on that I don't know about?"

I smiled.

"I know that look… You know who took the diamond, don't you?"

I shook my head. "No…but I have a good idea who it might be."

"But you're not going to tell me?"

"Maybe. But first let me hear what you've found out."

He looked at me intently for a moment or two before breaking into a smile and saying, "I detect a possible chink in your theory, Holmes… Because if you really have a strong idea of who might have taken the diamond, what's the point of hearing what I have to say?"

"Touché, Watson." I laughed.

"Well," Sebastian began, "I've found out how Misty knew her way around the museum so well last night."

I shook my head as I recalled our bizarre pursuit of one of the world's top supermodels through the labyrinthine staff corridors of the Met.

"She dated a chef," he continued, "who often did—and for all I know, still does—catering there. So naturally, if she was there for a fashion event that he was catering, they would meet up. She'd been seen disappearing with him into the corridors, and she would even pop into the kitchen on occasion. It's no big deal, but I was curious to know how she knew her way around."

"Good point, Watson. Thanks for that."

"On a more relevant note, it seems that Peter Van Oorst's father used to be a jeweler."

"What? Really?"

Sebastian nodded. "He later moved into dealing in antique silver, but he was trained as a jeweler, and for a large part of Peter's childhood, that was what he did."

Sebastian had done a thorough job of combing through everything he'd found on the Web—and he'd managed to find interesting facts about a few of the suspects. And while I wasn't sure that knowing Peter's father used to be a jeweler led anywhere, the information nevertheless added a new facet to Peter's character sketch. Now, for instance, I knew that Peter probably had a good idea of the real value of the Black Amelia. Whether that had induced him to take the diamond was another matter.

Sebastian had also found out that Peter was compiling a book of his photography—candid fashion shots, many of which were taken backstage during the fashion shows.

"Which is why," Sebastian explained, "he'll be backstage at so many shows this week—together with Brandon, who is very interested in his own photography. No one has seen much of his work, but they say that he'd like to move into fashion photography full-time at some point. He's thrilled to be learning so much from Peter, apparently."

Sebastian hadn't found anything drastically new or different from what I already had on Trish and Tom— although Trish did like antique jewelry. "If you check out her Instagram page, you'll see she's always wearing some sparkly piece when she's out on the town… And by the way," continued Sebastian, "her makeup line is very successful."

Interestingly, he had stumbled across rumors of a rivalry between Rafaela and Chandra—although only as unsubstantiated gossip on some blogs. And he'd also dug deep enough to find out about Chandra's supposed "theft" long ago at that shoot Ellie had mentioned. He'd thought that might be a good lead and looked a bit crestfallen when I didn't jump on it.

"So I haven't really given you anything new to go on, have I?"

I shrugged my shoulders. "Well, you never know…"

He shook his head as he looked at me. "I know you have something in mind, Holmes, so are you going to tell me what it is or do I have to drag it out of you?"

"I'll tell you." I smiled. "But I think you'd better hear this again first." I handed him one of my earbuds as I began to explain. "So, at dinner last night, one of the fashion editors was talking about her experience designing at Alexander Wang when she said something like: *'They were all so engrossed with finishing the top of the dress that I was able to quickly add my own little flourish to the skirt without anyone really noticing. When they finally stood back and looked at it, they loved it. Nobody had seen a thing…'* And that triggered my memory," I continued, "because listen to this…"

I searched my phone to find the section of the

recording I needed. "This was Chandra's answer when I asked her where she was when the alarm went off:"

I don't know. The mirrors by Trish and Tom, I guess. I'd just walked off the set, like Rafaela and Misty. I was waiting to get my makeup retouched, and then it went off. It certainly got everyone's attention. They were all engrossed in what was happening.

"Do you hear the similarity?"

"The engrossed bit, you mean?" Sebastian asked.

I nodded. "What's also curious about Chandra's version of events is that she makes no mention of seeing the old lady being wheeled into the ambulance. Why not?"

Sebastian shrugged his shoulders. "Maybe that just didn't capture her attention."

I shook my head. "I doubt it. I mean, *everyone* mentioned it. Even Peter and Brandon mentioned seeing the ambulance leave—and by most everyone's account, they ran to the windows later than the others because they were working at Brandon's computer. And Chandra's time is still less well accounted for than the others. So what was she doing? What else could she have been looking at? And again, if she did look out the windows right after the alarm rang, why didn't she mention the ambulance?"

"Okay...so the fire alarm goes off, and Trish and Tom are doing makeup and hair on Rafaela and Misty," Sebastian said. "Peter and Brandon are at Brandon's computer editing the photos they've shot so far, and

Cazzie is in the dressing area checking on the iron she thinks is burning… Is that right?"

I nodded. "Correct."

"And Chandra says she was just hanging out, waiting?"

I nodded. "And none of the others can remember where exactly she was or what she was doing after she walked off the set—while they pretty much remember what all of the others were doing. Trish and Tom did confirm that Chandra had been around their table for a while, but they didn't know where she'd gone once they started working on Misty and Rafaela."

"And presumably she saw Cazzie go into the dressing area?"

I nodded. "Cazzie remembers seeing her. She ran past Chandra on her way to the dressing area—and made eye contact with her."

"And Chandra knew Cazzie had the diamond with her?"

I nodded. "She was standing next to Cazzie when Cazzie slipped the diamond's case into her handbag. Although in all fairness, everyone else also saw Cazzie slip the case into her handbag and go into the dressing area with it. To my mind, what definitely works against Chandra is her lack of a solid explanation of her actions during the crucial few minutes before and after the fire alarm rang. And she made that comment about all the others being 'engrossed' by the action in the next building.

"It's as if she's standing somewhere observing them, instead of observing the fire like everyone else. Why? And she helped Cazzie pack up the clothes—something no model would ever do. So again, why?" I stopped for a moment and took a deep breath. "And her love—and knowledge—of magic tricks, something Cazzie herself has witnessed many times, means Chandra probably has an advantage over the others when it comes to actually stealing something..."

"And the rumor?"

"About the necklace she took?"

Sebastian nodded.

"As far as I'm concerned, it's just that—a rumor. I have no way of knowing if it's true or not. For all I know, someone could have seen her take something as one of her practical jokes and embellished the story a bit... But anyway, even without the rumor, right now Chandra is the best lead I've got. It all fits quite well."

Sebastian leaned back with a sigh. "So where's the chink?" he asked, running his hand through his hair.

I stood up and started walking south through the park with Sebastian following. With a glance at my watch, I saw that I only had three-quarters of an hour before I had to be at Lincoln Center for hair and makeup. Fortunately, it was only about a twenty-minute walk from where we were now.

"This is the chink," I said as I handed him my phone.

Quickly he read the text—the first one Cazzie had been sent yesterday morning, before the *Chic* shoot.

"I'm not following you—unless you don't think Chandra could have written something like that."

I shook my head. "I always run with the premise that, given the right set of circumstances, anyone is capable of anything."

"Do you have many friends?" He laughed.

"Very funny, Watson."

We turned off the main path and walked toward the Bethesda Fountain, the most famous fountain in the park according to my mom, who, on our last trip here, had insisted on taking my picture in this very spot. In fact, she keeps the photo on her bedside table at home, even though I'm half the size in it that I am now. Sebastian and I stood on the terrace, watching a colorful, lively assortment of grannies, joggers, children, lovers, and students wander around the fountain below and the edge of the large lake just beyond it.

"Anyway," I said, "presumably the text I just showed you—which Cazzie received yesterday morning—was sent by the person who stole the diamond, correct?"

"That would make sense…"

"Well, the text was sent at 7:30 a.m."

"And?"

"And at seven thirty, Chandra was apparently high in the sky between here and Miami, where she'd been shooting the day before. Obviously, I can't jump to any assumptions without all the facts, but if that's true, it seems unlikely she sent that text," I said. "I mean, maybe it *would* be technically possible—I need to find out for sure—but even so, it doesn't feel right. Why would she risk it when she could just wait 'til she landed?"

"But like you said, that text was probably sent by whoever has the diamond..."

I nodded. "So maybe Chandra is working with someone...or..."

I looked at him. Our eyes met, and for a fraction of a second, he looked at me in that way he had in Paris. Whatever we were talking about was forgotten. His blue-gray eyes darkened and I thought our conversation was about to head off in a totally different direction, but then Sebastian looked quickly away. It all happened so rapidly that I wasn't even sure of what I'd seen.

"Or," I continued, trying my best to ignore the confused feelings rising in my gut, "someone is lying big-time. Or someone else entirely—someone who's not part of the photo-shoot group—is responsible. Although nothing in the Juice Studios logbook backs that up." I sighed and looked up as a pair of courting pigeons cooed on a branch overhead. "Anyway, right now Chandra is my strongest lead, so I'm going to concentrate on her for the moment."

Sebastian's phone suddenly rang, and he answered it. I wouldn't have given it a moment's thought, but then he said, "Hold on a second..." to whoever was on the other end and walked far enough away that he was in no danger of being overheard.

Images of Cleo, the long-legged blond model I'd seen last night with her arms around him, came to mind—and the vision didn't make for easy viewing. And neither did the sudden memory of the text message he'd mistakenly sent me late last night. My stomach did a flip-flop—and not in a good way.

Great. Now I needed a strategy for how to act when he walked back. Uninterested? Smiling and happy? *Argh!* Why was everything so complicated? But in the end I was saved by Pat. Who would have guessed that I'd be thrilled to see her name light up on my phone?

Get going, Axelle. Jared Moor is waiting. And look sharp! SHARP!

I wrote back quickly:

Sharp as last season's stilettos!

To which she replied:

Better be. By the way, where have you been? We didn't have our fashion history lesson. You're lucky it slipped my mind because of the shows. Maybe tomorrow. Now walk well!

"You know what I'm looking forward to?" I asked Sebastian as I slipped my phone back into my shoulder bag and walked toward him. He'd finished his call and was waiting for me. Neither of us made mention of our respective conversations. "Holding the diamond. I really want to see it and hold it in my hands. But if I stand even a chance of getting that far, I have to speak with Chandra."

Sebastian and I had left the fountain and were now walking at a brisk pace toward Lincoln Center. I had twenty minutes before I was due at Jared Moor, and surprisingly, Sebastian was heading to the same place.

"I'm meeting up with someone," he said vaguely, studiously training his eyes on the path ahead.

Meeting up with someone? And would she, by any chance, happen to be called Cleo?

Then, with a sigh, I remembered what Ellie had told me about applying my own sleuthing advice to the Sebastian situation. She had a point, I thought somewhat sheepishly. I mean, maybe I was jumping to conclusions. Maybe he was going to meet someone else. Then again, if he really did want to spend time with Cleo, how much could our time together in Paris have meant?

Argh!

I took a breath. "That's nice," I forced myself to say.

"You said you wanted to speak with Chandra." Now he was changing the subject. Well, I was happy to go along with that.

I nodded. "Yes, and I think I'll try at the show. She's doing Jared Moor too. But she's not very easy to talk to. I hope I can get her onto the subject without making her suspicious or scaring her off. And I'd like to know whether she really was on a plane yesterday morning at seven thirty. Do you think you could manage to find that out—as soon as possible? I don't want to take anything for granted."

"Definitely."

"And if you could also find out as much as possible about where Peter, Chandra, Rafaela, Misty, and Brandon—"

"It was Brandon who danced with you last night, wasn't it? Although he seemed to be stepping on your feet more than dancing." He was smiling at me faintly, his eyebrows raised.

Now I was the one with my eyes glued to the path in front of us. "Uh, yes, that was Brandon. And, by the way," I went on, a touch more defiantly, "even if we didn't dance for long, I thought he was really good."

Sebastian shrugged his shoulders and an awkward silence hung in the air for a moment.

"Anyway," I continued, mentally shaking myself, "I would like to know as much as possible about where they've all been since the weekend—as well as what they have scheduled for this week until Friday morning. And be sure to include Cazzie—because like I said, given the right circumstances—"

"Anyone is capable of anything. And actually, we only have her word for it that the diamond is missing."

"Exactly."

"Anything else?"

I nodded. "Yes. More background information, please—but with an angle toward Cazzie. Assuming that she is telling us the truth when she says that the diamond is missing, and assuming that someone at Friday's shoot did indeed take it, there's still the possibility that the theft is revenge for something Cazzie did. In which case, I need to find a motive. Something she said or did to one of them, for instance… It would probably be something to do with their careers—although it might be something very personal… Do you think your sources can help with that?" As I asked, I realized that his main "source" was probably Cleo. How else had he known where to find me last night?

"I'm sure my source can handle your request," he answered cheerfully.

I didn't reply.

✳✳✳

Lincoln Center comprises a collection of several concert halls located around an open square a block away from Central Park on Manhattan's Upper West Side. Sebastian and I walked past the main entrance on Ninth Avenue, then parted ways on West Sixty-Second Street.

"I'm meeting someone at the café on the corner," he said, nodding toward a Mexican-themed restaurant across the street. "When should I give you a call about the research? Or do you want to meet right after your show?"

"How long do you need?"

"I should be able to pull something together in the next couple of hours."

"Then why don't we meet after my show? I should be done by about six… Can you meet me at the backstage entrance on Amsterdam and Sixty-Second?"

He nodded and turned to leave, but then paused. Looking back at me, he said, "You know, I'm happy I came… It's fun working together again."

I watched him, wondering if he might say more, but he didn't. "Yes, it is," I replied. Then I turned and left.

Our working relationship seemed to be on track. Sebastian and I had slipped into the pattern we'd forged last week in Paris…before the kiss. Maybe he wouldn't be such a distraction after all.

But was that what I really wanted?

✳ ✳ ✳

I received one of Ellie's Instagram selfies just after leaving Sebastian. She was getting her hair done backstage at Jared Moor.

I sent her a text saying I was on my way.

A few photographers were standing on the corner

of Sixty-Second Street and Amsterdam Avenue, which was where the backstage entrances to the shows were located. Lenses at the ready, the paparazzi were clearly hoping to catch sight of one of the famous models, like Rafaela or Ellie. Head tucked into the upturned collar of my trench coat, I walked past security, up the ramp, and into the hair and makeup tents put up especially for the shows. From there I was directed to Jared Moor.

Ellie was still having her hair done. She was going to be opening the show—and was therefore chronicling every aspect of her preparations for her Instagram and Facebook followers.

"You have to try these veggie wraps. They are so yummy," she enthused as soon as she saw me. Then in a whisper she added, "There's a new rumor going around that might be of interest to you—this one's about Tom." She nodded in the direction of the hair and makeup area, where, sure enough, I could just make out Tom's tall figure behind a cloud of hair spray. "He's hinted that he'd like to retire, move to a tropical island, and quit fashion—not that I believe for a moment that he could stay away for a long time, but…if he took what you're searching for, and it was valuable, maybe it could fund his early retirement."

"I'm surprised by you, Ellie," I said teasingly. "You're starting to think in the same suspicious way that I do—even about people you know and like!"

She smiled and took a sip from her drink. "Well, you did want information…and maybe some of your detective style is starting to rub off on me."

"I'll have to make you a partner."

"I thought you already had one," she quipped with an arch of her eyebrow and a giggle.

I opted not to answer, rolling my eyes before heading off to the buffet table.

On my way there I stopped to look at the wall that showed which models would be wearing which outfits and in what order they'd be walking out later. I noticed that Chandra was second to the last, while Misty would be closing the show. Hmm…that was good, because it looked like I was due to walk out for the last time a few outfits before Chandra, which meant that I could change, wait for her to change, and then try talking to her. And because she was nearly the last model on the runway, some of the other models and hair and makeup people should already have cleared out by then. I didn't want to make a scene—but with Chandra so cagey around me, I couldn't imagine it was going to be an easy conversation.

According to his show notes, Jared's collection was inspired by a mix of ballet, Richard Serra's metal sculptures, and "the iconic beauty" of Lee Miller (an American photographer and model of the 1920s and '30s). I read through further colorful references to everything from clouds and Rihanna to nineteenth-century whalers from Newfoundland. Then I looked at the dresses and trousers hanging on the racks and came to the conclusion that, despite all the talk of clouds and nineteenth-century whalers, Jared's clothes were basically smart and sexy.

"So are you still in denial?" Ellie asked when I joined her, two veggie wraps carefully balanced on one small plate and a chocolate cupcake and strawberries on another.

I rolled my eyes again as I stationed myself in the seat next to her, and the hairstylist, Laura, started brushing my hair.

"As Sebastian himself just told me, it's really nice working together."

Now Ellie rolled her eyes. "You two are such nerds. I wish you'd just get it together and admit you have the major hots for each other. I mean, trust me, Paris was not a fluke. Like, I was there. *I saw.*"

I shrugged my shoulders. "Well, his deal with my mom wasn't a fluke either."

"There you're wrong. Give the guy a break." Before she could say anything else, she had to leave for makeup.

As Ellie left, my phone vibrated. A text from Sebastian:

Chandra was definitely on the flight to Miami, and it left on time, so at 7.30 a.m. she was 33,000 feet above the sea. According to the airline's rules concerning electrical devices, she could not have sent the text to Cazzie. Now

I'm trying to find out if there was coverage where she was at that time in case she decided to break the rules.

I texted Sebastian back:

Great! Thanks. I'm going to try to talk to her backstage after the show, at around 6. Please wait outside for me until I appear. If she refuses to talk to me backstage, then I'll have to follow her out. So if you see her exiting quickly, please follow her. She hasn't been very talkative around me, and I imagine she won't be eager to talk to me later either.

He answered:

No problem, Holmes. I'll be on guard duty. And good luck with the show!

Thanks, Watson, I wrote back.

Have you ever noticed that your phone can be quiet for ages and then suddenly, within the span of a few minutes, everyone is trying to reach you at once? Sebastian's messages were quickly followed by messages from my mom, Pat, and Cazzie.

Hi, darling! I'm so excited about your fashion show. Jared Moor! That's brilliant, Axelle! Jenny and Kathy are coming over any minute. We're going to watch it live-streamed. So exciting! Miss you! XXX Mom

Kathy was Jenny's mom—and when she wasn't working as a pediatrician, she was my mom's number-one shopping partner.

> I'll be watching you on Fashion TV, girl. Look sharp! DVF casting tonight at 7 p.m. downtown at her HQ. Details to follow.

I think you can guess who that one was from. Cazzie wrote:

> Hi, Axelle. I just wanted to say that I still haven't heard anything…

I wrote back:

> Don't worry—you will. I think I've made a small break-through. Will tell you when I see you.

Of course, my small breakthrough regarding Chandra didn't yet amount to much, but I thought Cazzie needed something to hold on to, no matter how minor. Besides, I felt as if there'd been a slight shift in the rhythm of this case. Call me optimistic, but my small breakthrough had me buzzing, which was always a good sign.

I closed my eyes and let Nina, the makeup artist, work her magic.

✳✳✳

An hour and a half later, we were ready to go. In that last-minute preshow frenzy I was becoming accustomed to, my lips were glossed umpteen times, my face powdered, and my hair tweaked. I'd been slipped into my frock—a short, black wool-twill dress—and was adjusting the most amazing thigh-high leather boots when the music's decibel level shot up. It was showtime!

I walked out twice for Jared. One of those times I was on the runway with Misty. Ironically, she resolutely refused to look at me, instead walking past me with a sort of self-righteous *I'm the victim and you're the nasty one* look on her face. Had she really forgotten that I'd chased her because she'd been threatening *me* and that I'd found her, dusty and squirming, under cardboard boxes? Hardly supermodel-like behavior!

Misty also hogged the end of the runway, standing in front of the photographers and posing endlessly, so that I only had time to quickly turn and then head back. Not that I cared, but it was funny to see how she thought that giving me less time in front of the photographers would bother me. Whatever.

Chandra vaguely smiled at me when we passed each other on the runway, and Rafaela insisted on high-fiving me when we met. "Miss D!" she hollered above the beat of the music. Great. She'd shortened Ms. Detective to Miss D. Now I sounded like a rapper—although at least it was more discreet. Anyway, the photographers loved it. I heard the camera clicks increase tenfold as she continued down the runway toward them. Meanwhile, I breathed a sigh of relief as I slipped backstage. The whole runway thing still made me nervous—clearly I wasn't a natural. Then again, I thought, if it helped me solve more big, juicy cases...

Judging from the applause, the collection seemed to be a success. Jared dashed out on the runway in his sneakers and T-shirt to give a quick and modest wave of his hand before returning backstage where he was immediately swallowed by a swarm of media and well-wishers. I, meanwhile, quickly changed into my own clothes and then waited for Chandra.

Ellie came to say good-bye on her way out. She was about to head downtown to Juice Studios, where fashion shows for less established designers were often held. "It's a friend's show," she told me. "He's not famous yet—but he will be." Needless to say, having Ellie walk his show—as a favor, no less—was a real coup guaranteed to give him media coverage as an up-and-coming designer to watch.

I waited for Chandra near the exit, but she walked past, pretending not to notice me. At the bottom of the exit ramp she stopped to sign autographs for the group of die-hard fashion fans who waited in all kinds of weather for the models leaving the shows.

Out of the corner of my eye I could see Sebastian

standing across the street. It was still light out, although the sun was just beginning to drop. Chandra signed the last autograph and then turned left onto Sixty-Second Street. As she pulled away from the crowd I followed just behind her, and then caught up to her and told her that I'd like to speak with her.

She ignored me and kept moving, her long legs giving her an advantage in speed—and then suddenly she took off, catching me completely by surprise. In a few smooth, athletic strides, she bounded toward the curb of Ninth Avenue and disappeared into her waiting car just as the traffic lights changed. With a squeal of car tires, she was gone.

I was too slow, too late. I pulled back from the curb just as a yellow cab came flying past, its horn beeping loudly. The cab was followed by a zooming herd of cars, and I watched as Chandra's black Escalade disappeared in the fast-moving traffic.

Then I heard a car screech to a halt beside me.

"Axelle! Get in!" Sebastian was calling me from the window of a cab. He must have seen my struggle to keep up with Chandra and quickly hailed a taxi, thinking that she'd probably have a car waiting on Ninth Avenue. And he'd been right!

I jumped in and had just enough time to shut the door before the wheels screamed away from the curb and the cab started hurtling down Ninth Avenue at top speed. The black Escalade was not far in front of us—they must have had to wait at a light—so soon we were just behind them, about to catch up.

They must have seen us following them, though. If not, then Chandra's driver was the fastest in the Big Apple. But our cab stayed close and they never managed to shake us off.

"You know," our driver said, "I've been driving yellow cabs for more than thirty years, and no one's ever asked me to follow another car. I thought it was something that only happened in the movies!" He was thrilled with the chase and applied all his experience to keep us close to Chandra.

By the time we started crossing the West Village, we were no longer right behind them—at least not in any way that they could see. Our cabdriver was able to follow them discreetly by staying far behind and using streets that ran parallel to the ones they took.

The West Village is chockablock with tiny, narrow one-way streets. We met Chandra's car at intersections, but with Sebastian and I ducking down in the backseat, they had no way to recognize our yellow cab among all the others. So we were fairly certain they no longer thought we were tailing them. And sure enough, they started dropping speed and eventually came to a gentle stop on Centre Street in Nolita. From the back of our cab, parked sixty-five feet behind the Escalade, we watched as Chandra sprang out of her car and strode toward the Police Building, one of the most iconic downtown apartment buildings.

According to our taxi driver, "Back in the day, it actually *was* a police building, but it was converted into apartments years ago. You gotta be rich to live there, that's for sure. Lots of celebrities call it home. I reckon they must get a great view of the Williamsburg Bridge from the back."

The building's long, stone baroque-revival facade was impressive. Above the pediment over the entrance, an enormous dome glowed in the early evening light.

I handed some cash to our driver and thanked him. ("Anytime. I hope we meet again!" he said.) Then we slid out of the cab and stood on the sidewalk as I tried to decide how to proceed. "I have to follow her in," I said, as I watched Chandra disappear into the dimly lit depths of the cavernous lobby.

"But there's a doorman standing right there."

I turned to Sebastian. "Last night you managed to play a magazine vendor and dancing fashionista quite well…"

"So…?"

"So tonight, how about a lost tourist?"

He nodded and laughed.

"I'll go in and pretend Chandra's expecting me. Then you come in and distract the doorman. And while you're charming him—"

"Ah, so you *do* think I'm charming?" He was smiling.

"What I personally think of you, Watson, is immaterial to this case. In this instance, I only hope the *doorman* finds you charming."

"Have I mentioned that I like it when you're tough?"

Ignoring him, I continued, "And please try to charm him for a while—if you can. I don't know how long it'll take me to find her apartment in there." I was gazing up at the building. It looked like a mini version of the Met from last night's party.

I pulled a makeup compact out of my shoulder bag and checked myself out. Hmm…my makeup was fine, if a bit heavy, but my hair… I quickly ran my hands through my hair and ruffled it a bit. Ah, that was better. Then, stretching tall—as tall as I could in my Converses—I turned to Sebastian and asked, "Ready?"

"Yeah. How do I look? Like a tourist needing directions?"

Without thinking, I reached up and ruffled his hair. "Now you do."

"Are you sure you don't need to do more to me?" He was looking at me in that way again—only this time he held it long enough that I was sure I'd seen it.

I pulled my hand back before confusion got the better of me. "We have to go."

Double Trouble

G ood evening, how may I help you?" asked the
doorman as I strode into the building.

"I'm meeting Chandra—Chandra Rhodes—for
dinner. I think she's just gone up."

"Yes, she has," he answered as he picked up the internal phone. "May I ask who's here?"

"You can tell her that Misty Parker is here." As I lied,
the irony that Chandra's building was called the Police
Building was not lost on me, and I felt a twinge of guilt.

"I'm not getting an answer, but if you wouldn't mind
waiting, I'll try her again in a few moments."

"No problem," I said. Standing next to the front desk,
which was behind a high counter, I took my phone out
and feigned preoccupation with my messages. At that
moment Sebastian came in and pretended to be lost.
Good work, I thought, as I watched Sebastian maneuver
the doorman away from the desk and toward the grand
front door. As soon as the man had his back to me, I
stole behind the desk and looked at the various papers
taped to the inside wall of the counter. I quickly found

what I was looking for: a list of the tenants and their respective apartment numbers. Giving Sebastian the thumbs-up, I crept back out from behind the desk and quietly made a beeline for the nearest elevator.

Chandra was on the top floor, but when I got off the elevator, I discovered a problem. The apartment doors had no numbers on them! I suspected that was for security reasons because many of the people living in this building were famous, if some of the names on the list I'd seen downstairs were anything to go by.

I quickly walked up and down the corridor, trying to tell if I could hear anything through the doors. But no—nothing. The building could have been empty for all the noise I heard. But then someone suddenly turned some music on—opera, by the sound of it. I thought I could safely assume that it wasn't coming from Chandra's flat. The thought of her listening to opera didn't really sit well with her surfer-chick image.

But then I heard something else...something familiar...something I'd just been listening to myself... It was the music from Jared Moor's show! Surely that had to be Chandra. The music blared loudly from a door farther down the corridor. I walked up to the door, stood in front of the peephole, and knocked.

At first I got no answer, and the music continued to play. Again I knocked, and then I rang her bell—still no answer. In exasperation and hoping that she wouldn't call her doorman to report me, I had the idea of writing her a note. I could see light below her door. Surely I could slip a note underneath it. I took a small notebook and pen out of my shoulder bag and wrote:

Chandra, it's Axelle. Please, I'd like to talk to you…

I slipped the notepaper underneath her door and waited. The trouble was, for all I knew she could be in her bedroom or something. It could be hours before she came near her front door. But after another minute her phone rang, cutting through the music. I thought I heard her run past the door (at least that's how it sounded to me), and as she answered her phone, the music stopped. I knocked on her door again, hard. Surely she'd hear me this time.

A few seconds later I heard Chandra walk up to the door…and then nothing. Was she reading the note I'd written? Had she found it? A moment later I had my answer as I heard her undo the chain and lock. The door opened, and a tired-looking Chandra stood to the side and waved me in with her hand.

Without a word, she led me into a vast living room with soaring ceilings and enormous windows. Fleetingly I thought of what the taxi driver had said about the back of the building probably having a great view toward the Williamsburg Bridge. He was right. The bridge twinkled in the dusky light, adding a sparkly note to an otherwise uncomfortable encounter.

Her apartment looked more or less as I'd imagined the apartment of a mega supermodel would look: funky, sophisticated, colorful, and fun. I could imagine Taylor Swift feeling right at home. Apricot-colored walls were hung with all sorts of prints and pictures. Three surfboards stood upright against the wall to my right, and tie-dyed fabrics were draped over the enormous white sectional sofas that formed a long U shape. Above and to the left was an open mezzanine with a ladder leading to her bed. A colorful kilim carpet hung from the mezzanine railing.

A loud buzzer suddenly rang, nearly making me jump. Chandra quickly went to the intercom on the wall next to her door. It was the doorman downstairs calling to ask if she was okay and tell her that someone had been looking for her. She looked at me and I nodded, mouthing the words, "It was me." She didn't tell him I was with her, but just reassured him that everything was fine.

After hanging up with him, she disappeared into her glossy white-and-lime-green kitchen and I heard her blender start to whir. She still hadn't said a word to me, and I couldn't begin to imagine how this was going to play out. I quickly sent Sebastian a text to at least let him know that I'd made it in. He wrote back right away:

Well done! I'm off to dinner now. Let me know how you get on. See you tomorrow?

Dinner? He hadn't mentioned anything about dinner. I wrote back:

> Or we could meet up later to quickly discuss our game plan. I have a casting near here when I've finished with Chandra, but after that maybe?

Sebastian:

> Sorry, no, can't do. Busy all night. Tomorrow? Anytime is good.

Probably sending feedback to my mom, I thought. Or having dinner with Cleo.

Shut up. And stop jumping to conclusions.

I took a breath and wrote back:

> Fine. Tomorrow. We can make plans in the morning.

Chandra came out of her kitchen with two glasses of green smoothie just as I slipped my phone away. The fact that she produced her own smoothie mix—Chandra's Choice—came to mind. *This must be it,* I thought.

"I'm sorry—" we both started.

"You go first," she said as she put the glasses down on a large, low wooden table (literally, the table was a huge chunk of wood—driftwood, by the looks of it), then busied herself with watering an enormous potted palm that stood between two of the windows.

"Chandra, listen. I'm sorry I chased you here—and

please don't be upset by anything I'm about to say, but...I'd like to talk to you about a diamond you wore at the *Chic* shoot last Friday—"

"I knew you were in New York to do more than just model," she said, turning to face me. "But sure, we can discuss last Friday—although I think you'll find that following me here was a waste of your time."

I shook my head. "I'm not sure it was."

She glared at me for a moment, her eyes flashing.

"I think you know more than you're letting on," I insisted. I'd followed her here because the few vague clues I had pointed strongly to her. If she thought I was going to let go of this chance easily, then she was mistaken.

"That can be said about most people and most situations, don't you think?" she said mockingly. She'd finished watering her palm and was now sitting on the sofa across from me.

"Will you let me tell you what I think happened?" I continued.

She gave a slight shrug of her shoulders. "Suit yourself." I watched her profile as she picked at a thread on the back of the sofa.

Maybe I could shock her into admission, I thought. So I blurted out, "I think you took the diamond—as one of your well-known practical jokes or 'magic tricks.' Whatever you want to call it..." I thought I saw her flinch as I said it. "Even Cazzie said—"

"Cazzie?" She looked at me suddenly, her pretense of indifference slipping—even if only slightly.

I moved in quickly before she had time to regain her composure completely.

"Cazzie doesn't think you took it, but the fact is that the diamond is missing and she needs to find it… She called you, I think. Shortly after the shoot?"

Chandra nodded but said nothing. In fact, her stubborn silence seemed to highlight the trouble with this case so far. No one was saying anything; no one had seen anything; and no one knew anything. *Argh!*

I continued in a goading tone, "She thought you might confess that you'd taken the diamond, that you were playing one of your magic tricks on her— something she says you do regularly on fashion shoots. But when she called you, you didn't say anything…" I looked at her pointedly but was met with silence. "So," I continued, "Cazzie began to doubt you'd taken it because she says you never keep things for very long, and that in any case you like to draw attention to your tricks—neither of which you did in this instance."

I paused for a moment, waiting for all this to sink in. "Cazzie will have to go to the police, you know. At this point it really can't be avoided, but I was hoping you might help us first…" Surely threatening her with the police would make her crack? But still Chandra said nothing. I felt like I was sitting opposite a sphinx.

I kept going. "So Cazzie called me. You're right.

I'm here on her behalf to find it. And so far…" *Right, Axelle,* I told myself, *it's time to close in hard.* "So far all the evidence I have…" She was looking at me now, still sphinxlike, but at least I seemed to have her full attention. "…leads me to you. My trail goes cold at your doorstep. Anything you could tell me might help. I think you know much more than you're letting on. And like I said, if I leave here not having learned anything new, I'm afraid Cazzie will have to call the police…"

Basically, I'd stopped just short of accusing her of stealing the most famous black diamond in the world from one of the most prestigious fashion shoots in the world—but you'd never have known it from looking at her. If I'd expected a fierce denial, I was in for a surprise, because all Chandra did was take a long look at me and sigh. And when she finally spoke I had to question whether my dream of being a detective was really only that—a dream.

"I wish I could help you," she said, "but I'm afraid I don't have the diamond… Nor do I know where it is."

I raised my eyebrows as this registered. Of course, she could easily be lying—but my gut told me she wasn't. At the same time, if she really did know nothing of the diamond's whereabouts, as she claimed, surely she would sound more upset or angry at my accusation? But how could she not have the diamond? Okay, I knew I didn't have much to go on, and I'd jumped to some major conclusions based on a lot of tiny details—things she'd said and the recollections of others.

I had no hard evidence. But still… everything had pointed to Chandra! Even considering the chink that I'd pointed out to Sebastian—that Chandra had sent the text message to Cazzie yesterday morning while supposedly thirty thousand feet in the air… How could I have been that far off? I'd thought I was more than halfway to solving my second big mystery. Instead I seemed more than halfway to nowhere!

The case seemed to have more threads than haute-couture embroidery.

I took a few slow sips from my thick green smoothie, buying time as I rapidly went through all I knew about the Friday shoot. But again, everything pointed most strongly in Chandra's direction. I admit it wasn't a direct line…but it was much more so than for any of the others. With my last swallow of the thick green goop, a thought came to me. What was it she'd said?

"I wish I could help you…but I'm afraid I don't have the diamond… Nor do I know where it is."

Hmm…I repeated the words in my mind. If she hadn't taken the Black Amelia, wouldn't she have said, "I didn't take the diamond… I never touched it," or something like that? And wouldn't she have been angry at being falsely accused? But other than her simple statement, she hadn't defended herself, and she'd remained cool… Too cool, I thought now.

Suddenly, something my grandma had often told me rang in my ears: "Occasionally, Axelle, when your grandfather and his team were solving a tricky case, he'd say to them, 'Listen carefully to everything you hear… People often reveal more than they think by what they say.'"

If I took Chandra's statement literally, she'd only admitted to not *presently* having the diamond and to not *presently* knowing where it was.

Neither of those admissions relieved her of past possession of the diamond or of past knowledge of its whereabouts. So maybe I was right—maybe she did take the diamond after all.

If true, this might explain the absence of any anger or passionate denials in the face of my accusation. But then why didn't she have the diamond now? Where had the Black Amelia gone?

My mind spun as I went through likely scenarios. Either she'd gotten rid of the diamond, or she was lying and still had it and had some elaborate blackmail scheme up her sleeve, or… Suddenly, like a knot being slipped undone, I felt something shift about the way I needed to look at this case. An unusual theory had crept into my mind, and it was gathering momentum. Could it really be that? Maybe…possibly…

Why not?

I believed that Chandra no longer had the gem. She looked more uncomfortable with each passing moment, and I was inclined to go with what my instinct told me: that she was as bad at twisting the truth as she was good at playing pranks. I didn't think she could lie outright.

"I think we're finished here, so if—" Chandra was standing now, ready to show me out.

Quashing any self-doubt about myself or my new theory, and following my gut, I took a chance and quickly said, "Chandra, I believe that you don't have the diamond and that you don't know where it is…but I still think that you *did* have the diamond and that you *did* know where it *was*…"

She was looking at me, unwilling to give an inch.

Going out on a limb, I pushed forward. "*Until it disappeared for a second time…*"

This time I definitely saw her flinch.

"You had it, and then you lost it." I waited a moment before continuing. "Or perhaps *someone took it from you?*"

For a few minutes I sat watching as Chandra ran her hands through her hair and over her face. She was obviously tormented, her facade of indifference finally stripped away. Then she began to speak.

"If nothing else, it feels good to finally get it out in the open. This week has been a nightmare. I've been agonizing over whether someone would find out. And I've been terrified, because I *did* take the diamond— you're right. But I couldn't say anything, because I no longer have it! How could I possibly admit to Cazzie that, yes, I took the diamond, but sorry, I don't have it anymore? Even to my ears it sounds beyond ridiculous.

I mean, who would believe me?" She paused for a moment and seemed unsure whether to say more—and I had a feeling I knew why.

"I know why you're scared…" She looked warily at me as I continued. "I know about the rumor—the one from that shoot when you were starting out as a model…"

She sighed again and flushed, then leaped to her own defense. "I took a necklace from that shoot as a joke. I suppose I found the whole fashion business so *serious*, and I've always been a bit of a prankster, so I just couldn't help myself—stupid, I know. Anyway, I was working with another model on the shoot and she saw me take it, but by the time I gave it back, she'd already left for the day. So she assumed I'd stolen it and started spreading that nasty rumor. I should have fought back, but my agency was worried that I'd bring more attention to the incident and that it would cling to me, whether it was true or not.

"So you can imagine what would happen to me now if I told everyone that, yes, I took the Black Amelia, but guess what, I no longer have it. The nasty rumors would start all over again—and worse!" she said. "That's why I've been so rude to you. I'm sorry. When you showed up yesterday at the shoot, I was sure you must be there undercover to find the diamond. Naturally I wanted to distance myself from you. I'd been hoping that anyone looking for the diamond would find a trail leading straight to whoever actually has it and that I'd be bypassed. So I've been lying low. But it hasn't helped, has it?" She looked away, agitated and anxious. "But if I can help now…"

I nodded. "That would be great. I have some questions that I'd like to ask you." I was hoping against hope that she might be able to tell me something that could open up a new line of inquiry.

Before I pressed on with my questioning, however, she was at pains to clarify that she'd taken the Black Amelia as a trick, a practical joke, nothing else. It was something she liked to do—or, rather, *had* liked to do, she corrected herself. But this time it had gone badly wrong.

"First, did you have any idea of the diamond's value?"

She shook her head. "Not really. Cazzie had droned on about it while we were shooting, but I wasn't really paying attention. I mean, it's just a stone, isn't it?"

"Not to everyone." *Then again,* I thought, as I glanced around her enormous designer apartment, *everything is relative.*

She shrugged her shoulders. "Well, I honestly didn't think that anything would happen to it when I took it. The plan was just for it to sit in my handbag for a short while, and then I'd draw Cazzie's attention to it and watch as she freaked out because she couldn't find it."

"So how did you take it from Cazzie?"

"That was easy. As Cazzie left the set, I saw her put the diamond in her handbag. That was when I had the idea of taking it to make her panic. It seemed like a fun

206

idea at the time—the kind of thing I love to do—but totally stupid now. Obviously I won't be doing anything like that again. My days of magic are definitely over." I watched her face go a shade paler at the thought of what she'd done.

"I watched as Cazzie went to Brandon's computer and looked at the photos we'd shot... Then she suddenly dashed to the dressing area. I remember we smelled something burning and she thought it might be the iron. In the meantime I walked slowly toward the dressing area. Just as I neared it, the fire alarm suddenly rang and Cazzie appeared from behind the dividing curtain. I remember taking a quick look around the studio at that moment and realizing the noise was just what I needed.

"Everyone was so distracted by the screaming alarm that I was sure they'd never notice me slip behind the curtain into the dressing area. So I did just that. And then I simply reached into Cazzie's handbag and took the diamond. It was in a small box, so I quickly opened that to make sure I was taking what I wanted, then I slipped it into my bag. Anyway, once the diamond was in my shoulder bag, I quietly went back out and joined the others in looking out the windows."

So far, Chandra had only confirmed what I'd already suspected. She'd taken the diamond exactly when I thought she had. That was good to know, but I needed something new to work with. I had to keep digging.

"Did you take your shoulder bag with you to the window?"

"Yeah. It was on me."

"And as you were watching the commotion below, did you happen to notice where the others were? Can you remember if they were all at the windows too?"

"I think so, yeah…although I'm not sure I'd have noticed if they weren't. I was mostly excited about the joke I was playing on Cazzie. Even the fire took a backseat to it."

"Hmm…And after you'd finished looking out the windows, what did you do?"

"I went back to the dressing room and got ready to go home. Things were more or less normal again. Somebody must have turned the music off when the alarm sounded, but it had been switched back on and everyone was packing up for the day."

"Who else was in the dressing area with you?"

"Misty, Rafaela, and Cazzie."

"And then?"

"Well, I changed into my own clothes and then put my bag back over my shoulder. It was on the floor near me while I changed."

"Was that the only time it wasn't on you?"

She nodded. "I think so, yeah. But I had my eye on it. More or less, anyway."

I let the "more or less" slide for the moment. "Okay. Then what?"

"Then I said good-bye to Rafaela and Misty in the dressing area. But I did it really slowly because I was hoping that Cazzie would look for the diamond and not find it, and then I could surprise her. But Cazzie still hadn't noticed. So I went out to say good-bye to Trish and Tom and Peter and Brandon, thinking I'd circle back to Cazzie."

"And your shoulder bag?"

"It was still on my shoulder."

"Can I see it?"

"Sure." I watched us she unfolded her long limbs and strode across her living room. She came back a moment later with a large purple La Lune shoulder bag that was similar to mine.

"Did you have the top zipped?"

"No. I never do. It was unzipped."

"Hmm… And the diamond?"

She shrugged her shoulders. "Stupidly, I just put it into my bag, right on top of whatever I had in there. I was going to give it back, remember?"

I couldn't help looking sharply at her then. Her story was so childlike—and yet I was dealing with a supermodel who earned millions of dollars a year (and even had her own line of green goop), a world-famous diamond, and a shoot for the most prestigious fashion magazine in existence. It was close to surreal.

"Like I said," she continued, "I wasn't the least bit worried about the stone's safety. I mean, I never would have imagined that anyone from that group—presumably it's one of them?—would have taken the stone. Never. Ever. I've been working with all of them since I started modeling."

"You say you think someone from the group took the diamond from you. Are you sure it didn't just fall out somewhere? Dropped out of your bag while you were walking around saying good-bye to everyone?"

She shook her head. "No way. The stone was in a cloth bag that was in a box. Altogether it was about so big." She held her hands slightly cupped, one over the other, palms facing each other. "Trust me. I'd have heard it fall—and seen it."

I sighed, then stood up and said, "Can you please put the bag over your shoulder, turn some music on, and then come here and greet me?"

She looked at me questioningly, then nodded and stood up. With her remote, she turned her music on until it was suitably loud. Then she slipped the braided straps of her handbag over her shoulder and came to me.

"Now let's pretend you're saying good-bye to me."

As Chandra leaned in to double air-kiss me, I put my hand into her bag and pulled something out.

"Did you feel that?" I asked as I pulled back from her and held out the hairbrush I'd taken.

She shook head. "Not at all. Nothing."

"And in a real-life scenario, with more people around and all eager to leave, you would probably be even less likely to feel something… So if you're sure that nobody—from the moment you took the diamond and slipped it into your bag until the moment you left the studio—went near it, there's a fair chance the diamond might have been taken from your bag when you went around saying good-bye. It could have been done like I just did it now. It's the strongest theory that comes to mind, anyway. But it presupposes that someone saw you put the diamond in your bag to begin with."

Of course, the thought crossed my mind that Chandra could be lying to me about everything, but I'd look into that possibility later. Not now, not here. "So what happened next?" I continued. "You said good-bye to everyone, and then?"

"Well, I wanted to leave for home, and since Cazzie hadn't noticed anything yet, I thought I'd go to her and say, 'Can I see the diamond again?' or something like that—anything to prompt her to look into her handbag. But before I went to find her, I stopped by the makeup table to get the diamond ready so that I could quickly make it 'reappear.'"

"And?"

"And this was the horrible part. When I looked into my bag, it was gone. I don't think I've ever felt so awful. I searched and searched and couldn't find anything!" She was nearly crying now, her eyes beyond worry. "I can't believe what I've done to Cazzie, to *Chic*, to my career! And all because I was playing a stupid, childish joke. How could I have been so dumb? I might as well just disappear to an island somewhere and never come back."

"So what did you do then?"

"Well, I tried to help Cazzie pack up. I thought maybe I'd find it among her things. Don't ask me why. I was desperate. And I felt sick for not saying anything to her, but how could I? I didn't have it anymore! And maybe it was wrong of me, but the fact that I no longer had it made me feel as if I was no longer responsible for it… I mean, if it had just gotten lost somehow, it was bound to turn up in the studio somewhere. How could it have gotten anywhere else?"

Her voice dropped to a near whisper as she continued, "And if someone had decided to steal it, that wasn't *my* fault, was it? It's not as if I stole it myself. I only took it as a joke…"

The problem was that Chandra had trusted everyone at the shoot that day. She'd thought she was working with real friends. And while most of them probably were, one of them obviously wasn't.

And Cazzie, I thought, had believed that because she'd had her bag on her arm—at least until she'd dashed to the studio windows to look outside—the diamond was safe. And she hadn't thought to check on it until she was leaving—because again, like Chandra, she had trusted the small group of people she was working with.

So if I believed Chandra's version of events—and

so far what she'd said tallied with what I'd surmised—someone had seen her take the Black Amelia, and that someone had taken it from her.

So what next, Axelle? I asked myself. *What next?*

✱ ✱ ✱

I saw the doorman do a double take when I stepped off the elevator and back into the cavernous lobby. But before he could ask me anything, my phone started ringing. I smiled as I passed him, then stepped outside. I assumed Pat was calling to berate me about being late for my casting at Diane von Furstenberg, and I was surprised to be greeted instead by Miriam's breathy French accent.

"Axelle, I don't mind you being late—I will assume you've been working for Cazzie—but you must let me know. The clients don't realize that you have special extra work on the side—and as you know, neither does Pat. She had a dental appointment late this afternoon and went home early, so we've been lucky. She would have sent the police out after you by now, and I'm not joking."

"I'm sorry, Miriam. I was on the case and totally lost track of time. I can't believe how late it is!" I looked at my watch. The time really had flown. It was already eight o'clock, and my appointment at DVF had been for seven!

"Yes, well, don't worry this time. I've spoken with

DVF, and they're working late tonight in any case, so you can go there now—they are expecting you. But next time, please let me know."

"I will."

"As for your day tomorrow, I told Pat that I would give you the details myself. You have to go to the Condé Nast Building to see *Teen Vogue* in the morning—they definitely want to book you before you leave. And we've confirmed you for another two shows tomorrow; DKNY is one of them. Their casting scout saw you in Paris, so when I told them that you didn't have the time today to go by, they booked you anyway, which is fabulous.

"The second show is for Jorge Cruz, a young designer who has a great buzz about him. He's doing the most incredible things with cutting-edge synthetic fabrics. His show will be at an enormous Midtown loft and it should be fun. I'm going to see it—so look sharp, as Pat would say! I'll email you the times and addresses. Where are you right now?"

"Outside the Police Building."

"Good. You're only a short cab ride from Diane von Furstenberg. Do you have money for a taxi?"

"*Oui, madame.*"

"Then get going! I'll be home late, so *à demain, ma petite Axelle*!"

I hung up with Miriam and sighed as I stood on the pavement. New York was definitely a city with a buzz—and apparently the buzz never died down!

The next thing to come through as I hailed a cab was a text from Ellie:

I've finished with my show. Where are you?

I answered her back:

On my way to DVF for a casting. I'll be there in ten.

Ellie wrote:

Perfect! You'll be right around the corner from Juice— which is where I am. Dinner at my fave vegan place again?

I answered her back:

Great!

When I arrived at the casting, I realized that I'd met a few of the other models there either in Paris or at the Jared Moor show today. Plus, Thierry, the makeup artist I'd worked with a few times last week, was there—direct from the Paris shows.

He came at me with open arms and a look of concern on his face. "Axelle, I am thrilled to see that you are all right," he said, his French accent even thicker than I remembered. "How ghastly for you to have been dragged into Belle La Lune's disappearance! *Mon*

Dieu—what a nightmare! Anyway, you are safe now. The New York fashion world is too fast-paced for mysteries of any kind—trust me."

If only you knew, I thought.

Then he hugged me and we chatted for a few minutes about the shows.

Fortunately, the casting didn't take long. I was given a colorful, silk jersey wrap dress to wear (so light and easy to move in that I could have chased someone in it), then walked back and forth for the DVF team, after which I said good-bye and left.

Ellie and I met two blocks away from DVF Studio Headquarters. Fifteen minutes later, we were sitting at a rickety table in her favorite dive, waiting for our order. This time we had a seat right in front of the large window overlooking Abingdon Square. Ellie somehow always managed to look as if she'd just stepped off the plane from shooting in some exotic locale.

Tonight she was wearing a loose-fitting white blouse that looked like something the Three Musketeers would have worn. Over the blouse was a super-cool khaki-colored safari-style coat with large brass buttons. This was finished off with black leather trousers, ankle boots, and a very large Michael Kors bag in soft caramel leather. She looked sun-kissed and amazing—despite the long day of work she'd put in.

"Why aren't you with Sebastian?" she asked as soon as we'd ordered.

"I think he's having dinner with Cleo."

Ellie looked up at me from behind her long ruffled fringe. "And?"

"And nothing." I shrugged my shoulders.

She sighed loudly. "Like I said at Jared's, I can't wait 'til the two of you work it out. I have enough drama with Fashion Week going on."

"Thanks."

Ellie laughed.

By common consent we dropped the subject of Sebastian, and after going over our schedules for tomorrow, we moved on to the information and gossip she'd managed to gather for me.

"So…" She was about to start when our order number was called. We sprang up to get our food, then sat back down.

"I'm all ears," I said as I bit into my tofu burger.

"Well," she began again, leaning in and lowering her voice, "I found something out backstage at my last show." Here she stopped and pursed her lips for a moment as she looked at me. "About Cazzie, I think…"

"Cazzie?"

She nodded. "If what I heard is true, then she may have major money problems. But nobody here—in New York, I mean—knows."

"What do you mean?"

"Well, she's from London, right?"

I nodded, wondering where this was leading.

"So backstage at my last show, I overheard the two models sitting to my left while we were getting our hair done. They were talking about a casting that one of them had done in London. Now this model, the one who'd done the casting, happened to have some inside information about the London designer she'd gone to see. I think she said the information came from a friend who somehow works with the designer.

"Anyway, this designer is just starting out—and you know how big an investment it is for a young designer to start in fashion… Well, like many others in that position, he's having trouble with cash flow and manufacturing. And apparently, if this young designer doesn't get a large dose of cash soon, his whole business will probably go under."

"So?"

"So"—Ellie leaned in closer still as she continued—"the young designer is Cazzie Kinlan's brother." She paused for a moment. "The models didn't know that Cazzie and the designer they were talking about were related. Both of them were total newbies to the business and the designer is actually Cazzie's stepbrother, so they don't share the same surname."

"So how do you know that Cazzie has been investing money in her stepbrother's business?"

"Well, even though it's supposed to be a secret, some people in London know—which is how I know. I mean, people are careful—they don't want to gossip about Cazzie in case they incur her wrath—but eventually everyone will know that she and this designer are related."

"Hmm… If she wants to help him, why doesn't she just give him a ton of free publicity?" I asked. "Shoot his clothes for *Chic*, for instance?"

Ellie laughed. "If only fashion were that simple! Didn't you know that the more a designer advertises in a magazine—you know, pays for those glossy ads up front—the more likely his or her clothes are to be photographed for the magazine?"

"No, I didn't." But that was like bribery, I thought.

"Well, it's like that. The magazines don't just photograph any old frock. And it's much the same for beauty product placement in the magazines. To have your clothes or products photographed for the magazines, either you have to pay a fortune in advertising—something designers who are just starting out can't afford—or you have to be such a fashion-design genius that you're able to become a darling of a powerful editor-in-chief. The major editors have the power to fast-track a young designer to success—but the designer has to be good."

"Then why doesn't she make him her darling? Or isn't he good enough?"

"From what I've seen, his designs are actually pretty good—and I don't think Cazzie would invest in him if he wasn't talented. But Cazzie would be wary of showing that he's a favorite of hers in case that looks too much like family favors. That's not really looked upon well in fashion. Whatever else you can say about the fashion business, it really is a meritocracy."

"Did the models say anything else?"

"No. Just that the business was going under. Like I said, they had no idea that the designer was related to Cazzie. But when I heard his name, I thought you might like to know."

Hmm… While Ellie's gossip was intriguing, after visiting the Museum of Natural History I'd established that it was nearly impossible to sell a famous diamond on the open market without it being recognized, and cutting a large black diamond into smaller unrecognizable bits was also difficult because the stones were prone to breaking. Stealing the Black Amelia for money didn't really make sense.

Plus, so far I had no reason to doubt what Cazzie had told me about her actions last Friday—not to mention that they were in large part corroborated by the others. But I took a deep breath and made a mental note to have Sebastian look into Cazzie's situation with her stepbrother anyway. At this point in the case, it seemed important to make sure no stone was left unturned.

"You know, Ellie," I said, changing tack, "I wish I had a film of the day—Friday, I mean. I'd love to be able to see the sequence of events leading up to the theft, even if only from one angle. Time is running out fast now and I'm just not sure which way to go."

I continued eating distractedly as I mused. The tofu burger and sweet-potato fries were actually really yummy. And my meal reminded me of my grandma—not that she ever served tofu or anything else remotely like what was on my plate. But my burger had fresh chervil on it, and that was something she liked. She grew it in her garden and often put it on the soups she made, which she and I would have as a TV supper (together with a plate of toasted cheese sandwiches) when my parents were out for the evening. We'd sit in her cozy sitting room and watch the mystery programs she loved, the same ones I became obsessed with...

"Axelle? You've gone quiet."

I was thinking about the various detective programs we watched. Some I loved, but others were so-so. What always interested me, though, were the different methods the detectives used to solve the mysteries. And as I was thinking about this, I was reminded of a technique that could be just the one I needed to help me with this case.

In my excitement, I nearly overturned my glass of water. Ellie laughed as she put her hand out to save it.

"I know exactly what I have to do!" I said. "Do you have any time tomorrow? After the DKNY show?"

"Yes, I think so." She pulled out her phone and looked at her schedule. "I could squeeze in an hour or so just after it. Why?"

Carina Axelsson

"Could you do some acting for me?"

"Sure. But who do I have to pretend to be?"

"I don't know exactly—but someone from last Friday's group."

Ellie looked at me in total confusion.

"I have an idea for a little experiment. What would help me most right now is if I could see—literally *see*—everyone's movements on Friday afternoon. The only way to have that happen—"

"Is to have it acted out." Ellie smiled at me. "Good idea."

I nodded. I would start, I told myself, with the moments just before the fire alarm rang and go until the moment Chandra left the studio. It might just give me the answer I needed.

I was buzzing. I treated myself to a taxi back to Miriam's, ideas running through my mind as my cab flew up Tenth Avenue, skimming potholes and flying through the intersections.

Once we were near the park, the cabdriver caught my eye in his rearview mirror. "I think you're a very lucky person," he said in lilting French-accented English. He sounded as if he was from the Caribbean. "It is very rare to have so many green lights. We didn't hit a red one once!"

"Thank you." I smiled. "I'll know by Friday morning if I really am lucky."

"Huh?"

"Nothing." I said, laughing. "An inside joke. Thank you and have a great evening!"

I paid him and walked into Miriam's building.

Miriam was still out. Nicolette had put a few lights on, and I could hear the muted sounds of her television emanating from the corridor that led to her rooms.

I went to my bedroom and threw myself on my bed for a good stretch before checking my messages. Miriam had sent me my schedule details, and I had messages from Jenny and my mom—both simply wanted to know how I was doing. And there was another frustrated-sounding email from Cazzie: still nothing from the thief.

Why were they taking so long in sending the next riddle?

For a moment I was tempted to write back and ask if Cazzie could help me get the same studio at Juice for my little experiment, but that would be too big a production. I needed somewhere quick and easy.

Suddenly an idea came to mind: maybe I could do it at Chandra's apartment. It was smaller than the studio, but not that much. And it had those huge windows that wrapped all the way around—and even faced the same directions as the ones in the studio at Juice. If I hung some fabric across the opening to her kitchen, I would even have a pretty good simulation of the dressing area at the studio.

It was late…but not that late, especially considering it was Fashion Week and Chandra would be working pretty much nonstop and well into the night.

I quickly sent her a text and had an answer within minutes:

> Hi, Axelle. No problem—I'd be happy to help. Do you need me to be there?

I answered back:

> That's great, thanks! You don't have to be there, but it would help. Do you think you could squeeze it in? I would need your help for about an hour to do a reenactment of Friday afternoon. And would you mind if I have two friends along to help? I trust them completely.

To which Chandra answered:

> If I move my hair and makeup time for Calvin Klein back a bit, I could squeeze an hour in. I'll have my booker do it tomorrow. How about straight after DKNY? I think you're doing that too, right? We could go down together in my car after the show. So let's say I'm yours from 12:30 to about 2 p.m. at the latest. Does this work? And friends are okay. If you trust them, I do too.

Awesome, I thought—and told her so.

Sebastian had said he'd be free to help all day, and Ellie had said she could give me an hour of her time, which was great. Right now, though, I needed to get some sleep.

I always felt better when I had a plan, so as I ran through what I needed to do tomorrow, I began to relax. After taking a deep breath, I stretched one last time before getting ready for bed.

As I slipped between the sheets, my last thoughts were of Sebastian. Where was he? How had his dinner gone? And was he still out having fun…without me?

Rogue Rumors

My phone was ringing again. *Argh! Pat!* I thought. But I sat up with a start when I saw it was Cazzie. Despite having slept long and well, I was engulfed by a sense of anxiety and frustration when I saw her name.

"Axelle," she said in a brittle voice when I answered. Her fear was palpable through my phone—even at this early hour. "I need you to go online."

"Okay," I said as I jumped out of bed and went to my laptop.

"Go to the fashion blog called 'The Unfashionable Truth,' then look under today's news. You'll see what I mean."

I did just that and found the blog post Cazzie was referring to. It was only a couple of sentences long, but I understood why she sounded scared.

What's going on with Cazzie Kinlan? The Unfashionable Truth hears that she's lost more than just the plot... Is she stumbling in her stilettos? Is a certain young model helping her find her way out of trouble? Does Chic *know?*

It was, of course, suitably vague and named no

sources—which I guessed was the point. But the grains of truth buried in what was written made me feel more than uncomfortable. It was almost as if it was written in code targeted at Cazzie and me: Cazzie had lost something, I was helping her find it, and might her career suffer? *Argh!*

"Axelle," Cazzie said, "if this catches fire, I'll face serious consequences from Sid Clifton and *Chic*—and by the end of this week…"

And that's probably exactly what the thief wants, I thought. And then, although I'd already asked her once on Monday, I repeated, "Think, Cazzie. Please, it's vital that you're honest with me. Is there someone in your past who you've upset? Someone who could have a motive for hurting your career?"

"No," she answered emphatically and without hesitation. "I honestly can't think of anyone I've angered enough that they'd want to hurt me like this. No one. Of course, during my career—and especially since becoming editor-in-chief of *Chic: New York*, I'm sure I've stepped on some toes—who hasn't? And occasionally I do have to throw my power around. But I've never intentionally hurt or angered anyone enough to inspire this kind of revenge. No. No way. At least, not that I'm aware of."

I sighed. I'd have to carefully comb through everyone's backgrounds yet again. Maybe I'd missed something, a small detail that might tie one of them to

Cazzie. On the other hand, time was closing in on me. Noah was expecting to fetch his diamond tomorrow evening—giving me about thirty-six hours to find it.

Hmm... What had my gut told me early on? That this case would boil down to some minute detail. And while I still believed that to be true, with time closing in and a lack of a strong motive or lead suspect, it was definitely time to change tack. Maybe I'd missed some detail elsewhere. Maybe the reenactment I'd organized for the afternoon would throw up some new possibilities. I quickly sent a prayer to the detective gods, hoping that was exactly what would happen.

"The thief is clearly trying to make you crack, Cazzie. So stay as calm as you can. The riddles are slowly leading me to whoever has the Black Amelia. And if we can solve the riddles by tomorrow, then hopefully we'll find the treasure at the end of our hunt."

"Maybe they're tricking us, though! Maybe they won't give it back. Maybe by this time tomorrow, I'll have to call the police—and tell Noah and Vanessa that I've lost their gem, that their trust in me was completely misplaced," she said, sobbing. "And what will I tell Sid Clifton? He'll never trust me with anything again either."

"I will find the Black Amelia, and I'll find whoever is behind all of this," I promised Cazzie. "Please stay as calm as you can. Keep showing up on time for the shows, keep paying attention to how you dress, and keep smiling. Don't let them win. Okay?"

I hung up with Cazzie and sat on the edge of my bed for a few moments, thinking about the online blog. Its writer had sounded relatively convinced that I was helping Cazzie. Was that pure conjecture? If not, how did they know? Had someone been observing me? Was it Misty again? Who had guessed? Rafaela had, but would she do something like this? I didn't think so…but then nothing made sense.

A glance at my watch told me I had to get going. My *Teen Vogue* appointment was in under an hour, and from there I had to go straight to DKNY. My morning schedule left me little time to work on the case. Like a swimmer lost at sea, I clung to the hope that the reenactment I'd planned for this afternoon would yield a lead of some kind.

I dressed in what had quickly become my New York City outfit: skinny jeans, T-shirt, and pullover sweater. Although today I chose to throw the fashion rule book to the wind and reached to the back of the drawer for my oldest, stained, moth-eaten lucky sweater. I'd brought it with me even though my mom had begged me to throw it out—and this case demanded all the good luck and good vibes I could get.

A fluffy rock-star scarf to wrap around my neck, my new trench coat, and another pair of my DIY-decorated Converses finished off my look. Taking my phone, I went into the kitchen for breakfast. Today Nicolette had a fresh cinnamon-raisin bagel, toasted and buttered, waiting for me—along with some fruit salad. With my phone in one hand and my yummy bagel in the other, I started organizing my day.

I called Pat and made sure to tell her that I needed an hour or so left free after the DKNY show. Lying through my teeth, I told her that Chandra Rhodes had offered to help me with my walk.

"That's great, Axelle! Any off-time you can spend perfecting your work will only help. And Chandra has one fierce walk."

Just as I hung up, Miriam made an early appearance in the kitchen. "The shows," she said, stopping my curiosity in its tracks with a flourish of her hand. "Only for the shows." Then she paused as she looked at my torso, eyes wide.

Oh no, I thought, *my sweater*. Like a true fashionista, Miriam had homed in on the one thing that wasn't fashionably perfect about my outfit—even first thing in the morning.

But I had no time to waste—the last thing I wanted at this moment was to get into a fashion discussion—so before she could ask anything I said, "Tie-dye. It's not a stain. It's tie-dye. From a London specialist. He sells his sweaters at Glastonbury," I added for good measure, knowing the famous music festival's aura of cool would impress Miriam, even if I'd just made it up.

"Ah *oui*," she answered. "From where I'm standing, it really looks like a stain of some sort. It must be the light in here." She stepped back, narrowed eyes on my sweater.

"Probably," I said. "Indoor lighting can be funny." I took another bite of my bagel and turned away.

Then, as Nicolette busied herself elsewhere, Miriam came up to me and whispered, "Are you close to solving the case? Cazzie looks as if she's about to crack, and the fashionistas are starting to comment on it."

That's not all they're commenting on, I thought as I remembered the blog. Whispering back, I said, "I'm getting closer, Miriam. I am…"

I wished I felt as confident as I sounded. Before she could ask me anything else, I took a last bite of my bagel, slipped my phone into my shoulder bag, bade Miriam good-bye, and left.

***

The *Teen Vogue* offices were downtown, which was an easy trip on the subway. As I left Miriam's apartment building, I received a text from Sebastian asking what time and where we should meet, and what, in the meantime, he could help with. I sent him back a text briefly explaining Cazzie's morning call and my plans for later at Chandra's. Then I asked him to comb through the pasts of the suspects again in case we'd missed a revenge motive. Plus, I asked him if he thought he could get me everyone's contact details and, importantly, find out where they all would be working today and tomorrow.

I had just under thirty-six hours before Noah Tindle flew back into the city to collect the Black Amelia. The chase was on, and my instinct told me that knowing everyone's whereabouts for the next day and a half might prove crucial later. I also asked Sebastian to look into the rumor Ellie had told me last night about Cazzie's financial loss.

He quickly wrote back:

> **You're right. Better to be safe than sorry. I'll got on it right away ;-)**

Then we made plans to meet outside the back entrance of Lincoln Center at about twelve thirty, just as soon as I'd finished the DKNY show.

***

The *Teen Vogue* appointment went well, and the offices were fun and colorful. I met one of the junior editors and tried an Anna Sui dress on. Then I was back on the Upper West Side and at the Lincoln Center fashion tents by my appointed hair and makeup time of 10:00 a.m.

Tom Urbino—he was doing the hair for the show— was one of the first people I met backstage. Cowboy hat firmly in place, today with a bright orange strip of sheer fabric wrapped around its crown, Tom was not easily missed.

"Getting ahead with your case?" he whispered as he sat me down to start my hair.

His question totally took me by surprise. Firmly I said, "Like I told everyone at the *Chic* shoot on Tuesday, I'm here to model—not for a case."

He laughed. "That's not what I hear. The little fashion birds are twittering, and they're saying that you're here to solve a crime."

He read the surprise on my face and laughed. "Here," he said. "Take a look at this. It was just released. And I don't know if you know this blogger, but they're usually right." He pulled out his phone and showed me a short entry on one of the popular fashion-gossip blogger sites—a different one from the Unfashionable Truth:

Word on the street says that Cazzie Kinlan has a huge problem... So will she find the root of her trouble? Maybe a certain young model presently in the Big Apple is helping her?

I swallowed hard. I had to stop these rumors—but how?

I looked Tom in the eye as I handed back his phone. Then I shrugged my shoulders, laughed lightly, and said, "Well, you know how people are... They love to make stuff up—even when it's miles away from the truth." Then I changed the subject by asking him about his inspiration for the hair he was doing for the show. I had hoped to ask him a few questions about how and when the group had left the studio on Friday afternoon, but after his comment, I didn't dare push my luck. I wasn't about to feed the rumor mill.

We talked for a few minutes about the shows and then, once he was totally absorbed with showing his assistant what to do with my hair, I took my phone out.

Sebastian had already made some headway in finding out about everyone's schedules. So far the entire group—including me—was here at the DKNY show. Trish and Tom were doing hair and makeup, and Peter and Brandon were taking more candid backstage shots for Peter's upcoming coffee-table book. Cazzie was expected to see the show, and Misty, Chandra, and Rafaela would be on the runway.

He continued:

It also seems they'll all be uptown at the Ralph Lauren show this afternoon. I'm still looking into the middle of the afternoon—although I know Trish and Tom have another show then. And I think some of them will also be at the Jorge Cruz show later today. Should know more by 12:30.

I grabbed my phone to text Ellie about meeting at Chandra's, but as I started writing, she found me in person. It was time for her to have her hair done by Tom too. She sat down next to me and handed me a plate loaded with goodies from the backstage buffet table.

"I was sure you'd be glued to your phone and plans and whatnot and wouldn't have given your stomach a thought. So I brought you this. The sushi is especially good," she said. "And are we still on for after the show?" she added in a whisper as Tom started brushing her hair.

"Thank you," I said, as I bit into the sushi. It was good. "And yes for later." Out of the corner of my eye, I saw Rafaela give me a wave from the other side of the tent. She was wearing about five gold chains around her neck—each one as thick as a belt.

Tom's assistant was busy working some texture into my hair when my phone rang.

"*Teen Vogue* loved you—you're booked for tomorrow. You're looking sharp, girl. Now keep it up! I'll send you details later. In the meantime, though, I have more good news…"

Oh no. Pat's good news always translated into my bad news. *What now?* I thought desperately. *I need every free minute I can have today.* But the fashion gods were smiling on me.

"The Isle has also just confirmed you for their show tomorrow at Juice." I was so relieved when she said "tomorrow" that I physically slumped in my chair. Tom's assistant gently reminded me to sit back up. Whew! I'd really thought Pat was going to wipe out my free time this afternoon!

"This is great news, Axelle! The Isle is *the* hot NYC brand at the moment. H-O-T. Your passion for fashion is pushing you to the top! At this rate, you'll never need to go back to London!"

Just after I hung up with Pat, Cazzie called me. Again, her anxious voice hit me like a cold, clammy wave.

"I'm finding out who my real friends are. Since the online rumors have started to spread, I've already gone from fashion maven to fashion pariah. People who would have crossed burning polyester to talk to me last week are now suddenly busy on their phones when they see me. You'd think I was wearing white socks with Birkenstocks." Her voice was jagged and had a hard edge to it. "Do you really think I'll have the diamond by tomorrow? Otherwise I'll have to go to the police—as much as I don't want to. But if I'm going to go down, I at least want to go down doing the right thing."

"You will have the diamond, Cazzie. I'm sure of it. So far the rumors are only online. You'll have to ride this out, but it will all end well."

"I'm just so incredibly stressed. I want this all to be over. I want to hand Noah his diamond back and pretend this never happened." She was close to weeping.

"Cazzie, listen, whatever else we can say about the thief, they've stuck to their plan. They said they'd give us three riddles and so far we've had two—both of which we've correctly answered. I'm sure we'll get the third one soon, and I have no doubt that we'll be able to answer that one too. We just have to believe we'll get to finish this treasure hunt and that the prize at the end is the one we're hoping for."

***

The show went well, although I was on automatic pilot for most of it. Our hair had been left more or less natural—just nicely textured, really. Some of the girls had been given loose, messy chignons that looked as if they'd pinned them up themselves—never mind the fact that it had taken a professional hairstylist an hour to achieve the look. The makeup was pretty, young, and shiny. For once I didn't feel too overly done up.

I'd just finished changing into my own clothes and had stepped back out into the general backstage area when I bumped into Chandra. We'd signaled to each other from a distance during hair and makeup, but we hadn't had a chance to talk.

In stark contrast to when I'd first met her, she now seemed relieved to see me. *What a difference a clear conscience can make*, I thought.

"Thanks again for last night, Axelle. I'm sorry I was so rude to you before, but now you know why. Have you made any progress?"

"A little…"

"Maybe you'll make more now at my place," she said

as we headed toward the exit together. "I won't be able to sleep until you've found it."

"I'll let you know as soon as I do."

"And you still haven't told Cazzie anything—about me, I mean?"

I shook my head. "No, not yet, but I'm afraid I'll have to as soon as I have the whole mystery solved."

She looked away as she answered. "That's okay. I'll be able to bear it once I know you have the diamond and have figured out who took it from me. But to just tell her that I took it as a joke, and that we still don't have it… I couldn't bear that."

Me neither, I thought. *Me neither.*

✱✱✱

"Hey, Axelle, how's it going?" It was Peter, the photographer, and he (together with Brandon) was photographing the contents of Misty's shoulder bag. Fortunately she was busy removing her makeup. She'd ignored me all through hair and makeup, as well as out on the runway.

Photographing the contents of a model's handbag was something Peter liked to do for fun and was somewhat known for. He claimed that what a model kept in her handbag revealed her personality. Out of the corner of my eye I saw that Chandra had been cornered by a journalist and was answering questions. Peter and I chatted while I waited for her.

"I've heard you've been busy since Tuesday's shoot," he said. "I tried to option you for something for tomorrow, but you're shooting *Teen Vogue*. That's great!"

Peter was as upbeat as ever, his camera strung around his neck, and dressed in his usual dandy manner. He was a pro at simultaneously taking photos and carrying on a conversation. "What else have you got lined up for today?"

"Well, I've got Jorge Cruz later, and until then I have some different appointments scheduled," I answered.

"Good, good. Then I'll see you at the Jorge Cruz show. But not backstage like here—I'll be in the audience. Jorge is a friend of mine. It should be good fun. See you there!"

I finally managed to leave the backstage chaos and had just stepped outside when I heard a familiar voice call my name. It was Brandon.

"I tried calling you yesterday," he said after catching up to me. Today he was wearing a black sweater and ripped jeans. The casual ease of his clothes set his tall, athletic build and long, dark hair off to perfection. I saw more than a few people glance at him as we stood talking. "But I didn't have any luck getting through. How are you? I saw you walk the show," he added with a nod toward the tents, "and I thought you did super well— although I have the feeling that doing well at modeling isn't something that interests you too much." He was smiling as he said this.

"I thought I'd ask if you have any time to catch a movie, or maybe I could show you around the city a bit," Brandon said as he took a step closer to me. "Or maybe I could take your portrait. I'd love to photograph you."

Great. I was in the middle of solving what seemed to be an unsolvable case—I had to find the Black Amelia by seven o'clock tomorrow night—and I was being asked out! Spending time with Brandon was out of the question. But what was I supposed to tell him?

Basically, there was only one thing. "I'm sorry, Brandon, but I need to take another rain check. I have a ton of work for today, and I have to talk to my agency about my schedule for tomorrow…"

Brandon smiled at me and shook his head. "Don't worry. I had to try. But, listen…I may be way off base with this, but if you want my help—with anything—just let me know, okay?"

Now I felt really lame. I'd brushed this totally sweet, gorgeous guy off twice, and yet he was telling me that he'd be happy to help me with anything—"anything" being a clear euphemism for my detective work. At least that's how I read it, although Brandon was too discreet to say anything more direct. But why would he want to help me?

"Like I told you Tuesday night, it's because I think you're interesting."

"I didn't ask why."

He laughed. "You didn't have to—I could read it on your face. And don't worry about the two rain checks. I'm patient." His eyes were now serious.

I suddenly saw Sebastian waiting for me at the bottom of the exit ramp.

So did Brandon. "Right. I won't keep you. See you later." Then he turned and vanished.

Back to the Drawing Board

"Was that your dance partner from Tuesday night?" Sebastian asked when I reached him.

"Yes."

The wind was blowing his already tousled hair every which way. I allowed myself to be distracted by him for a moment. Then I forced myself back to the task at hand. From his jeans pocket, Sebastian took out a piece of folded paper and handed it to me. On one side he'd written a timetable with names and columns that showed, more or less, where everyone from the group would be working tonight and tomorrow, and on the other side he'd made a list with every suspect's contact information.

"I think it's pretty accurate," he said. "I got most of it by phone—I spoke directly with the agencies." Remembering how he'd passed himself off as a cobbler for the case in Paris last week, this didn't surprise me. "And the rest of it," he continued, "I found online."

I quickly perused the schedules while we waited for Ellie and Chandra to come out, but annoyingly, everyone's time seemed to be well accounted for over the next day and a half. I'd been hoping to find a large gap of time that might indicate a dramatic diamond delivery. If indeed the last riddle led me straight to the diamond, surely the thief would need a block of time to hide it somewhere.

But nothing obvious could be gleaned from the schedules I had. I didn't see how any of the group would be able to keep on top of their agendas, let alone discreetly drop a diamond off somewhere as well.

Wishful thinking, Axelle, I told myself. *Did you really think things would suddenly be so easy?*

When Chandra and Ellie finally appeared, the four of us climbed into Chandra's waiting Escalade. Twenty minutes later, we drew up to the curb outside her building.

The next hour flew by. Sebastian, Ellie, Chandra, and I took turns standing in for one or another of the group. Chandra's large sofa cushions stood in for the others. I kept my earbuds in, rewinding and fast-forwarding the recordings I'd made on Tuesday as needed. I literally listened to everything again, starting with Cazzie. Then I placed myself, Ellie, Sebastian, and Chandra into position according to whatever I heard.

And while it was impossible to replicate the experience of being in the studio last Friday exactly, I hoped the exercise could shed some light on who might have seen Chandra disappear into the dressing area just after the fire alarm rang. Someone had to have seen her take the diamond to know it was in her handbag and then steal it themselves.

So those were the crucial few minutes of Friday that I was focusing on with this reenactment—and I hoped that having Chandra present might bring more information to light.

But in the end, that wasn't the case.

Chandra claimed that before slipping into the dressing area, she waited until Cazzie, Trish, Tom, Rafaela, and Misty were at the windows looking at the scene below.

"And what about Peter and Brandon?"

She walked to the chair we were using as a substitute for Brandon's computer station and sat at it, facing what would be the set area of the studio. "Peter and Brandon were still at the computer like this, with their backs to the windows everyone was looking out and to me," she explained. "They wanted to finish whatever they were doing before getting distracted by everything going on outside—they said as much. The others were looking out the windows at the bottom of the studio, also with their backs to me. At that moment I was standing in between the two groups of people. And I'm sure it was like that because I remember thinking, *Perfect, no one will see me. None of them are looking my way!*"

Frustration swept over me like a cold wind. This was no help at all!

"Plus, all the commotion and the ringing alarm

masked any noise I would have made crossing the wooden floor. The thing is, if I'd noticed someone looking at me, I probably wouldn't have gone into the dressing area." She shrugged her shoulders.

Next, we reenacted the moments after she stepped back into the studio from the dressing room. But, again, it didn't tell me much. Chandra didn't really remember where the others were, except to say that some had walked back near the set and others were still standing at the windows.

"So if someone had walked past the curtain divider, because, for example, they were walking away from the windows and back toward the set or hair and makeup area, could they have seen you?" I asked.

"I doubt it. The divider was pulled shut," she answered.

I thought of how, at the studio on Tuesday, Cazzie and I had looked out through the tiny space between the curtain and the wall as we'd watched Misty walk over to Brandon. If we'd been able to look out through such a narrow space, then unless the curtain had been pulled completely up against the wall, someone could have looked in and seen Chandra at the table, taking the diamond out of Cazzie's bag. But who?

As befitted the fashion world, the diamond seemed to have been stolen discreetly, simply, and stylishly— and I was unable to find a chink in the thief's armor. No clumsy explanation, no out-of-place step.

So far my plan to re-create the Friday session had

245

failed spectacularly. Okay, maybe not spectacularly—after all, I did have a better idea of how things must have happened within those few minutes. But I was certainly no closer to having a clear suspect.

And just when I thought things couldn't possibly get any worse, they did.

"I'd love to stay and help some more, but I really have to get going," Chandra said.

"Me too," Ellie added. She was putting her things back in her shoulder bag with one hand while applying moisturizer to her face with the other. "I've got to baby my skin or it won't survive the week. Do you know how rough it is on our faces to go through three to five makeup changes per day? And for a whole week? I mean, one Fashion Week for any face is, like, equal to at least four non-fashion weeks condensed into one. It's murder—no detective pun intended, Axelle."

"Thanks, Ellie."

I watched as she left, the door shutting behind her with more certainty than it seemed I'd ever feel.

As Chandra moved about the living room, straightening her chairs and cushions, Sebastian and I talked through what we'd learned one more time, but nothing came of it except more repetition of what little we already knew. I was wondering how to move forward when my phone vibrated. I'd received a new text forwarded by Cazzie.

One last riddle: See the work of Azzedine Alaïa, Missoni, and Ralph Lauren at the Fashion Institute of Technology. You'll understand what I mean when you're there. This should keep your undercover model entertained in between shows. But never fear—you'll see the diamond later.

Below it, Cazzie had added a message for me:

Axelle, I have no idea what this is about! Off the top of my head, I can't think what the work of these three fashion houses have in common. I'm sorry! Once you're at FIT, let me know if you need more help. It must be something obvious that has to be seen.

I'm also sorry that you're mentioned in this. The thief is clearly aware that you've been helping me. I have heard rumors going around that you're here in NYC to solve a case. Thank God no one seems to know precisely what it is yet, though. Although with those blog entries today, I'm worried that it won't be too difficult for someone to make the connection to me.

Presumably I'll get the diamond back once this riddle is answered. I tried writing back to the sender as soon as I could—I wanted to make sure I'll get the diamond by 7 p.m. tomorrow—but I was in the basement of a building for a show when it was sent, so I only got the message when I was back on the street. I wrote back right away, but I was too late—the account was already closed!

So the rumors about me working a case were indeed spreading…and the thief was personally baiting me on this one. That was new.

There was nothing to do but go to the Fashion Institute of Technology. Sebastian shrugged his shoulders when I asked him where FIT was, so I quickly asked Chandra for directions.

"You can take the subway up and get off at the Twenty-Third Street station on Seventh Avenue," Chandra said. "The FIT is only a few blocks from there."

It was now two o'clock, which meant I still had two hours before I had to be at Juice Studios to start my hair and makeup for the Jorge Cruz show.

"Then let's go," I said as I slipped into my trench coat and grabbed my shoulder bag.

Chandra went down with us, and I promised to send her word about the diamond as soon as I heard anything.

"Thanks," she said. "I won't relax until I know you've seen it with your own eyes."

But would that ever actually happen?

✳ ✳ ✳

"You're thinking something, Axelle. What is it?"

Sebastian and I had quickly walked to the subway station Chandra had mentioned and were now on an uptown train. We only had a few stops to make, but I'd sat down because a thought had come to me as we got on the train.

"Hmm…I'm not sure, just that this last message is a bit off—compared to the others, I mean. It's as if the style is different or something…"

"You mean because the thief mentioned you personally?"

"Yes, but…I think there's more to it than that." I was scrolling through my phone, reading Cazzie's forwarded messages with the riddles. I couldn't really put my finger on what I was looking for, just that something about this new one seemed different.

Sebastian sat next to me, and together we dissected them.

"The others have more precise directions. Like this one here," I said, as I scrolled back to the very first riddle:

**There are two lions outside, but there is also one inside—
and she has a certain allure. Find it and photograph it…**

I then scrolled to the second riddle. "And this one…"

**Donna Karan
Marc Jacobs
Céline
Rhymes with power, find the…and photograph it. I'll text
you again at 9:30 p.m.**

"Do you see what I mean? The thief ended both of those riddles with a command because they wanted a specific answer."

"I think you're on to something. And the third riddle?"
"Here."

See the work of Azzedine Alaïa, Missoni, and Ralph Lauren at the Fashion Institute of Technology. You'll understand what I mean when you're there. This should keep your undercover model entertained in between shows. But never fear—you'll see the diamond later.

"This last riddle doesn't ask for anything specific, does it?" I continued. "Just 'see' and 'You'll understand what I mean when you're there.' That sounds more like a threat than a command. It's not driving us toward a specific answer in the way the others do…but why not? Besides, Cazzie couldn't think of anything that linked the three fashion houses in any obvious way… And why 'This should keep your undercover model entertained in between shows'?"

"You're right," Sebastian said. "That is odd. It doesn't fit with the style of the others. And what does keeping you entertained have to do with anything?"

"Exactly. What does keeping me entertained have to do with anything? Unless…"

"Unless what?"

"Unless they want to keep me away from someone or something… But what? And I don't even know who they are. Why would they worry?"

At that moment we arrived at our stop. Gathering

our things, we jumped off the train and bounded out of the station.

"Can I see that schedule you made again?" I asked as I strode to the side of the nearest building, out of the flow of the foot traffic.

From the inner pocket of his leather jacket, Sebastian pulled out and unfolded the same piece of paper he'd shown me after the DKNY show. As he held it against the side of the building with his hands, I quickly scanned it—and my stomach fluttered with nerves.

Everyone from the suspect group was at this moment all the way uptown at the same show, Alexander Wang. Trish and Tom were doing hair and makeup, and Cazzie was there to see it. Peter was there shooting more backstage photos for his book—with Brandon's help—and Chandra, Rafaela, and Misty were walking the show.

But they'd all been together at the same show this morning—DKNY—and I had been there. So why did I suddenly feel that the thief was now trying to keep me away… And away from what? I stood silently while Sebastian spoke.

"But if I was able to find out all this information about their schedules," he said with a wave of his paper, "then surely the thief must know that you *weren't* booked to do Alexander Wang. So why would they worry that you may show up? Like you said, it doesn't make sense, because you don't even know who they are."

Nothing had made sense so far…and yet I was buzzing. There was something about this message…

"Unless maybe they thought there was a chance you'd go to the show just to keep tabs on the group. And then maybe they thought you might see something you shouldn't," he continued vaguely.

His words caught me by surprise… *See something*… Could that be it? With a sharp intake of breath, I turned to Sebastian. Finally, something in this frustrating case made perfect sense—and I couldn't believe the simplicity of it all.

"You're a genius, Watson."

"Are you changing your mind about me?"

His eyes told me he was flirting again. But I was too hot on the trail to be derailed. Ignoring his question, I said, "You suggested that maybe the thief didn't want me to *see* something I shouldn't see."

"Yeah, but what? Like you said, you don't even know who they are."

"You're right, I don't. But maybe the thief is trying to keep me away from seeing something…something they must feel could give them away. Why else would they need to lead me off course?"

I glanced at my watch and shook my head, frustration beginning to claw at me again. *Argh!* The thief was always one step ahead of me! According to Sebastian's schedule, the Alexander Wang show was now in full swing at the Neue Galerie uptown. And afterward, the entire group—even Cazzie—would be heading back-stage, which meant that the thief would be rubbing shoulders with everyone from last Friday's shoot while they were congratulating the designer or preparing to leave and saying good-bye.

A shiver ran through me as I ran the last phrase through my mind. *Preparing to leave and saying good-bye.* Why did that scenario sound familiar to me? What did it remind me of?

Argh! The reenactment I did with Chandra at her apartment suddenly came back to me, nearly making me choke. But not the second reenactment—the first one. The one when I'd been alone with her at her apartment and had shown her how the diamond had most likely been taken out of her shoulder bag after she'd *prepared to leave and was saying good-bye.*

I'd asked her to turn the music up and to put her bag on her shoulder exactly as she'd worn it in the studio at Juice on Friday. Then, when I'd leaned in to air-kiss her, I'd reached into her shoulder bag and taken out her hairbrush—in the same way I was sure the thief must have taken the diamond.

I silenced Sebastian with a wave of my hand and continued to stand while thoughts whirled through my mind. *Faster, Axelle, faster. The thief is way ahead of you. You're going to have to move more quickly if you want to catch up. Take a deep breath and go through your thoughts one by one.*

I still believed the thief had stolen the Black Amelia from Chandra's handbag while they said good-bye to each other. And the thief now clearly knew that I was on their trail. They'd also been threatened by Cazzie with a deadline for delivery, and if they didn't hand over the gem, they knew Cazzie would report the theft.

Assuming the thief felt they'd had their fun with Cazzie and wanted to return the Black Amelia before the "game" turned more serious and they had the police breathing down their neck, was it too far-fetched to think that the thief might return the diamond in the same way they'd taken it? While saying good-bye with people around, just slip it into a handbag? Theoretically, why not? They'd done it once, to great effect. And stylistically, it fit. It also explained why the thief had thought to keep me away—although if they knew how far behind them I was, they wouldn't have had to worry.

So whose handbag would the Black Amelia be placed in?

As far as I could see, only one handbag made any sense—Cazzie's. And backstage, with all of the suspects present—and bound to greet her—she wouldn't be able to say which of them had given her the diamond back. Cazzie would never notice a thing.

I was furious with myself for not having been quicker. Of course, for all I knew, I was clutching at straws, but my hunch told me I wasn't—and at this point it was the best theory I had.

"I have to call Cazzie," I said. "Maybe, if I can reach her and tell her…" Frantically, I reached for my phone and dialed her number. But I got no answer—just her voice mail. I left her a message and tried again anyway—with the same results.

"I'm sure I'm too late, but we've got to try anyway," I said to Sebastian. "Come on! Forget the FIT. We need to get to the Neue Galerie!"

We ran to the intersection of Twenty-Third Street and Park Avenue to catch the uptown train. Traffic was building and the subway would be faster than a cab—or so I thought.

What I hadn't counted on—surprisingly, considering how often it happened at home in London—was that a "technical difficulty" would leave us stranded, sitting on the train for a good forty minutes. Despite reassurances from the conductor that they were doing their best to get things moving again, time seemed to stand still. By the time the engines started and the train pulled forward with a lurch, I was furious with myself for missing the only chance I was sure I'd get.

"According to your information," I said to Sebastian, "if the show started on time, it should be finished by now. They're probably all backstage—and within striking distance of each other. *Argh!* I could really kick myself for not seeing this ploy. Some fashion detective I am!"

✳ ✳ ✳

As soon as we got off on the uptown platform of the Eighty-Sixth Street and Lexington Avenue station, I felt sure we were too late. Elaborately turned-out fashionistas, phones in hand, were already filing into the subway station on their way to their next shows.

Come on, come on, I told myself as Sebastian and I ran the few blocks west on Eighty-Sixth Street to the Neue Galerie at Fifth Avenue.

The show must have started unfashionably punctually, I thought, as we came in sight of the gallery. I spotted Trish and Tom stepping out of a side door and reached for Sebastian's arm to stop him. Their assistants followed them, pulling various black suitcases packed with supplies. They were all laughing and talking. Clearly the show had gone well and they were happy to have another one done.

Following just behind them was a pack of long-legged, slim, giraffe-like creatures, their long necks and long strides marking them as models. In the midst of the group I easily made out Rafaela, Misty, and Chandra. All three—along with Ellie—stopped to sign autographs for the fans gathered outside.

Behind them I saw Peter and Brandon walk out together with the last wave of hairstylists and makeup artists. Peter paused to photograph the models as they signed autographs. Then I watched as Brandon said something to him. Peter stopped what he was doing and they hurriedly disappeared into a black Escalade and drove off. They were no doubt going to their next show—which was also the one I was due at, the Jorge Cruz show.

But first I had to find Cazzie. Ellie and the other models were leaving now. I continued to watch as a few more makeup artists and models trickled out. Finally the famous bloggers, journalists, and editors appeared. I recognized the one from *Teen Vogue* who I'd sat next to at the *Chic* party. I also recognized a couple of famous fashion bloggers.

Then, finally, I saw Cazzie. I asked Sebastian to wait for me and made a beeline for her, catching up to her just as she walked past the paparazzi and slid into her waiting car.

When she noticed me, she beckoned me into her car. Then she asked Ira to step outside for a moment.

I took a deep breath and asked Cazzie to look in her handbag.

It took her a moment to find it. I watched as her hand moved around…but it was there. As her hand felt the diamond's hard case, her eyes lit up with surprise and disbelief.

"No, no, no…is it?" Then she inhaled sharply as she pulled the cloth bundle out of her bag. Her fingers were nearly shaking as she untied the cord, yanked open the bag, and let the diamond fall into her hand. Her relief was palpable. She leaned back in the plush leather seat and let out a very long breath.

The afternoon sun streamed in through the car window, making the diamond glow like a burning ember. All around us, hundreds of tiny sparkles danced as the Black Amelia reflected the sunlight off its faceted sides.

Then Cazzie threw herself at me and hugged me. "You did it! You did it, Axelle! You found the diamond. Thank God!"

* * *

I stood on the pavement and watched as Cazzie's car pulled out into the street. I couldn't remember any mystery ever leaving me feeling so gutted and just plain awful. Sure, Cazzie had her (or rather, Noah's) diamond back…but how much of a hand had I had in that? Honestly?

And I still had no clue who'd stolen it! Naturally, while basking in her sense of relief, Cazzie had started to ask me about the who, what, and whys of the theft. But—thank the fashion gods—then she'd realized that she had to be at a show in fifteen minutes and asked if we could meet in her office as soon as possible instead so she could give me her undivided attention. "Besides," she said, as she pointed out the window, "I'd also prefer that Ira didn't have to stand outside for hours. He might start to wonder what's up. I've been acting strangely all week, after all."

She didn't have to ask me twice. I'd already started to wince inwardly at the thought of answering her questions. As far as I was concerned, this case was still marked "Unsolved." It would remain that way until I managed to outwit the perpetrator of the crime. And who knew how long that would take? Or if I would ever manage it.

I quickly sent Chandra a text message as promised, telling her that Cazzie had the diamond but asking her not to say anything to Cazzie, should she see her, because I hadn't had time to explain anything to her yet.

Chandra then asked me who'd taken the diamond. I answered that I'd see her at the Jorge Cruz show and explain things there. Then I slipped my phone into my shoulder bag and wrapped my trench coat tightly around me.

"Don't beat yourself up, Axelle." It was Sebastian. He'd crossed the street just after Cazzie's car pulled away.

"I can't help it. I've been totally outwitted. And I missed the only chance I had to possibly catch the thief in action because I fell for their fake riddle and was too slow to pick up on their real intentions. *Argh!*"

"When do you leave New York?"

"My flight leaves on Saturday night. Why?"

"Because that still gives you forty-eight hours to solve the mystery." He was smiling now. "And my flight doesn't leave until Saturday night either. Which means…"

"Yes, Watson?"

"That I am your able and willing assistant until then." He laughed.

Whether he was really my mother's spy or not, the trouble was that Sebastian's blue eyes and ruffled hair were beginning to distract me on a regular basis again. *But it's not like we have to hang out together, right?* I told myself.

"And I have another idea," he said.

"Yes?"

"Could we maybe hang out together for a little while after your next show?"

Now he was being seriously distracting.

✳ ✳ ✳

Music was blasting out of the speakers, and my hair was being back-combed—yet again—as a stylist strapped a pair of bright pink, patent leather stilettos onto my feet. Plus I had Pat on the phone.

Sebastian and I had taken the subway from the Neue Galerie to the midtown location of the Jorge Cruz show. I was now standing in a huge industrial loft space, behind long black curtains that separated the backstage area from the runway. The ceiling soared an easy twenty feet above us.

"*Teen Vogue* will be shooting on location in Central Park tomorrow," Pat was saying in my ear, "as long as the weather holds. If it doesn't, then I'll call you first thing in the morning—*as if she didn't every day anyway*, I thought—"and give you the address of their alternate location. But the forecast is for wind and sunny skies like today, so I think you'll be lucky. Central Park is beautiful at this time of the year. But forget about the park—*you* better be beautiful, girl! I expect you to go straight to Miriam's to get some beauty sleep after Jorge's show."

I thought of Sebastian and the dinner plans we'd made a little earlier. I could get out of them now that Pat had handily given me the perfect excuse.

But did I want to get out of our plans?

"Axelle? Are you there? We also need to talk about some options I have for you for next week—and next month. Girl, speak up! I can't hear you!"

Ellie was right—I did still like him. A lot.

And Ellie was also right about my not hearing him out—or to put it into detective speak, I'd jumped to conclusions about him and his actions without looking at all the evidence first. I mean, honestly, for all I knew, he could have had a good reason for talking to my mom.

Not that one exactly leaped to mind, but still…

I took a deep breath as the makeup artist powdered my nose.

"Axelle?" Pat brayed into the phone.

Grrr! Would I ever get a moment's peace from Pat and her eternal options and castings and bookings? "Pat, I can't hear you because of the music and hair dryers. Can you email me and we can talk more about my options tomorrow? I have to concentrate on this show. You know how important it is to my career," I quickly added.

"Ooh! Good, Axelle. Your passion for fashion is shining through yet again! You're right. So, yes, why don't we talk tomorrow? And look sharp on that runway, girl! I'll be watching you on the Fashion Channel!"

***

"What are you thinking about? You look all distracted." It was Ellie. We were standing backstage together, waiting to walk out. "It's not a great look—but it's better than the one you had on your face earlier."

I'd told her about Cazzie finding the diamond in her bag. Like Sebastian, she'd asked immediately how much longer I was staying and then said that I still had forty-eight hours to work on solving the case, so why was I fretting?

"Don't forget, during the collections they're often sewing the last stitches on a dress minutes before we walk out, right?"

I rolled my eyes. "And?"

"My point being," Ellie continued, "that sometimes

you have to take it to the limit. The frock isn't finished until every last sequin has been stitched on. I'm sure you'll solve this case before you leave. Just don't lose focus."

She had a point.

"So what are you thinking about?" she asked again, snapping me back to the here and now. "The diamond?"

I shook my head and she looked at me through narrowed eyes.

"Don't tell me you're actually—finally—thinking about *him*?"

I shrugged my shoulders.

"And?" she persisted.

"And...not much. We're going to have dinner tonight."

"And kiss and make up?"

"No." I laughed. "We're going to discuss the case."

"Not according to the trail of clues I've seen."

"Very funny, Nancy Drew."

✳ ✳ ✳

The show went well, even though I couldn't stop thinking about the case. My pride couldn't let go of the fact that I'd been stumped. But at least that had the advantage of keeping my mind off the photographers and TV cameras, not to mention the assorted A-listers in the front rows. They still freaked me out a bit if I looked at them too much. But as long as I didn't think about them watching my runway effort, I was okay. I'd seen

Miriam smiling at me in the front row, though, and that had been nice.

Backstage, I quickly changed into my own clothes. I was just slipping my trench coat on when Brandon and Peter came up to me.

"That trench coat looks great on you, Axelle." Peter was snapping away as he spoke to me. "It's a natural match for you, isn't it?" Pleased with his little witticism, he winked and turned to start photographing Chandra, who was next to me.

Brandon quickly greeted me. "How are you doing? Everything okay?"

I nodded. "I'm getting there."

"What does that mean?"

"It means that sometimes things don't go according to plan."

"I know exactly what you mean," he said, his eyes on mine. I thought of how I'd turned him down twice when he'd asked to spend some time together. I had the feeling that was what he was referring to. But then he broke into a smile. "You never know, though. Things can change faster than the snap of a camera. Speaking of which, I'd better get back to helping Peter. I'll see you later." And he was gone.

Chandra caught up with me as I was leaving. "Thank goodness the diamond has been found!" she whispered. She looked more relaxed and happy than I'd ever seen her since meeting her—and no wonder. With her innocent practical joke, she had not only placed her own career in the line of fire, but Cazzie's as well—not to mention *Chic's* reputation. But now the diamond was back in Cazzie's hands (or rather, in the *Chic* safe at the Sid Clifton Building)—and by tomorrow evening it would be returned to Noah Tindle.

The only reputation now hanging by a couture thread was mine.

"Are you going to figure out who took it? Does it still matter?" Chandra asked as she adjusted a beanie on her head. She was in full surfer-dudette early-spring style and looked amazing: navy blue pea coat, skate-boarding sneakers, sweater, and jeans. And her thumb rings, of course.

"I have to, Chandra—and I will." My confidence was coming back. For my own peace of mind, I had to solve this case. There was no way I was going to allow the thief to get away with it. My friends were right—I still had forty-eight hours. I would go back over the evidence again and again until I found a chink in the armor. There had to be one. There had to be one tiny, crucial detail somewhere that I'd overlooked.

Confessions and Fries

As I stepped out of the industrial building, Sebastian was waiting for me.

"Hungry?" he asked.

"Starving."

"Burger and fries?"

"Perfect."

We took a subway uptown, Sebastian promising to show me the best burger joint in the city. After walking a few blocks from the station, we entered the elegant lobby of an enormous hotel. I was about to ask him if he knew of something a bit less grand, but he motioned for me to follow him and didn't stop walking until we reached a large, heavy, red velvet curtain. He pushed it aside just enough for us to slip behind it and then led me into the tiniest burger joint I'd ever seen.

It also had the shortest menu of any place I'd ever been. You could order a burger with all the toppings or a burger without all the toppings. And you could decide whether or not you wanted fries. That was it. Nothing else.

The kitchen was open to the tiny seating area. While

we stood in line, I gazed at the walls. They were covered from top to bottom with scribbles (in ink) left by customers. We ordered and slid into a booth in the back corner. I loved it!

Right away we started discussing the case. I even took my earbuds out and we listened to my recordings again—not that we gleaned anything new. But finally we drifted away from the case and on to other things...

He told me he'd spoken with my mom and promised to keep an eye on me for her.

"It sounded like you promised to do more than just that," I said pointedly, reminding him that he'd agreed to derail me from my detective work and push me into doing more modeling.

"Yes, okay, I admit I told her I'd do that—but have I? Besides, what was I supposed to say to her? I mean, she *is* your mom. And I want to keep seeing—I mean, I want to keep helping you." We both looked away from each other, pretending to ignore that slip of his tongue. "And I honestly never thought you'd see those texts or I would have told you about them sooner. I forgot you're a detective," he added, "and that you feel no compunction about looking at things that aren't intended for you." He was looking at me again. "Do you?"

I rolled my eyes. "When were you planning on telling me about them?" I asked.

"Probably here, now. Or sooner. I don't know. But I would have."

Grrr!

We even hashed out the matter of Cleo.

"But I told you I was going to be staying with my aunt. I am, and Cleo's my cousin. She lives on her own now, but we meet up whenever we can."

"How was I supposed to know that?" I wondered if I sounded jealous.

"Well, it's not my fault you didn't ask. And you didn't want me calling you anymore, remember? So how was I supposed to tell you?"

He had a point.

Annoyingly, Sebastian was just as funny and cute and smart as he'd been in Paris—even more so, I thought, as I watched him run a hand through his hair in exasperation during my cross-examination.

When things finally simmered down, he leaned back in his chair and smiled at me, his eyes teasing. Then he asked, "So? What next, Holmes?"

✳✳✳

On this trip to New York, nothing was working out as planned, I thought, as Sebastian and I stepped out of the burger joint and back onto the street. First the case, which I still hadn't solved—which I was fumbling through, in fact—and then *him*…

We walked to Miriam's in silence, each of us busy with our own thoughts. When we reached her building we stood nervously looking at each other, unsure how to proceed.

But there was only one thing to do really, wasn't there? As we stood in front of Miriam's building, our hands in our pockets, weight shifting from foot to foot, our eyes finally met and held.

"I'm sorry—" we both started at the same time.

"Me first," Sebastian said. "I'm sorry I didn't tell you about your mom right away. I should have. And even if you didn't want to speak with me, I should have texted and told you about all that, and about Cleo too. Maybe—in fact, most definitely—you wouldn't have answered"—he smiled—"but at least you would have known."

The incessant noise of the city ceased to exist. The honking, screeching, vivacious buzz that was a background constant was relegated to a place far away, as Sebastian and I stood close together.

"I'm sorry too," I said as I looked at him. "I should have heard you out before jumping to conclusions that weren't entirely true."

Gently, his hands found mine. Then as our eyes locked once more, he carefully pushed my hair behind my ears and slowly ran his finger down my face. He smelled amazing, and the feel of his body so close to mine made me go weak. The disappointment and frustrations of the day melted away until I was only aware of him. Slowly, Sebastian lowered his head toward mine and I reached up to meet his lips.

"Axelle? Is that you?" A familiar voice cut through the romantic New York night, stopping us just as our lips were about to meet.

Pat! I could have strangled her.

"What are you doing still up?" she continued as she walked up to us. "You should be in bed! And who is this?"

Embarrassment swept through me, and as Sebastian and I pulled away from each other, I was blushing.

"Pat's my booker," I whispered to Sebastian.

"She's got great timing," he replied.

Miriam was just behind Pat. They'd obviously had dinner together—something they did regularly when Miriam was in town—and were walking home. Pat, apparently, lived only a few blocks away from Miriam.

"I tried to hold her back," Miriam whispered to me as she approached. "But you know Pat—and you're her favorite right now, so she feels extra-protective."

Great. Thanks, Pat.

After a few minutes of chitchat, Pat finally left. And then Miriam, with a glance at her watch, said, "I think we should go up now, Axelle. You have that shoot for *Teen Vogue* tomorrow and I want you to look fresh. And after the day you've had…" she added lightly.

I looked at her with raised eyebrows and dug my hands into the pockets of my trench coat.

"Cazzie spoke with me. She is very grateful." Then after a short pause, Miriam added, "But she didn't tell me who did it…" She had a twinkle in her eye as she looked at me.

She knows why, I thought. She—unlike Cazzie—had guessed that I didn't know who did it. Miriam has always been savvy, so I wasn't surprised, but she was waiting for me to tell her—which I did right away. "That's because I still don't know… I haven't figured it out yet."

My disappointment hung like a wet coat in the crisp night air.

"Ah! So the case is not finished." She watched me quietly. "Well then, I suggest you call it a night, *ma petite Axelle*. Knowing you, you'll want this case solved by the time you leave, in which case you're definitely going to need all the sleep you can get." She was smiling at me now. "And don't worry, I have a feeling that the solution will come to you like this," she added, with a quick snap of her fingers. Then Miriam said good night to Sebastian, turned, and headed inside.

I watched as she walked into her building, heels clicking, fur-trimmed stole around her petite shoulders. In one swift movement, Sam (who was on night duty) pushed the grand old door open for her. I continued to watch, my back to Central Park across the street, as Miriam walked into the lobby and the door swung gently shut behind her.

Now when I think back to this moment, I see it all in slow motion. I can remember Sebastian standing to my left, suddenly reaching for his pocket and saying something about wanting to let his aunt know that he'd be on his way back to her apartment soon.

I can also clearly remember that I continued to stand, feet planted firmly, watching as the door to Miriam's building stopped swinging and came to a complete halt. And in that very moment after Sebastian stepped away and I continued to stand watching the door, a lady walking her dog went past behind me—*and I saw her even though my back was to her.*

Suddenly my heart stood still, and I felt as if someone had kicked me in my gut. I was nearly sick. Eyes wide, I turned quickly and looked behind me. The lady and her dog had indeed walked past me. I could see their backs as they continued up the block.

In shock, I turned back and looked at the door to Miriam's building.

Like Miriam had said—and who else? Ah yes, Brandon. Things can change quickly, they'd told me.

And they were right.

In the space of a moment, I was pretty sure I'd cracked this case.

In fact, I was certain I had.

"Good evening, Miss Axelle. Can I help you?"

I didn't blame Sam for thinking I needed help. I'd stepped up to the door and stood in front of it, staring at it—probably somewhat wildly. I must have been a strange sight.

"No, Sam, I'm all right, but thanks," I answered as,

without thinking, I walked past him and into the building's lobby. I walked straight to one of the chairs lining the walls and sat down. I needed to think.

A few seconds later, Sebastian came into the lobby looking for me. "You disappeared," he said.

I nodded.

"What's happened?" he asked. "You have that look… Oh no. I've missed something, haven't I? You've had a breakthrough."

Again, I nodded.

"And you're not going to tell me?"

I shook my head.

He was smiling. "I didn't think so."

My phone vibrated. It was Cazzie:

> Sorry to text you so late, Axelle, but I just wanted to thank you again for today and to say that I look forward to handing Noah back his diamond tomorrow. Call me a coward, but I doubt I'll be able to say a word to him about anything. I hope I'll be forgiven in my next life. I'll call you tomorrow. And many, many thanks again.

"Now why are you smiling?" Sebastian asked.

I put my phone away and looked up at him. "The element of surprise, Watson, surprise. The thief is secure in the knowledge that I haven't figured out who they are, right?"

He nodded.

"So I look forward to using that to my advantage."

"I have the feeling that solving this tricky case might just make everything you've been through so far worth it, Holmes. Don't you think?"

"You'll have to ask me again tomorrow, Watson." I smiled.

✳ ✳ ✳

Sebastian and I quickly parted ways. Under the bright lights of the lobby and Sam's watchful eye, any thought of a romantic good-night kiss was now definitely off the agenda.

But we made plans to meet right after my *Teen Vogue* shoot tomorrow and then go downtown together to Juice Studios for The Isle show. My idea was to confront the thief after the show—which, if it went according to plan, would fittingly take place at the same studios where the diamond had been stolen.

But before that happened, I had some preparation work to do. *So much for Pat's idea of beauty sleep*, I thought, as I pulled the chair up to the desk in my bedroom, turned on my laptop, and quickly wrote a list.

The first thing I have to do, I thought, *is contact Cazzie*. I fished my phone out of my shoulder bag and wrote her a text. Then I took out Sebastian's paper with the group's schedules written on it and flipped it to the other side where he'd written contact information for everyone. There I found the number I was looking for and wrote another text. As I pushed the send button, I began to relax. My plan was taking shape…

Before getting into bed, I shut my computer down. I shook my head as I looked one last time at the screen. *How could I have missed it?* I thought.

Sewing on the Last Sequins

I awoke with a start. I'd forgotten to draw my curtains shut the night before, so by 7 a.m. the sun was streaming in through my windows.

I reached for my phone and checked my messages. Cazzie had answered late last night:

Studio 7 will be yours from 6 p.m. onward. And yes, the images were dark. See you tomorrow.

Then I saw that I'd already received an answer to the other text I'd sent last night, also positive.

Perfect, I thought, yanking on my robe and heading to the bathroom. As I stood in the shower, I started writing notes to myself on the steamed glass:

9:00 a.m. Teen Vogue

4:30 p.m. Sebastian meets me in Central Park after shoot

5:00 p.m. Hair and makeup call time for The Isle at Juice Studios—all suspects present

7:00 p.m. (approximately) Finished at The Isle show

Immediately afterward Meet with suspect at Studio 7

Seen this way—in the friendly, steamy environment of my shower—my plan looked short and tidy. But how, I wondered, would it all end?

✳ ✳ ✳

The good weather held for the *Teen Vogue* shoot. The sun that had streamed through my window at 7:00 a.m. was still shining at nine, so Central Park it was; no alternative location needed.

The clothes were all summer outfits, colorful and bright. This meant that, with the cool breeze and crisp spring temperatures, I'd be chilly while shooting outdoors. But I knew from the location shoot I'd done in Paris last week that I'd be able to warm up between shots in the comfort of the heated location van, and the stylist would no doubt have a large coat of some sort that I could throw over myself while my hair and makeup were retouched or the lighting was tweaked.

Makeup and hair were easy and light, with pretty lipstick colors allowed to make a summer statement. The various tones of bright pink popped off the computer screen, I noted when, between shots, we all went back to the location van parked (thanks to a special permit) on one of the winding roads that crisscrossed the park.

The van was large and comfortable, with a dressing area in the back. Regular hissing sounds emanated from the steam machine the stylist's assistant was using to iron the clothes I'd be wearing. In the kitchen area, a buffet breakfast had been laid out on the tiny countertop when I arrived in the morning, and later lunch was brought in too, delivered by a caterer direct to the van.

The photographer, Blue Koslowski, along with her digi-tech assistant and the *Teen Vogue* editor, held regular strategic huddles at the dining room table about their ideas for the shoot. Meanwhile, Olaf the makeup artist and Tiina the hairstylist worked on my look at a table set up for that purpose between the kitchen and dressing areas. And even though we were in a van, this area looked pretty much like it had in the studios where I'd worked.

Over the table, which was set against the wall, hung a large mirror—as large as the wall allowed anyway—with strong lights all the way around it. A comfortable folding chair was at my disposal. Olaf and Tiina's respective assistants had carefully placed their various tools (hairbrushes, hairpins, hair spray, eye shadows, blushes, foundations, makeup brushes, and so on) in neat, tidy rows on the white towels they'd first laid on the table.

Even though I was the only model on this particular shoot, I still had plenty of downtime. *Teen Vogue* didn't like to rush things, and their main concern was that the images looked good—however long that took. But they knew I had to be at Juice Studios for The Isle show at 5 p.m. We spaced the shots accordingly, the weather held, and (for once!) everything went according to plan.

After a fun day of shooting around some of the park's more famous landmarks—including the Bethesda Fountain I'd walked past with Sebastian the other day and the Alice in Wonderland statue—we finished the seven shots for our story and called it a day.

"Send me an image if you can," Pat had ordered me by phone at lunchtime. "I want to see what the story looks like. And I'm going to ask them in exactly which issue it will run. Believe me, Axelle, a shoot like this will propel you to the top in no time! I'm telling you, girl, give me another week and you'll be, like, 'London, where?' You are going to have such an exciting year!"

I also got a text from my mom:

> **Axelle! Darling! Wonderful news about shooting *Teen Vogue*! I am so proud of you! And remember, if your career starts to really take off, don't think you have to rush back to London. I'm sure we can organize a tutor for school. I'll call you later. Love, Mom**

I silently prayed to the fashion gods, thanking them that my mom and Pat were separated by a very large ocean. The thought of the two of them together on the same continent, working to propel my modeling career, was too much to bear!

✳ ✳ ✳

Sebastian met me at the van at the end of the shoot. Both Olaf and Tiina checked him out through the windows before giving me their approval.

"He's really cute," Tiina gushed.

"And I love his leather jacket," Olaf added.

There were some laughs and teasing from Blue and the rest of the crew as I blushed and bounded out of the van.

Sebastian and I were happy to see each other, the air finally cleared after last night. But there wasn't any time to pick up where we'd left off before I had a call from Pat. I had to be at Juice in twenty minutes.

We ran to the nearest subway station and jumped on a downtown train. On our way, I explained to Sebastian that I had an appointment just after the show. I also asked if he'd mind waiting for me until I was out.

"An appointment? This has to do with the suspect, doesn't it?"

I shook my head.

"I don't believe you," he said. "I have the feeling you're planning much more than you're letting on— but you're not going to tell me anything, are you?"

I shook my head. "No. I have to do this alone. I'll be fine. Just wait for me outside the studios."

"Of course I will. But why don't we call the police? Just so they know. Or maybe Cazzie can call them."

Again, I shook my head. "Why would they come? I don't have proof that any of this ever happened. The diamond is in the *Chic* safe, soon to be reunited with its owner—and he has no idea that it was ever stolen. Cazzie won't call them, not as long as I have nothing concrete to tell her. And there's no way Sid Clifton and *Chic* will want to call in the police unless I have proof— something I doubt I can get now."

"You sort of have a point…"

"Like I said, just wait for me outside the studios. If I need to reach you, I'll text you. Okay?"

Sebastian nodded.

✳ ✳ ✳

The Isle was clearly considered one of the hottest fashion shows of the week. I could see that as soon as we approached Juice Studios. The street was packed with cars and paparazzi. Bloggers were already crowding the pavement around the studio entrance, and onlookers were swiveling their heads in every direction, hoping to catch a glimpse of a famous face. And the show wouldn't start for at least another hour!

But I still didn't have a moment to spare—I was already ten minutes late. Sebastian and I parted ways in the middle of the excited crowd on the street. After a quick wave, I turned and cleared security before disappearing through the studio doors.

Chandra and Ellie were waiting and motioned for me to join them where they were having their makeup done. Tom's assistant—the same one who'd worked on my hair the day before at DKNY—greeted me enthusiastically before sitting me down and starting to prep my hair.

"You look more like yourself," Ellie whispered to me under the din of the hair dryers. "That must mean you've solved the case."

I nodded. "I think so. I'll know for sure after the show."

"I don't suppose you're going to tell me anything?"

I shook my head and smiled. "You know my policy."

"Then maybe we can meet up later. See how it all goes, but this is my last show of the day, and The Isle is giving an after-party at the Mercer Hotel. Everyone will be there, but they have plenty of quiet corners where we can catch up."

Chandra, sitting on my other side, also asked whether I'd solved the case yet. When I told her that I'd know later, she asked me to please keep her posted.

"Because if you do know who did it and Cazzie goes public with it all, I'll look like the biggest idiot in the fashion world," she fretted.

"I wouldn't worry too much, Chandra," I said. "First let me nail the thief—if I can—and then we'll speak with Cazzie. Don't forget that *Chic* won't want this story going public any more than you will."

❋ ❋ ❋

Peter and Brandon were backstage, and although we waved at each other, they were concentrating on the famous faces: Misty, Rafaela, Chandra, and Ellie, among many others. I did catch Brandon watching me at one point, though, and he smiled when our eyes met. I wondered what he was thinking.

A little later, Rafaela and I were seated next to each other at the makeup table.

"Miss D! How are you?" she said as she high-fived me. I started trying to count her tattoos again, but this time I only made it to six before I lost track. She was effervescent and looked incredible. "Rumors, rumors, have you heard them? And are they true?" She laughed.

"You see, Axelle, I knew you were here working on a case. I knew it. Didn't I say it? 'She's here on a case,' I said. 'Be careful!' And it turns out I was right. The only thing I don't know is what it could be about. But it must have been something that happened at that *Chic* shoot on Friday, because on Tuesday you were asking us so many questions about that day."

I rolled my eyes and took a deep breath. "Rafaela, has anyone ever told you you're prone to dramatics?"

"Prone to dramatics? Hmm…I like it. 'Prone to dramatics,'" she repeated. "I think I could make a new tattoo out of that." Then she high-fived me again and left, trailing a cloud of glittery powder behind her.

Cat and Mouse

The show finally started. From the runway, I saw Cazzie wink at me. Because of the text I'd sent her last night, she knew I was up to something, but not what. I hadn't wanted to get into details until I spoke with her in person. And that didn't seem likely to happen until after I'd finished solving this case.

Brandon and Peter were sitting in the front row, snapping away, while Chandra, Misty, and Rafaela wowed the crowds with their style. Trish and Tom were backstage, quickly retouching the models between their turns on the runway.

All the suspects were present, and with a bit of luck—and if my instincts hadn't failed me—I'd soon be on my way to downloading my case notes to the folder named "Solved."

As soon as I'd done my last turn on the runway, I changed into my street clothes. Then, taking my shoulder bag, I left the backstage area without saying good-bye to anyone. I found my way to the stairwell—the elevators had too many people around them—and began to climb to the seventh floor. Glancing at my watch, I saw it was 6:45 p.m., which was perfect. I wanted to be in Studio 7 ahead of the meeting time I'd scheduled with the thief.

The eerie green-tinged fluorescent lighting of the windowless stairwell did nothing to boost my confidence. *Everything will be fine*, I told myself. *You have the advantage of surprise.*

Finally I reached the seventh floor. As promised by Cazzie, the door to the studio was unlocked. I pushed it open and walked through. Twilight was just giving way to night. The studio glowed as the sun set, the last of the day's light streaming in through the enormous windows. I looked at the huge spotlights standing around. More than ever, they looked like misplaced dinosaurs. I carefully stepped over their electrical cables as I moved beyond the lights and past the set.

The desk for the editing computer was standing exactly where it had been last Friday and on Tuesday, with the executive chair in front of it. Ditto the hair and makeup table; everything was placed as I remembered it. So far, so good.

Now I wanted to check the dressing room. The wide-wooden-plank floor creaked as I crossed the room. I slipped behind the curtain and took a long careful look around. Here, too, everything was as it should be. Then I half sat, half leaned on the long table under the windows and waited.

Finally, I heard someone come in.

"Axelle? Are you here?"

"I am," I answered. *Stay calm, Axelle,* I told myself, *stay calm.* "And you made it. That's great," I said as I stepped out from the dressing area.

"Of course I did. Did you doubt me?"

We met and greeted each other. Our voices rang out in the cavernous studio, at odds with the still surroundings. "Are we going to stay here?" asked the person I thought was the thief. "It's a bit creepy, isn't it? I thought we could maybe join the others at the Mercer or something."

"Actually, I have something I'd like to show you first. Do you mind?"

"Of course not."

I took my laptop out of my shoulder bag and carried it to the digi-tech table by the set. There I opened it up and placed it exactly as Brandon's had been placed last Friday.

My computer quickly hummed to life and the screen lit up. *Now it's time for my surprise,* I told myself. *Do it now.*

"I thought it might interest you to know how I figured out that you stole the diamond," I said in as normal a voice as I could.

I was about to turn and face them. I wanted to look squarely into the face of the diamond-stealing shadow I'd been chasing all week. I wanted to watch the thief try to come up with an excuse.

But before I could turn and finish what I wanted to say, a flash of movement in the computer screen caught my attention. It happened in exactly the same way it must have happened last Friday afternoon, when the thief sat facing the computer and saw Chandra's reflection as she stole into the dressing area to take the diamond.

My reflexes took over, and I moved without thinking. Thanks to the reflection in the computer screen, I had the advantage of being forewarned. With a rapid turn, I ducked and managed to deflect the hard blow of Brandon's fist.

But not quite quickly enough—his hand brushed against my shoulder and we both lost our balance and fell to the floor. I rolled away from him and scrambled as quickly as I could in the direction of the door, but he was grabbing at my shoes and clawing at my legs. I kicked him hard and tried to pull myself up, but it wasn't easy. Finally, with a swift kick at his hand with my heel, I got up and ran. But instantly he was up too, already just behind me. As he reached for my back, I swept down and grabbed one of the electrical light cables from the floor, pulling it up to trip him. As he fell, I toppled the nearest light onto him for good measure.

At that moment the door burst open and I heard Sebastian. "Axelle!"

"I'm here."

He ran to me and held me. "Are you okay? Where's Brandon?"

I wanted to ask him how he knew it was Brandon, but the words got stuck in my throat. A scream rose up instead as, over Sebastian's shoulder, I saw Brandon getting up, his face enraged. He'd managed to free himself from the light and was coming at us.

"Behind you!" I yelled as I dived toward Brandon's legs.

But Sebastian hit him first. He pivoted and, with a hard punch to the face, knocked Brandon back down.

I grabbed at the cable nearest my feet and dragged it, along with the attached light, toward Brandon. Then, with Sebastian pinning him down, we started tying him as tightly as we possibly could. Brandon struggled madly for a moment—but then all the fight suddenly seem to dissolve out of him... And that was when he started to talk.

By the time Cazzie dashed in, with Ellie and Chandra just behind her, Brandon had confirmed everything I'd suspected.

***

I was at the *Chic* building near Times Square. But this time I hadn't been ushered into Cazzie's white office. Sid Clifton himself had opened the door to a conference room on the penthouse floor of his building. Now Cazzie, Chandra, Sebastian, and I sat with him around one end of an enormous table. This present meeting, however, had been convened only after we'd spent a long time answering questions at Juice Studios for the discreet police unit sent to untangle our mess.

After Cazzie had come running into Studio 7, she'd called Sid straight away. It was time to tell him what had happened and to ask for his help in dealing with it. He had the power to keep the story from leaking—at least until his publicists could hear all the facts and come up with a less sensational way of presenting the story to the press.

Sid had directly contacted someone he knew within the police force, and that officer and his team were the ones who'd showed up at Juice Studios about half an hour after Cazzie first called Sid.

After each of us, including Ellie, had told the police our version of events, along with all of our contact information, we were free to leave—but with a warning that we might be needed for further questioning. Brandon was arrested on a charge of theft.

As the only one of the group who wasn't directly concerned with the case, Ellie had opted to go home, while Sid had requested that the rest of us meet him here.

Somehow, with all of this going on, I'd remembered to call Miriam to ask her to tell Pat not to worry that I hadn't checked in with her after The Isle show. I quickly brought Miriam up to date and was more than relieved when she promised to look after everything for me— including Pat—and that she would try to keep my day tomorrow as free as possible.

"You have one show in the afternoon—Carolina Herrera has confirmed…although I suppose I could cancel it if you really need me to."

"No. I'll do it. It will give me a break from all this."

"And at some point, Axelle, you should come to the agency so that we can discuss how you want to handle the press, should the story leak. It's Saturday tomorrow, but we'll be open because of the shows. We could meet in the morning, perhaps? Before your show? And then you could have the late afternoon and evening all to yourself."

I agreed and thanked her.

"You deserve it, *ma petite* Axelle. And tell me, did it happen like I told you it would?"

It took me a moment to realize she was talking about how I solved the case. "Absolutely," I said. "It happened just like that." I remembered her gesture last night and snapped to myself. "You were right."

✳✳✳

Sid was as commanding a presence in his conference room as he'd been at his *Chic* party on Tuesday night. He was studied and methodical, and his gray eyes seemed to miss nothing. As I watched him listening to Cazzie, the thought occurred to me that he'd probably make a good detective.

He seemed a bit disappointed with Cazzie—not

that he said anything. But I had the feeling he would have liked to be made aware of what was happening at his magazine much earlier. Of course, everything had turned out all right, and with a bit of luck and some strong-arming, Sid would probably manage to keep the story out of the press. And no doubt Cazzie's career would continue on its upward trajectory.

Chandra appeared to feel relief and guilt in equal measure. I wouldn't have been surprised if she decided it was time to sail off around the world again. I also doubted whether she'd ever play another practical joke.

Sid Clifton did seem curious about me, though. He knew the La Lunes well and had heard from them about how I'd found Belle and her brother Darius. He asked question after question about my hunt for the diamond and its thief.

"I admit this case was an odd one," I said, "starting with the fact that I couldn't find a single concrete clue—not one. And because it was a double theft, the tracks of the second theft were nearly impossible to find because the first theft hid them for so long. Not that I really think of what you did as a theft, Chandra," I added with a nod in her direction.

"I still can't believe it was Brandon," Cazzie said, rubbing her hands across her face in exhaustion. "Then again, I'm glad it's him and not one of the others. Considering I've known them all for so long, I'd be devastated if it were one of them. But still, why Brandon?"

I shrugged my shoulders. "Revenge, first and foremost. Remember, you yourself said you've stepped on some toes and that occasionally you've thrown your power around—and apparently Brandon felt you'd done that to him. While Sebastian and I tied him up, he spoke bitterly about the unfairness of the fashion world. He'd presented his photography portfolio to you numerous times, only to be flatly rejected every time."

"But I only remember him submitting once! And I told him nicely that he needed more experience, needed to refine his technique and style."

"Ah! But do you remember what else you said after telling me you might have stepped on some toes?"

Cazzie shook her head.

"I'll tell you. You said: 'I've never intentionally hurt or angered anyone enough to inspire revenge… At least, *not that I'm aware of.*' And there lies the distinction— because you were unaware that Brandon had in fact submitted his portfolio to you numerous times *anonymously*, only to be soundly rejected each time."

Cazzie stared at me wide-eyed from across the broad conference table.

"And don't forget," I continued, "that Brandon was responsible for most—if not all—of Peter's photo retouching. I'm not saying it was an even partnership, but sometimes it must have come close. And Brandon never got much credit for what he did. That's bound to give rise to frustration, isn't it? Especially when, all day, every day you're surrounded by people who are so successful in such tangible, visible ways. Remember, he is the only one of the group not to have yet succeeded on his own merit. But success needs a strategy and lots of hard work too, doesn't it? I think he may have lost sight of that along the way...and cracked a bit."

"Wait, aren't we jumping the gun a bit here? Start at the beginning. How did you work out that Chandra took the diamond originally?" Sid asked.

I smiled. "Frankly, it was through repetition."

Sid looked nonplussed.

"I mean by listening repeatedly to my recordings. It was a good lesson in learning how the smallest vocal inflections can, in fact, give a lot away."

"But how did you get them all to talk in the first place?" Sid asked.

"I found out from Cazzie that a fire alarm had gone off that Friday. So on Tuesday's shoot, I took that as my starting point for a bit of undercover detective work—not that I ended up fooling everyone. Rafaela in particular—and Brandon too, by the way—were quite vocal about me being present to solve a crime, not to model. Although in hindsight, I suppose this gave Brandon an ostensibly innocent way to find out whether I really was looking for him or not.

"But, regardless, I managed to get some questions in while recording their responses. And then I literally listened to everything I'd recorded again and again.

That was how I got onto Chandra's trail. I remembered something odd that she'd said—triggered by something similar that I'd overheard during dinner at the *Chic* party."

"And then?" Cazzie asked.

"And then I realized that if she had taken the diamond—and I totally believed she had—she didn't have it anymore."

"Because?" Sid asked.

"Honestly? Well, first because she told me she didn't have it, and I was inclined to believe her. But also because of a text Cazzie received on Tuesday morning from whoever had the diamond. It was sent at 7:30 a.m.—exactly when Chandra's plane was midway between here and Miami. When I realized that, I knew that she was either working with someone—"

"Or the stolen diamond had been stolen again." Sid finished my sentence for me.

"Exactly. A double theft… And that's when my confidence really took a nosedive."

Sebastian got up and poured water for everyone, while I stretched my legs.

"Why?" Cazzie asked. "You've done brilliantly."

"Thanks, Cazzie, but if you'd spoken to me yesterday afternoon, you'd have found out otherwise. I was frustrated beyond anything I've ever known—and I was really beginning to believe I'd bitten off more than I could chew. Don't forget that I had no tangible clues to go on. The studio had been swept clean; the diamond had been stolen three days before I landed here; and for the sake of discretion, I couldn't *openly* investigate its disappearance."

I stopped and took a deep breath. "I have to backtrack for a moment. One thing I did glean from finally confronting Chandra about her part in the diamond's disappearance was that we could substantially narrow the time frame during which someone could have seen her take the stone—because, of course, that was crucial. Without Brandon having seen Chandra slip the diamond into her shoulder bag, how would he have known where to take it from later when they said good-bye?

"And based upon what Cazzie told me about when she had last seen the diamond, I knew that it must have been taken the first time—for Chandra's prank—within a few minutes of the fire alarm going off. Ironically, Cazzie"—I turned to look at her—"kept her handbag on her arm for the rest of the afternoon, thinking the diamond was still in it and safe on her arm. Only it wasn't—because it had already been taken by Chandra and then stolen from her."

I saw Cazzie slump slightly in her chair at this recollection.

"Then—together with Chandra, Ellie, and Sebastian—I even did a reenactment of that all-important time frame, but nothing, absolutely nothing, came of it."

"It was a real-life game of shadows and phantoms, wasn't it?" Chandra said.

I nodded. "At times I definitely felt I was grasping at fog. A fog of revenge—although I didn't know it then. Brandon's ultimate purpose was simply to make Cazzie sweat. Stealing the diamond was a convenient way to make her feel what it's like to have your career held in the palm of someone else's hand. It was a spoiled rich kid's game taken to the extreme. And of course, he felt quite certain that you wouldn't go to the police—at least not right away, because it would be such an embarrassment. He boldly assumed he'd have some time to play with you, and he was right."

Cazzie began to protest. "But his career wasn't—"

"I'm not saying that's what you did, Cazzie. I'm saying that's how Brandon felt. It came out very clearly in the way he talked after Sebastian punched him."

"I'm sorry I dumped everything on your shoulders, Axelle," Cazzie said.

"Don't worry," I said, "I asked you to. Besides, I had Sebastian's help. Unfortunately, the texts Brandon sent didn't give anything away. It wasn't until we got to the last one that I really understood how simple the plan was—that he really did intend to return the diamond to Cazzie and in precisely the same way he took it, slipped back into a handbag just as it had been slipped out. It was all quite stylish and surprisingly simple—as befits a crime of fashion, I suppose…"

"But up until yesterday afternoon you still didn't know who was responsible, right? So how and when did that click for you?" Sid asked.

I tipped my head back and sighed. I quickly glanced at Sebastian and saw the corners of his mouth lift into a small smile. Like me, he was no doubt thinking of last night's near kiss and Pat's untimely interruption.

"That was a stroke of good timing—or luck—whatever you want to call it," I continued. "Last night I stood in front of the door into Miriam's apartment building and watched Miriam—she's my agent," I added for Sid's benefit, "walk in. I continued to watch as the door swung shut behind her. The top half of the door is glass, and as I stayed standing there, I saw *in the glass* a lady walking behind me. I had my back to her—it was her reflection that gave her away. That was my 'aha' moment, and suddenly everything shifted very dramatically.

"The people who I'd most believed couldn't have seen Chandra—those with their backs to her, those facing the screen of a large computer—were now the suspects with the best view of her! I'd simply forgotten that a computer screen is reflective. Especially if the image on the screen is dark—and last night Cazzie confirmed for me that the shots Peter and Brandon would have been looking at on-screen were indeed dark. Again, the basic style and simplicity of the theft are surprising."

"Of course," I continued, "it was another stroke of luck for Brandon that he saw Chandra take the diamond. When he caught sight of her in his computer screen, sneaking into the dressing area just as everyone was dashing to the windows because of the activity on the street below, he saw the perfect chance. He was well aware of her reputation as a prankster and guessed what she was up to from her furtive movements. He would have taken the diamond no matter what, but stealing it from Chandra and having her confuse—or even cover up—his tracks was too good a chance to pass up."

There was a brief moment of silence while everyone digested this. I took a sip of water and then *I* asked a question. Looking at Sebastian, I said, "How did you know that I was facing trouble?"

In answer, Sebastian took his cell phone out of his pocket, searched for something on it, and then passed it to me. "Read that," he said.

I've lost my phone! Borrowing this one. Am heading back to Miriam's. Meet me?

This was Brandon's one and only really dumb move, I thought as I looked at the text message he'd sent Sebastian.

Sebastian agreed. "It might have been better for his purposes if he hadn't sent anything," he said. "It's not that it doesn't ring true—in fact, he does a fairly good approximation of your brief style. It's more like *why?* I can only think that he must have been very nervous by this point. And obviously he felt unsure about what might happen at your meeting. Regardless, he clearly wanted me out of his way. He must have seen me and assumed I was going to look for you."

"But how did he get your number? And when did he see you? You were outside the studios, and he was inside the entire time."

"He got my number from Ellie. He simply asked her. And since she thought it might have something to do with the case—if only she'd known how right she was—she didn't hesitate to give it to him." Sebastian paused before continuing. "As for when Brandon saw me... After you and I parted ways, I didn't stay outside the studios." Sebastian suddenly looked sheepish and nearly blushed. "I got a call." He smiled awkwardly.

I had a good idea where this was leading. "From whom?" I asked.

"Uh...from your mom. She was concerned. She hadn't heard from you all day and just wanted to make sure you were all right," he quickly added. "She made me promise to check on you."

Exactly as I'd thought. Since the possibility was quite high that Sebastian's conversation with my mom had saved my life, I would sound like the proverbial shrew if I ever said anything about their chats again.

Score one for my mom and Sebastian, I thought.

"So I thought I *should* check on you," he continued. "After all, I knew you had some kind of plan going, but you hadn't told me exactly what—beyond meeting with 'someone,' which was worrying. So I sent Ellie a quick text asking where you were, and she answered that she didn't know, that she couldn't see you. So I asked her to get me past security, which she did.

"I don't remember seeing Brandon, but I was walking around looking for you, and then two minutes later I received the text. That's when I knew you'd need help because something was already wrong or was about to go wrong. By then I was certain you'd be up in Studio 7 with the thief. I sprinted up the stairs and arrived just as I heard the light fall on Brandon."

I then explained about the final "riddle" not being a riddle at all, but rather a ploy by Brandon to ensure that I wouldn't be anywhere near him when he slipped the diamond back into Cazzie's handbag. We slowly wound down our discussion. All questions had been answered, for the time being anyway, and it was late, nearly 1:00 a.m. Plus, as Cazzie pointed out—and Pat likes to say—fashion never sleeps. Tomorrow was another busy day of New York Fashion Week. It was time to get some shut-eye.

Cazzie wanted to drive me home. Despite knowing that Sebastian wanted to speak with me—and I with him, I also knew Cazzie needed to speak with me so I accepted her offer. Sid Clifton, meanwhile, offered to drive Sebastian back to his aunt's, and Chandra's car was still waiting for her. "One in the morning is nothing!" she said with a laugh.

But before we all left, Sid asked to have a quick word with me—alone.

"I'm not really sure what to say—which you'd realize is unusual, if you knew me." He smiled. "So I'll start by saying thank you so much. I'm indebted to you. You've saved me and my corporation from a lot of potential embarrassment and maybe even a future similar crime. Had he not been caught, Brandon may have tried something like this again. I'll be in touch with your agency tomorrow about proper remuneration. Miriam's, I believe you said?"

I nodded.

"You must be overwhelmed by this evening's turn of events, so I'll let you go, but I'd like to say that I'll be doing my best to keep this out of the press."

His implication was clear: he was hoping I'd do the same. "Don't worry," I said. "I'd like to keep this out of the press too. I can't call myself an undercover model when everyone knows what I've been doing, can I?" I smiled.

"Thank you." Then after a short pause he continued. "By the way, I know you said that you will be staying in New York until tomorrow evening. Is there anything I can get you tickets to? Anything at all that you'd like to see? My office can arrange anything you'd like."

I was about to thank him and say that I couldn't think of anything, but at the last moment something came to mind. When I told Sid what I wanted, he threw his head back and laughed a deep laugh.

"You're amazing," he said. "If everyone else I dealt with was as easy to please, my life would be heaven. Consider it a done deal. You'll have them first thing in the morning." Then we shook hands and I left.

✳ ✳ ✳

The text came just as I hit my bed:

Good job, Holmes.

I wrote back:

You too, Watson. See you tomorrow?

To which he answered:

Absolutely. But do you think we could arrange it so that Pat can't surprise us?

I smiled and then fell asleep before you could say DKNY.

A Sky-High Surprise

The tickets arrived first thing in the morning, messengered by bike from Sid Clifton's office. And for the first time since arriving in the Big Apple, I had a leisurely breakfast: no emails, texts, clues, missed chances, or anything else to distract me. Nicolette fussed over me like a large French hen.

After breakfast I packed my bags for my flight home that night. I wanted that out of the way because I definitely didn't want anything distracting me later. I had the tickets; the weather was gorgeous; I'd solved my case; and my only obligations now were a meeting with Miriam and one last fashion show. After that I'd have my final few hours to myself—and Sebastian.

Miriam was waiting for me when I showed up at the agency, and she immediately whisked me into her office. There I told her about all that had transpired last night. She listened, entranced, and was delighted to hear that Sid Clifton had finally taken charge.

"He should be able to keep the story from leaking. And I'm sure that Cazzie will be okay. He must be furious with her, of course…but what matters is how it's ended, which—thanks to you—is very well indeed." She paused for a moment before adding, "Poor Brandon, though. You know, there is a famous European designer who says—I'm paraphrasing now—'Fashion is unfair. And if you can't accept that, then you shouldn't be in it.'

"That sounds quite harsh," Miriam continued, "but there is some truth to it. Many of the usual rules of business—and even ethics, I sometimes think—don't apply to fashion. That can be difficult for many to understand, especially you young people."

With a delicate Gallic shrug of her petite shoulders, she sighed. "C'est la vie. Anyway, you came out of it well, and that is all that matters to me and your family. Speaking of which, I must report back to your mother. She is waiting on pins and needles to hear about yesterday's outcome."

What? Miriam too? I looked at her with wide eyes. Was everyone a spy for my mom? And why was I always the last to know?

"Ah! Axelle, I see that this upsets you, *non*? Ignore it. You know how mothers are. They always worry and want to know how their children are. Besides, you are an only child, so you really have no escape from this parental scenario. And it could be worse."

"How could it possibly be worse?" I asked.

"Well, you could be related to Pat too!" Miriam laughed. Very funny.

✳ ✳ ✳

My last New York City show, for Carolina Herrera, took place at Lincoln Center, and it all went according to plan. The only problem was that I kept feeling like I'd forgotten something. I finally realized that was because, for once, I didn't have anyone to question, or any clue to follow up on, or anything else to race off to.

I managed to say good-bye to Chandra and Ellie, who both were doing the show with me. Ellie, however, was quick to remind me that I'd see her in London next week. "I can't wait to be home—not that I'll be there for long. But at least I'll have enough time to repack my suitcase and meet you for a gluten-free veggie burger." She laughed.

Then, finally, it was time to meet Sebastian.

We met in Central Park, which was glowing in the late-afternoon sun.

"You've been more mysterious than any diamond thief about where we're going," he said, laughing.

After a long meandering walk through the park and down Fifth Avenue, I clasped my hands over his eyes and made him promise not to open them until I said so.

When he did—admittedly after a few minutes of tricky doorway negotiations and a couple of stumbles—it was with a huge smile.

"Holmes, where are we?"

"On top of the Empire State Building, Watson," I

answered. "You said you didn't want Pat or anyone else interrupting us, so I thought that from here we'd be sure to see her coming." I laughed.

The view was amazing. New York City lay before us like a lustrous sunset tapestry of glass, greenery, cars, and lots and lots of teeny-tiny people crawling everywhere. The sky was made up of dazzling streaks of orange and red. Puffs of purple and blue clouds scuttled across the horizon, brushing against the top of the Statue of Liberty's torch.

But soon all I saw and felt was Sebastian. As his hands pushed my hair back from my face and I drew him to me, our lips met with an intensity that we'd been circling around all week.

And if you've never kissed your own super-cute, super-sweet guy on top of the Empire State Building... well, just so you know, it's definitely worth solving a mystery for.

HOW TO SPEAK SUPERMODEL

Axelle's guide to surviving in the world of fashion

If you want to blend in with the fashion set, it's worth learning the lingo. Here's a handy guide:

*BIAS-CUT: A special technique used by fashion-designers to cut fabric on the diagonal. A dress cut on the "bias" gives an impression of great fluidity.

*BOOK: This is another word for the all-important portfolio models have. A book or portfolio is used to show clients and designers both how a model looks in photos, and what kind of work they've done.

*BOOKER: A staff member at an agency whose job is to handle requests from clients and to represent and set up appointments for models.

*DIGI-TECH: The digi-tech is responsible for regulating exposure, color, and light conditions of the photos taken by the photographer on set. The digi-tech checks and corrects the images in real time as they are imported into her or his computer.

*FITTING: A session that may take place

before a fashion show or photo shoot where the clothes to be modeled are fitted onto the model.

*GALA: A large and lavish social event. Dress code leans towards formal, so long dresses and black or white tie.

*GO-SEE: An appointment for a model to see a photographer or a client. Unlike a casting, there is no specific brief.

*LIGHT METER: A device used to measure the intensity of light for a photo. Photographers or their assistants will hold a light meter up in front of the model before taking the photograph.

*LOCATION VAN: A vehicle that has been specially outfitted to drive a fashion team to a location, and serve as HQ when working outside of a studio. Besides a kitchen, dining table, and lavatory, you'll also find a special area for makeup and hair, and styling.

*OPTIONS: An option is put to a model by a client to see if he/she would be available for their shoot. Options are then either confirmed as a booking, or released.

*TEAR SHEETS: These are photos which are literally torn from magazines, and which a model can use in her book. Tear sheets from magazines like *Vogue* and *Elle* are what every model hopes to have in her book.

*TEST: Resembles a normal photo shoot, but

organized by a modeling agency in order to provide a new model with photos for her book and practice in front of the camera.

*ZED CARD or COMPOSITE CARD: This is basically a business card for models. A5 in size, zed cards or composites normally show at least two photos, as well as basic info such as a model's hair color, eye color, height, and agency contact details.

And if anyone's still suspicious that you don't belong, just throw in one of these handy phrases...

*"DIY Converse is **so awesome!**"*

*"I still haven't decided if the **midi-length** is for me."*

*"Sometimes I just need to wear a **statement** belt."*

*"**It's all about** a ladylike bag right now."*

*"**I'm loving** patchwork jeans."*

*"Did you **self-style** for the gala last night?"*

*"Cool **cross-body!**"*

*"OMG, orange is so **the new black**."*

*"Beanies **aren't just for winter**, you know..."*

Now don't forget the air kisses, darling! Mwah, mwah!

THE NEW YORK LIST

Carina's favorite places to visit in the city of romance and fashion

"I was lucky enough to live in this inspiring, extraordinary city for a few years when I was working as a fashion model. And while the city demands the best of everyone and everything—no doubt about that—it also offers up a world of dazzling delight and wonder. So here's a list of some of my favorite Big Apple sights and experiences."

CENTRAL PARK: Whether you're in the mood for a brisk morning run or a romantic stroll at sunset, this is the big-city park that dreams are made of. Romance, beauty, a sense of escape, and cute, bushy-tailed squirrels: this park has it all. I dare anyone to spend some time in this sylvan fantasy of fountains, vistas, and wooded trails, and not fall in love with it.

THE METROPOLITAN MUSEUM OF ART: We all need to feed our minds, and the Met, as it's known, is the ultimate grocery store for brain food. From intricate Egyptian jewelry that's thousands of years old to the famous painting of Madame X, prepare to be dazzled. Afterwards, take a break on the grand stone steps outside.

NEW YORK PUBLIC LIBRARY: Right. So there are libraries, and then there are libraries. Where else can a book lover experience the thrill of having two iconic stone lions waiting to greet them, awesome architecture, a leafy terrace upon which to read the books you just checked out, and a snack bar in an elegant marble hall? Not to mention having one of the finest and largest book collections in the world at your fingertips? Nowhere but here, that's where.

EMPIRE STATE BUILDING: Go at sunset, on a clear, warm evening, to the viewing platform on the 86th floor, to enjoy what has to be the most romantic view in the Big Apple! Plus this sumptuous and sleek art deco building is straight out of Batman—even the elevators are amazing. So don't forget your camera. And don't forget to brush your teeth before going—you never know when romance might strike, and if it happens at the top of this building, you definitely want to be prepared!

BALTHAZAR: Let's face it, sightseeing works up an appetite. So if you're craving some French-via-New-York brasserie food, feel like you're oozing style, and want to do some major people-watching in the heart of SoHo, Balthazar is the place for you. I find lunch is best—and don't forget to order the fries. Oh, and if you see the Beckhams, try not to stare!

THE HIGH LINE: Need to escape the gritty NYC pavement, and maybe stop for an ice cream while listening to songbirds trill? Want to experience Downtown NYC at its funkiest best? Then the High Line is the place to go. This park of tall grass and blossoming shrubs is built on a former elevated train track. How cool is that? Every city should have one. Seriously. You'll love it.

BENDEL'S: Although every floor of this enchanting department store oozes glamour, I have a special weakness for Bendel's chic toiletry bags. Covered in the iconic Bendel's brown and white stripe, they may be pricey, but they are worth it – they instantly add a touch of Manhattan pizzazz to any bathroom!

STREET ART: Keep your eyes peeled, girls, because NYC has the most amazing street art! While wandering around, you're sure to walk into or past all sorts of fab graffiti; you'll see walls, sidewalks, and even the sides of trucks that have received clandestine art treatments. And all of those sleek skyscrapers and the miles of gritty cement pavements really make the perfect backdrop to the colorful, vibrant street art you'll find. Take photos!

__PREMIUM LACES :__ Like Axelle, I have a weakness for a cool pair of sneakers, and in NYC you'll find oodles of fun, fab ones. You'll find them everywhere, although I can say that, as of this printing, there's an especially fantastic collection of sneakers at the tiny shop, Premium Laces, in SoHo. Definitely keep a bit of extra space in your suitcase for the trip home!

HAVE FUN

Acknowledgments

THANK YOU:

Peter Usborne, and your fantastic team at Usborne Publishing, for making the journey to publication such an amazing, fabulous ride! Jenny Tyler and Rebecca Hill, for your expertise, faith and enthusiasm! Anne Finnis and Sarah Stewart, for being such wonderful editors. Anne, I never quite know what to expect, but it's always good! Amy Dobson, Anna Howorth, and Sarah Aspinall, I can't tell you how much fun it is to work with you, and to be the lucky recipient of so much of your talent and time.

To Dominique Raccah, and the zesty team at Sourcebooks, for all of your support and encouragement. Steve Geck, for your keen eye and unflappable charm—even when faced with deadline changes and last minute tweaks. You have all been absolutely lovely!

To my agents, Jenny Savill and Andrew Nurnberg, of Andrew Nurnberg Associates, for your unfailing support through so many false starts. Jenny, you are yet again the recipient of the gold medal prize for patience!

Marc, for your quick answers to all sorts of questions concerning the technicalities of fashion photography. You've been a star!

Alexandra, for all of the support and enthusiasm you've shown me since the beginning of this endeavor. You've been a rock!

Helle, for understanding so much.

To my family, for your constant encouragement and love.

Gustav, for everything…

CARINA'S FASHION CREDENTIALS

Carina Axelsson is a former fashion model whose jet-setting career saw her starring in advertising campaigns and fashion magazines across the globe, including shoots for *Vogue* and *Elle*.

After growing up in California, Carina moved to New York, and then later to Paris, where she studied art and rounded off her days in fashion with a short stint working as a PA to international fashion designer John Galliano. Her experiences—along with a love of Scooby-Doo and Agatha Christie—inspired her to write *Model Undercover*.

And as for her character's unusual name...

"Sometime before I wrote the first notes about this girl detective there had been posters up all over Paris with a cut, spunky-looking, long-haired singer named Axelle. I think they were advertising her concerts or new album. It was the first time I'd seen the name Axel—which I only knew as a man's name—feminized and in French. I loved it straight away! And, obviously, the name became lodged in a corner in my brain because as soon as this girl detective came into my mind the name attached itself to her—she never had another. And just so you know, it's pronounced with the accent on the second syllable, like the verb 'excel'—not like the car part!"

Carina now lives in Western Germany with her partner and four dogs. She writes and illustrates full-time. You can find out more about Carina at http://www.carinaaxelsson.com.